Pelican Library of Business and Management
Advisory Editor: T. Kempner
The Multinationals

Christopher Tugendhat was born in 1937 and
educated at Ampleforth College, and at Gonville
and Caius College, Cambridge, where he was
President of the Union. Until 1970, when he was
elected Conservative MP for the Cities of London
and Westminster, he was a feature and leader writer
for the *Financial Times*, where multinational
companies was one of his special subjects. He was
Opposition spokesman for Employment (1974–5) and
on Foreign and Commonwealth Affairs (1975–6).
Mr Tugendhat was for several years a Director of
Sunningdale Oils and Phillips Petroleum
International (U.K.) Ltd. His publications are *Oil:
The Biggest Business* (1968) and *The Multinationals*
which won the McKinsey Foundation Award in 1971.

The Multinationals

CHRISTOPHER TUGENDHAT

PENGUIN BOOKS

Penguin Books Ltd, Harmondsworth,
Middlesex, England
Penguin Books, 625 Madison Avenue,
New York, New York 10022, U.S.A.
Penguin Books Australia Ltd, Ringwood,
Victoria, Australia
Penguin Books Canada Ltd, 2801 John Street,
Markham, Ontario, Canada L3R 1B4
Penguin Books (N.Z.) Ltd, 182–190 Wairau Road,
Auckland 10, New Zealand

First published by Eyre & Spottiswoode Ltd 1971
Published in Pelican Books 1973
Reprinted 1974, 1976, 1977, 1979, 1981
Copyright © Christopher Tugendhat, 1971
All rights reserved

Made and printed in Great Britain by
Richard Clay (The Chaucer Press) Ltd,
Bungay, Suffolk
Set in Monotype Baskerville

For Julia, my wife

Contents

Tables and Figures

Preface

The relationship between multinational and international companies on the one hand and governments on the other creates difficulties everywhere. But this book concentrates almost exclusively on the countries of Western Europe and North America. Together they account for the greater part of the companies' investments and activities. They include most of the world's largest and richest markets, and generate the bulk of international trade. Their economies are closely inter-related, and they share many of the same problems. Japan is in a class of its own with a unique culture and industrial structure. Moreover, the companies' interests in Japan and their role in its economy are much smaller than in the West. The Third World has been excluded because the problems and needs of the developing countries are in this, as in so many other ways, quite different from those of the industrialized countries. Another book would be required to do them justice.

My main problem in preparing this text has been the dearth of reliable statistics, and the reluctance of companies to reveal information which they regard as confidential. 'If you believe their figures,' a Geneva stockbroker has said of the Swiss international companies, 'they earn so little they couldn't afford to have the annual report printed.'* The Swiss provide an extreme example of secrecy, but most continental companies reveal as little as they can. Indeed they are so secretive that the European Institute of Business Administration has to make do with second-hand U.S. case studies because it cannot get enough from Europe. British and U.S. companies are, on the whole, much better in this respect; but they too are reluctant to divulge information that does not appear in their annual reports, or which they consider has political implications. Many of the issues dealt with in this book, such as the movement of funds between different currencies, the allocation of

* *Men and Money* by Paul Ferris (Hutchinson).

9

export markets to subsidiaries, and the way decisions are taken on where to locate new plants, are regarded by all companies as top secret. They never discuss them in public, and only with governments under severe pressure.

Government statistics are usually worse than those of the companies, and the governments themselves more secretive. When the secretariat of the European Free Trade Area prepared a report on member countries' direct foreign investments Switzerland refused to cooperate. When the Organization for Economic Cooperation and Development (OECD) was gathering statistics of a similar nature some years ago Holland, Italy, and Belgium, as well as Switzerland, either would not or could not provide details. By far the best official figures are the American followed at some distance by the British, although these too have many gaps.

An additional problem arises from the rapidity with which changes take place in international business. Men move suddenly from one job to another, and companies alter the pattern of trade between their plants, and the responsibilities of their national subsidiaries, as circumstances demand. Some of the facts in this book are bound to have been overtaken by events between the time they were researched and the date of publication. The reader is asked to be tolerant when he discovers examples of this kind.

As so often happens with a new subject, the study of the relationship between governments and multinational and international companies is surrounded by far too much jargon, and there is not enough precision of language. There is no universally accepted definition of a multinational company, nor of the words international and transnational, which are also widely used. Not content with these, some writers like to categorize companies as to whether they are 'ethnocentric', 'polycentric', or 'geocentric'. So let me define my own terms. This book is about the activities of manufacturing companies which produce and sell their goods in different countries. I shall generally use the word international to describe them, and reserve multinational for very large companies with especially far-flung interests, such as Ford, IBM, and Shell. Often the two words are interchangeable.

In recent years an increasing number of economists have become aware that the growth of international business has profound implications for their subject, and necessitates a re-examination of many basic propositions. This has led to numerous controversies. If I attempted to deal fairly with each point of view that has been expressed, my own task of explaining how international and multi-national companies work and how their activities impinge upon governments would be impossible. Consequently I have decided to plough my own furrow without seeking support from other writers, or attacking their conclusions.

London, 1 January 1971   CHRISTOPHER TUGENDHAT

Acknowledgements

I owe a special debt of gratitude to Sir Gordon Newton, the former Editor of the *Financial Times*. For most of the time that I was writing this book I was on the staff of his newspaper. He allowed me to work out many of my ideas in its columns and responded generously to all my requests for help.

Throughout my researches I have relied heavily on Colin Abson, the Deputy Librarian at the *Financial Times*. He has provided me with much invaluable help in unearthing facts and figures, tracking down references, and preparing material for the illustrations.

I should also like to express my thanks to the Royal Institute of International Affairs, Chatham House, which held two private conferences in 1968 and 1970 on the problems arising from the spread of international companies that played an important part in shaping my ideas. In addition, I have benefited considerably from my membership of their Study Group on International Economic Relations in the 1960s, which has enabled me to see the growth of international business enterprise in a wider context.

Since I began writing about industrial subjects ten years ago I have enjoyed the friendship of many people employed in international companies at every level. To those who have helped me in this task I extend my grateful thanks.

Neither this book nor its predecessor, *Oil: The Biggest Business*, could have been written without the assistance of my agent, Miss Deborah Rogers. She encouraged me to start writing books and through her professional brilliance has ensured that I have had the financial incentives to continue doing so.

I cannot find words adequate to express my thanks to my wife. She has put up with my locking myself away at weekends and with the bad temper and tiredness that usually result from my writing, with patience and generosity. She has given me all the support and love a man could hope for. This book is dedicated to her.

Introduction to the Pelican Edition

Since this book was first published in July 1971 the problems posed by the growth and spread of multinational companies have become much more widely appreciated. Dangers, which then seemed rather esoteric and futuristic, have become urgent matters of public concern. The argument is no longer between those who believe that multinational business can be accommodated within the framework of the customary powers and operating procedures of national governments, and those who believe that new initiatives are needed. It is now between the exponents of different types of initiative. The need for change is widely accepted, and this is as true of the United States as it is of Europe.

The companies' role in international currency crises has played a large part in bringing them to the attention of governments and the general public. The companies did not cause these crises. They result from the combined effects of government policies throughout the western world, and from deep seated social and economic imbalances. But the ability of corporate treasurers to move vast sums of money across frontiers and from one currency to another within a matter of days has enormously exacerbated the basic difficulties. Before the floating of the £ in June 1972, for instance, some $2,500m. left London in about a week.

Governments and trade unions have also become more aware of the companies' power to determine trade flows between states. The proportion of Britain's exports accounted for by internal transactions, such as sales by Ford of Britain to Ford of Germany, or by ICI in Britain to ICI in Belgium, has risen to over thirty per cent. Consequently, when companies decide to transfer export sales from their factories in this country to their plants elsewhere, the impact on the industries concerned, their suppliers, and the economy as a whole can be substantial. Ford provides a case in point. Since the first edition of this book was completed it has transferred the responsibility for supplying its important U.S., French, and Italian markets from its British to its German subsidiary. This move followed a period of ten years during which Ford and General Motors increased their net fixed assets in Germany at four times the rate of those in Britain.

Decisions of this kind exert a major influence on the level of industrial investment and job opportunities in the countries concerned. This issue is causing growing controversy everywhere, and particularly in the United States, the home of more multinational companies than anywhere else. American unions claim that between 1966 and 1969 some 400,000 jobs were lost to American workers as a result of U.S. companies shifting production to their foreign plants.

The reality is more complex. The location of a plant is only one factor among several that must be taken into account when assessing the effect of a new investment. Decisions on how export markets should be allocated, and where supplies of components and raw materials are purchased, must also be considered. So too must the provision of expert services, like banking, advertising, and construction engineering. But this does not alter the fundamental fact that the normal business decisions of multinational companies have far-reaching effects on the countries where they operate.

This brings me to a point in the original edition that requires a change of emphasis. In Chapter 2 I suggest that the pace at which U.S.-owned companies expand in Europe will be less in future than it was in the past. I now think it will be substantially less. The pressures from American unions and politicians, fearful of unemployment in the U.S. and the decline of many traditional industries, is one important reason. Another is the deterioration in the U.S. financial position relative to the other industrial countries. The U.S. Government is no longer prepared to tolerate a massive outflow of investment funds. U.S. companies abroad will continue to grow. But they will have to rely much more than in the past on re-investment and locally generated funds. At the same time the extent to which they repatriate profits to the U.S. will increase.

The desire to secure what they regard as their fair share of the fruits of multinational enterprise is not confined to the Americans. In this book I describe how some countries try to woo internationally mobile direct investments, and make themselves attractive places in which to site export plants and earn profits. I warn against the dangers of governments embarking on competitions with each other to secure the favours of the multinationals so that their investment and other incentives become mutually destructive.

This threat has been recognized by the European Economic Community. Although member countries are still pursuing a number of competitive policies, especially with regard to regional development, proposals for harmonization are being considered. It will not be easy to reach agreements that satisfy the aspirations and requirements of all nine member countries. But the evolution of common policies in these fields could be one of the first fruits of the enlargement of the E E C.

The enlargement will also encourage European companies to work more closely together. In this context, however, it is vital to distinguish between mergers and cooperation. In this book I explain how difficult it is for companies of different nationality to merge with each other. I suggest that cross-frontier mergers will be extremely rare, and this view has, so far, been borne out by events. It will now be possible to tackle the crucial underlying problems relating to company law and taxation, stock exchange procedures, and accounting principles on a Europe-wide basis. But many years will be needed to work out a common framework within these areas, and I expect the annual rate of cross-frontier mergers to remain in low single figures for a long time to come.

Meanwhile cross-frontier cooperation will become increasingly common. Since the publication of the first edition of this book, substantial progress has been made in industries as diverse as nuclear power, aviation, shipbuilding, and computers. Although the emphasis in future will be on trans-European cooperation, there will continue to be considerable scope for European companies to form links with North American and other overseas concerns. In oil, the doyen of multinational business, this pattern has been commonplace for some years.

Developments in multinational business are mirrored in the trade union movement. Workers from different countries employed by the same companies have recently been forming themselves into groups to discuss matters of common interest. For the present they are concentrating on non-economic issues rather than rates of pay. Hours of work, production line speeds, manning schedules, safety standards, and re-training opportunities are typical examples. There has also been a growing tendency among trade unionists to try to help colleagues in other countries who are engaged in strikes or other disputes. The international trade union federations and at least some national trade unions regard these limited understandings as being the first step towards the international negotiation of labour agreements. That day is a long way off. But progress towards it will have to be made if trade unions are to go on fulfilling their traditional role.

In the light of experience I am happy to stand by all the recommendations put forward in these pages for government action, both at the national and international levels. I have, however, become convinced that the most effective measures will be those designed to create a common framework within which companies and governments can work.

For as long as governments, especially in Europe, pursue

differing, and frequently inconsistent, legal, tax, investment, industrial safety, and other policies the scope for tension and conflict between governments and companies will increase. National differences provide the spur for companies to find ways round laws and policies they do not like, and the profits for those that succeed. If the anomalies could be eliminated, companies would have less incentive to follow policies of this sort, and it would be much easier for governments to prevent them from doing so. This does not mean that all governments, either within the EEC or a wider area, must adopt the same laws and policies. But it does mean that they should endeavour to legislate and to pursue policies that are based on the same general principles.

In my conclusion I discuss some of the initiatives that governments and companies should take in their relations with each other. I now feel that my net should have been cast wider. The international repercussions of U.S. economic policies have underlined the extent to which the national economies of the industrial countries have grown together. When one large country or group of countries imposes capital movement controls or import restrictions the rest are immediately affected. The same applies to anti-trust and monopoly policies. Governments must be prepared to take more account of each other's interests than in the past if they are successfully to tackle the problems of multinational business that cross all their frontiers.

Introduction

The time has come for governments everywhere to decide what to do about the great multinational companies that have grown up in the last twenty-five years. Their emergence is one of the most dramatic developments of the period, and of more than just economic and industrial significance. Their position profoundly affects the role of governments in the exercise of their responsibilities, and the relationship between states.

Their operations span the globe. They build their factories and sell their products in many different countries. They transfer vast sums of money between currencies as the need arises, and they employ people of numerous nationalities. General Motors and Ford cars, Shell and Esso oil products, IBM computers, SKF bearings, Alcan aluminium, Philips electrical products, Bayer drugs, Unilever and Proctor & Gamble detergents, Olivetti typewriters, and Dunlop–Pirelli tyres, to name only a few examples, cannot be identified with any single country. They are not made in one place and exported to others. They are manufactured simultaneously in several different countries, and sold through integrated distribution systems which transcend national frontiers. The companies concerned are among the most complex and successful examples of international cooperation known to history.

They are also extremely large. Already, as the table overleaf shows, several have annual sales worth as much in money terms as the gross national products of the smaller European nations, and their rate of growth is much faster.

Apart from this measure it is difficult to be precise about

A comparison between the sales of some multinational companies and the gross national products of some countries

Gross national products 1970 ($000m)		Sales 1970 ($000m)	
Holland	31·28	General Motors	U.S.	18·75
Sweden	30·77	Standard Oil (N.J.)	U.S.	16·55
Belgium	25·88	Ford	U.S.	14·98
Switzerland	20·31	Royal Dutch/Shell	Holland–U.K.	10·79
Denmark	15·57	IBM	U.S.	7·50
Austria	14·37	Unilever	U.K.–Holland	6·88
Norway	11·39	Philips	Holland	4·16
Finland	10·22	Imperial Chemical Industries	U.K.	3·50
Greece	9·39	Hoechst	Germany	1·42
Ireland	3·89	Alcan Aluminium	Canada	1·36

The source of the corporate figures is *Fortune*, which each year publishes lists of the 500 largest industrial corporations in the U.S. and the 200 largest outside the U.S. The companies listed are a representative selection of large companies with substantial international interests. Japanese companies have been excluded because the vast bulk of their manufacturing takes place within their home country. They do not have significant manufacturing interests in Western Europe or North America.

Source of GNP figures: OECD Main Economic Indicators.

the scale of international business enterprise since the statistics on the assets and operations of companies outside their home countries are extremely scarce. Those that are available are invariably out of date, and no better than approximate. Another problem is that national accounting methods vary so much that it is difficult to compare like with like. The most comprehensive published data was prepared* by the Organization for Economic Cooperation and Development (OECD) in 1968. This showed that in 1966 the book value of the companies' investments outside their own countries amounted to about $90,000m. About two-thirds was in the industrialized countries, and the remainder in the less developed nations. In the industrialized countries the most important category was manufacturing at $28,000m. followed by petroleum at $14,000m.

These figures are now out of date. The total has been growing at an estimated twelve per cent a year,† and must currently be over $150,000m.

Impressive as they are the figures understate the real scale of international industry. Research carried out by Judd Polk ‡ suggests that every dollar of book value investment generates two dollars a year of sales. On the basis of this admittedly rough and ready calculation international companies produced over $300,000m. of goods outside their own countries in 1971, or more than the total value of world trade. There is some double counting in this since Ford cars produced in Britain or Germany, for instance, and exported to a third country are counted twice over, but it is

*The figures were compiled from OECD-DAC (68) 14, Annex C, 23 April, 1968. They were first published by Sidney Rolfe in 'The International Corporation, with an epilogue on rights and responsibilities'. This was produced as a background report for the 22nd Congress of the International Chamber of Commerce, held at Istanbul, in June 1969.

† The logic of economic growth. Remarks by Arthur K. Watson, then president of the International Chamber of Commerce, to the first plenary session of the chamber's 22nd congress, Istanbul, 2 June 1969.

‡ 'The New World Economy' by Judd Polk. *Columbia Journal of World Business*, January–February 1968.

still an awe-inspiring measure of the enormous and pervasive influence possessed by international companies.

They are frequently thought of almost exclusively in American terms, and their growth and influence considered in the context of America's relations with its allies. This is understandable. More of them are based in the U.S. than anywhere else. The American share of the total of international direct investment is, however, not more than about sixty per cent, and some of the leading multinationals are non-American, such as the Anglo-Dutch twins Shell and Unilever, the Canadian Alcan, the Swedish SKF, the Italian Olivetti, and the German Bayer. Although the Americans will remain well ahead of the field during the 1970s the part played by companies from other countries will increase steadily. Some indication of this is given by the sharp jump in their direct investments in the U.S. itself, which expanded by a third between 1966 and 1969.

Quite apart from this it is wrong to think of the companies in conventional national terms. The overriding aim of each one of them is to pursue its own corporate interest which is separate and distinct from that of every government, including the government of its country of origin. There is, of course, an overlap between a company's interests and those of the governments of the countries where it is involved, and in most cases that overlap is greatest with its own home government. But the companies' attitude to themselves has been aptly put by Dr Max Gloor, directeur of the Swiss Nestlé Alimentana. 'We cannot be considered either as pure Swiss,' he said, 'or as purely multinational, i.e. belonging to the world at large, if such a thing does exist at all. We are probably something in between, a breed on our own. In one word we have the particular Nestlé citizenship.'*

Each company functions as a centrally directed and co-ordinated body. In some the individual subsidiaries are allowed to exercise a good deal of initiative, and in others

---

* From a talk given at a conference on 'The Multinational Company', organized by the British Institute of Management, on 10 July 1968.

practically none. But whatever the system employed for the time being, the head office is the brain and nerve centre, while the subsidiaries are limbs carrying out their appointed tasks. IBM, for instance, does not manufacture complete computers anywhere outside the U.S.; it makes components in different countries that are combined into multinational end-products. Ford is aiming to coordinate the activities of its British, Belgian, and German subsidiaries as closely as those concerns already coordinate their own local factories. SKF diverts orders to whichever of its subsidiaries needs them most so as to maintain a more or less uniform level of work throughout the group. In these, and all other, multinational and international companies the purpose of the subsidiaries, like that of our arms and legs, is to work on behalf of the body as a whole, and their interests are subordinated to that end, as defined by their respective head offices. The bonds which companies create between nations when they link their operations in different countries are not readily apparent, like those of a treaty between governments, but they can be tighter and more durable.

The nature of the international company has far-reaching implications for the men who manage them. W. J. Kenyon Jones, the chairman of the U.S.-owned Ronson's British subsidiary, defines the duty of an executive in these words.* He 'must set aside any nationalistic attitudes and appreciate that in the last resort his loyalty must be to the shareholders of the parent company, and he must protect their interests even if it might appear that it is not perhaps in the national interest of the country in which he is operating. Apparent conflicts may occur in such matters as the transfer of funds at a period of national crisis, a transfer of production from one subsidiary to another, or a transfer of export business.'

This blunt enunciation of the doctrine of company before country is one to which many executives would take excep-

*'The Shape of America's Challenge' by Rex Winsbury. *Management Today*, February 1967.

tion. They often argue that real conflicts of interest between their companies and their countries cannot arise because, in the long run, the two are synonymous. Sometimes this is true, but not invariably. Charles Wilson's famous remark, on the occasion of his move from the presidency of General Motors to the U.S. Secretaryship of Defense, that, 'I have always thought that what was good for the country was equally good for General Motors – and vice-versa,' was received in America with the laughter and derision it deserved. But even if it had been true, one must stretch the imagination to believe that the interests of General Motors, or any other company, could invariably be the same as those of the U.S., Britain, Germany, Belgium, and all the other countries where it operates.

Kenyon Jones identified the most sensitive issues. International companies can influence exchange rates by moving funds from one currency to another, and affect national balance of payments by altering the prices at which goods are transferred from one subsidiary to another. They can switch export orders from plants in one country to those in another, and they can have an important impact on national growth rates by putting their investments in new plant and machinery in one place rather than another. Every decision involves a choice in which various national interests are involved.

In these circumstances there is a natural and inevitable tension between companies and governments. The purpose of this book is to examine the nature and background of that problem, and to make some preliminary suggestions about how it might be resolved. It would be agreeable to think one could put forward a definitive solution, but that will have to wait until far more is known about the principles and practices involved. This is one of those questions where we are still at the stage of gathering information and trying to interpret its significance. If this book can contribute to that process it will have succeeded in its objective.

It is divided into two parts, which can be read either

separately or in sequence. The first provides the background to the present situation by describing how modern multi-national business has evolved. The second explains how the companies work today.

Part One:

The Growth of Multinational Business

1. Historical Background

In June 1969 the International Chamber of Commerce held its fiftieth anniversary congress in Istanbul. To mark the occasion the organizers wanted to find a suitably momentous theme. So the chamber's president, Arthur K. Watson,* who was at that time chairman of IBM's World Trade Corporation,† proposed 'The Role, Rights, and Responsibilities of the International Corporation'. The choice proved a good one. More than 1,800 delegates turned up, among whom were the heads and other senior executives of most of the world's leading companies. There can be no doubt that in business circles the importance of the growth of large international companies, and the gravity of the resulting problems, is fully appreciated.

Yet Watson's choice came in for some criticism. Several of the larger multinationals felt it was dangerous to stir up debate on this subject. Leroy D. Stinebower, a vice-president of Standard Oil (New Jersey), expressed concern lest 'all this talk lead host countries to believe that international companies are something completely new from what we've had in the past, which will cause them either to welcome or discourage investors because they fit some description they've read of multinational companies'.‡ Another delegate was more succinct: 'We do ourselves a disservice,' he said, 'if we emphasize the newness of this subject too much.' ‡ The critics represent a substantial segment of business opinion. Many industrialists feel it is

* Arthur K. Watson is now the U.S. ambassador to France.
† The IBM subsidiary responsible for the company's non-U.S. interests.
‡ *Business Week*, 14 June 1969.

dangerous to discuss the implications of the rapid growth of international companies in public. They argue that it tends to alarm governments and public opinion, and will therefore provoke political action that will be harmful to their interests.

They prefer to argue that international companies have a long history, and that, despite their rapid growth in the postwar period, the novelty of the present situation is being exaggerated by politicians and writers. They have plenty of ammunition to draw on. Banking has been conducted on international lines since the Middle Ages; some academics trace the origins of international trading companies back to the Mesopotamians, and even if that thesis is rejected it is true that the East India Company, which at one time ruled India, was established in the reign of Elizabeth I; in the nineteenth century companies from Britain, the U.S., and several European countries were conducting huge international trading operations, while others were running public utilities, such as tramways, and gas and electricity undertakings in foreign countries; also in the nineteenth century companies from several countries, notably Britain and the U.S., exploited the raw material and natural resources of Latin America, Asia, Africa, and Australia on a vast scale; from about 1860 onwards manufacturing companies began to establish production facilities outside their own countries, and by 1914 many of today's giants were already operating in several countries.

International companies are certainly not a new phenomenon. But to list these examples is to evade the issue.* The

* Comparisons are also sometimes drawn between the enormous international investments of Britain in the nineteenth century, and those of U.S. and other international companies today. These are based on a misconception.

Britain was indeed an enormous foreign investor, and at the outbreak of the First World War its overseas investments amounted to some £4,000m. compared with about £1,200m. for Germany, and £600m. for the U.S. But international companies comparable with those whose operations are discussed in this book played a negligible role in this total.

present situation is quite different from the past, and it is important to be clear about those differences.

The most striking characteristic of the modern multinational company is its central direction. However large it may be, and however many subsidiaries it may have scattered across the globe, all its operations are coordinated from the centre. Despite frequent assertions to the contrary, the subsidiaries are not run as separate enterprises each of which has to stand on its own feet. They must all work within a framework established by an overall group plan drawn up at headquarters, and their activities are tightly integrated with each other. They are judged not by their individual performance, but by the contribution they make to the group as a whole. Thus a subsidiary which records a loss but whose operations prevent a rival from moving into one of its parent company's more profitable markets may be fulfilling a more valuable task than a subsidiary with a better financial record.

Central direction of this sort only became possible in the last two decades. It depends for its effectiveness on rapid and reliable air travel, an efficient telephone, telegraph, and telex system, and computers capable of handling a mass of information. When trans-Atlantic and trans-European journeys

Some forty per cent of the British investments were in the shares of foreign or imperial railway companies, thirty per cent in government and municipal bonds, ten per cent in raw materials, and eight per cent in banking and finance. These were portfolio investments undertaken for the purpose of financial gain. They did not involve control of the operations in question, as the history of the U.S. railroad companies, much of whose stock was owned by Britons, so amply demonstrates. Nor did they evolve ownership of physical assets, except in cases of default. Contemporary international companies, by contrast, make direct investments, which means they establish or take over subsidiaries and factories in foreign countries which they own and control.

Portfolio investment still flourishes on a very large scale, as the enormous European holdings on Wall Street, and huge investments by Britons and Americans in Australian shares, show. But there is all the difference in the world between buying shares in a foreign company, and establishing a subsidiary in a foreign country.

took several days, and most communications were by letter, it was impossible. Subsidiaries had to be left with a large measure of independence, and their operations had to be kept separate. Each was established to serve its local market, not as a link in an integrated network.

Another factor preventing closer integration, especially between the wars, was the absence of any commonly accepted set of rules governing international trade. Countries signed separate and often mutually exclusive trade agreements with each other. Thus a factory in one country might be used to supply components to a plant in another, but it could not do so on the same terms to a plant in a third. As a result of the establishment soon after the war of the General Agreement on Tariffs and Trade (GATT), to which all but the Communist countries subscribe, this problem has been immeasurably reduced.

After central direction, the most notable feature of the modern multinational companies is their importance, which is increasing all the time, in the industrial and economic life of the most powerful nations. This is shown by their leading positions in key manufacturing industries, and their influence on the flow of trade among developed countries. In the past the main impact of international companies, except in banking, insurance, and finance, was felt in the colonial and semi-colonial territories. The companies themselves were generally involved in trade, the running of public utilities, or the exploitation of raw materials through mining, plantation, and ranching ventures. In the more advanced countries the role of international companies was very small until after the Second World War, as the figures for U.S. direct investment in Europe show. In 1929 their total book value, including ventures of every sort, amounted to only $1,400m.; by 1946 it had fallen to $1,000m. Then came the post-war boom, and by 1969 it had risen to $21,554m., of which manufacturing companies accounted for $12,225m., and oil companies for $4,805m.*

* Department of Commerce.

The vast and rapid expansion of the last twenty years has brought momentous changes in its train. In the past it was a characteristic of an independent country that the most powerful economic interests in the state – at first the great landowners and later the great manufacturing companies – should be citizens. Today these interests may just as easily be foreign-owned, and even if they are domestically owned they may have interests and commitments abroad that are greater than those they have at home.

The forerunners of the modern multinationals began to expand beyond their home countries in significant numbers in the 1860s. Among the pioneers was Friedrich Bayer, who took a share in an aniline plant at Albany in New York State in 1865, two years after establishing his chemical company near Cologne. In 1866 the Swedish inventor of dynamite, Alfred Nobel, set up an explosives plant in Hamburg. In 1867 the U.S. Singer sewing machine company built its first overseas factory in Glasgow. Singer was the first company to manufacture and to mass-market a product in basically the same form and bearing the same name across the world. It has the strongest claim to be regarded as the first of the multinationals.

Each company that went abroad in search of higher profits had its own particular reason for doing so. But there were a number of factors that influenced them all. Industrial enterprises were becoming larger, and mass markets were beginning to develop. The improvement in transportation and communications through the development of the steamship, railways and the telegraph drew the attention of manufacturers to foreign opportunities, and made it possible for them to exercise some control over distant subsidiaries. They discovered that it could be cheaper to manufacture in a foreign market near the final consumer than to do so at home and pay the cost of shipment. It was for this reason that Bayer decided to invest in the U.S. and Singer in Scotland.

The spirit of nationalism also played a part. Companies

began to realize that it was often more effective to supply local needs through local managements who understood their customers far better than an export manager in the home office. Direct pressures of various sorts emphasized this point. The U.S. Westinghouse Airbrake was induced to establish manufacturing facilities in France because of stipulations in railway contracts that supplies had to be made locally. Edison built a plant in Germany because it found that 'national feeling' resulted in local suppliers receiving preference over imports. In addition governments could in effect force importers to set up local plants by insisting that patents should be worked in order to maintain their validity.

However the most important reason for the growth of international companies in the last thirty years of the nineteenth century was the spread of protectionism, itself a manifestation of nationalism. Except in Britain, then the world's leading manufacturing and exporting nation, governments everywhere introduced tariffs in order to reduce imports of manufactured goods, and to foster the growth of local industries. Sometimes the tariffs were specifically designed to encourage foreign companies to invest in the country concerned. This was the case in Canada where the government wanted U.S. companies to establish local plants rather than supply its market from over the border. More usually the object was to encourage the local citizens themselves to create new industries. But as there were no currency restrictions and few regulations preventing foreigners from establishing factories if they wished to do so, the more tariffs were imposed the more international business tended to become.

The effect tariffs could have on a company's thinking was explained in 1902 by William Lever (later Lord Leverhulme), the founder of the Lever Brothers soap empire: 'The question of erecting works in another country,' he said, 'is dependent upon the tariff or duty. The amount of duties we pay on soap imported into Holland and Belgium is

considerable, and it only requires that these shall rise to such a point that we could afford to pay a separate staff of managers with a separate plant to make soap to enable us to see our way to erect works in those countries. When the duty exceeds the cost of separate managers and separate plants, then it will be an economy to erect works in the country that our customers can be more cheaply supplied from them.' *
Other companies responded to tariffs in the same way. In 1887 Bismarck introduced a tariff designed to protect German agrarian interests against imported food, and to encourage a German margarine industry. Within a year the large Dutch margarine manufacturer, Jurgens, had built a factory in Germany, and by 1914 Jurgens and Van den Berghs, the other principal Dutch margarine company, each had seven factories in Germany. High import duties also prompted Bayer to set up dyestuffs factories in Moscow in 1876, at Flers in France in 1882, and at Schoonaerde in Belgium in 1908.

Most of the leading European countries had companies of their own involved in the new move, but from quite an early stage U.S. companies began to play a particularly prominent role. In the 1880s and early 1890s the U.S. went through a period of intense industrial concentration. Over 5,000 companies were consolidated into about 300 trusts, and, although a great many small companies remained, these giants dominated the industrial scene. Some, such as Standard Oil, United States Steel, and International Harvester, are still household names today. Most had no desire to extend their activities beyond North America, except to export their surplus products and to secure raw materials, but those that did provided formidable opposition to the Europeans.

They knew how to think and plan on a much larger scale. Their management was frequently more efficient, and because of their large profits at home they could afford to allow a foreign subsidiary to run at a loss while it established its

* *The History of Unilever*, Volume 1, by Charles Wilson (Cassell).

position. When a U.S. company went abroad it often did so in a massive fashion. In 1901 the British were surprised to learn that the local American-owned Westinghouse factory was the largest single industrial plant in the country. John D. Rockefeller's Standard Oil was the largest oil company in Europe, and by 1914 Ford was producing a quarter of the cars made in Britain.

Moreover the American emphasis on research and innovation coupled with the high cost of American labour often meant that the U.S. secured a lead over other countries in some of the most technically advanced industries of the period, such as telephones, heavy electrical equipment, sewing machines, and cars. Many of these had been invented in Europe, but were first mass-produced in the U.S. The result was that Europeans and others frequently went to American companies with suggestions that they establish a foreign subsidiary. The early expansion of the Ford Motor Company occurred in this way. Within a year of its establishment in 1903 Henry Ford was approached by the Canadian Gordon MacGregor with a proposal for a Canadian subsidiary, and in 1906 the British Perceval Perry went to Dearborn with a scheme for a British Ford Company. These approaches enabled Ford to build up its overseas network far more quickly than if it had to rely entirely on its own efforts.

The movement across the Atlantic was both ways. Some European companies secured very important positions in the U.S. By the outbreak of the First World War, to take only three examples, the British Courtaulds dominated the new and rapidly expanding U.S. rayon industry through its subsidiary the Viscose Company (later and better known as the American Viscose Corporation), that dynamic Dutchman Henri Deterding had established Royal Dutch Shell as a force to be reckoned with in the oil industry, and Lever Brothers was prominent in soap. In dyestuffs, the forerunner of much of the modern chemical industry, the U.S. producers were hopelessly outweighed by the Germans and to a lesser extent the Swiss. U.S. producers supplied only about ten per cent of their own domestic market, and even for this small output they imported about ninety per cent of their intermediates.

In both the U.S. and Europe foreign companies aroused controversy. But the U.S. was so large that beyond their particular industries foreigners did not make a great impact on public opinion. In Europe, by contrast, the U.S. companies by virtue of their size in relation to the markets aroused widespread fears. In 1902 F. A. McKenzie wrote: 'America has invaded Europe not with armed men, but with manufactured goods. Its leaders have been captains of industry and skilled financiers whose conquests are having a profound effect on the lives of the masses from Madrid to St Petersburg.' Nothing, he felt, was safe before this onslaught: 'Our aristocracy marry American wives, and their coachmen are giving place to American-trained drivers of American-built automobiles. ... Our babies are fed on American foods, and our dead are buried in American coffins.' * McKenzie was referring as much to the flood of imports from the U.S. as to the establishment of U.S. subsidiaries in Europe. But his outcry was to be the forerunner of many similar attacks on American business abroad down to the publication in 1967 of Jean-Jacques Servan-Schreiber's *Le Défi Americain*.

By 1914 the concept of the international company was firmly established. This was especially true of those industries, such as cars, oil, chemicals, and aluminium, which are so important today. But the scale of the international companies' operations in relation to total economic activity in the industrialized countries was very small. In what were then the most important industries – coal, railways, iron and steel, engineering, shipbuilding, textiles, and above all agriculture and agricultural products – international companies played an insignificant role. All the main companies in the

* *The American Invaders* by F. A. McKenzie (Grant Richards, 1902).

leading countries were locally owned. Relevant figures are almost impossible to produce since countries drew no distinction between direct and indirect investment in their statistics. But it has been estimated by Professor John Dunning that in 1914 ninety per cent of all international capital movements took the form of portfolio investment* by individuals and financial institutions, whereas today seventy-five per cent of the capital outflows of the leading industrialized nations are in the form of direct investment by companies.† Another indication of the small scale of pre-First World War direct investment is that in 1914 Britain, the main recipient of U.S. investment, had only 12,000 people employed by U.S.-owned companies.‡

During the inter-war period a number of companies continued to expand their international interests. They were mostly in the new technologically advanced industries of the day, or producers of goods for which there was a mass consumer demand. General Motors and Ford were particularly active in establishing manufacturing facilities in Europe and elsewhere, while the oil companies created petrol distribution networks to keep pace with the growth in car ownership. Hoover, Remington Rand, and Procter & Gamble all crossed the Atlantic in this period, and by 1939 more than half the employees of the Dutch Philips Electrical were outside Holland. Another notable international investor was the German IG Farben chemical trust. Initially in the 1920s it set out to recover as much as possible of Germany's pre-war position in the industry after the expropriations and sequestrations of the allies. In the 1930s it went on to become the most powerful chemical company in the world. But the trend was not all one way. Many companies disposed of

*For an explanation of the difference between portfolio and direct investment, see the footnote on pages 30–31.

† 'The Multinational Enterprise: Some Economic and Conceptual Issues.' Speech by Professor John Dunning at a conference on the multinational enterprise held at Reading University, 28–30 May 1970.

‡ *The American Take-Over of Britain* by James McMillan and Bernard Harris (Leslie Frewin).

their international interests to concentrate on their domestic markets.

In the inter-war years conditions were not favourable for a rapid expansion of international direct investment, or the growth of international companies. There were many factors to discourage the expansionist. What might be described as 'war psychology' was the most pervasive. People were not only living in the shadow of the 1914–18 holocaust, they also believed for most of the period that another war of some sort would probably break out. This simultaneously deterred companies from investing abroad, while encouraging governments to aim for industrial self-sufficiency and to discriminate against foreigners.

Nationalism was strongest in Nazi Germany where the government required companies to 'swear' that they were 'pure German', and not under 'foreign, Jewish or Marxist' control. But it was to be found everywhere. In the U.S. the American Viscose Corporation, which was the world's largest rayon producer and owned by Courtaulds, was hounded in Congress and the Press until in 1941 the U.S. Government insisted that it should be sold at a knock-down price as a condition of lend-lease aid to Britain. In France, when the Czech Bata company wished to construct a shoe factory, the Poullen Law of 22 March 1936 was passed forbidding the opening of new factories or ateliers for shoe manufacturing, or the enlargement of existing ones.

The currency situation was another major deterrent to international investment. Before 1914 currencies were based on gold, funds could be moved easily from one country to another, and inflation was not a serious problem. After the war chaos took the place of certainty. In Germany and Austria in the early 1920s inflation reached the point where money became worthless. Nowhere else was it so bad, but every country suffered to some extent. Inflations were followed by deflations, currencies lacked confidence, and exchange controls began to appear.

Finally there was the Great Depression, which brought

The Multinationals

with it a catastrophic decline in the level of world trade and
sent company profits tumbling like the walls of Jericho. In
the light of all these factors it is perhaps surprising that
international companies were able to expand as much as
they did.

The most characteristic form of international industrial
enterprise in the inter-war period was the cartel. There were
many variations on this theme from a straightforward exchange of information on prices and investments at one end
of the scale to common marketing arrangements at the
other. The specific aims of each cartel varied, but the
underlying objective of all was to maintain prices and profits, and to provide some mechanism whereby companies
could reconcile their conflicting interests without loss of
blood. Inevitably this tended to reduce the level of investment undertaken by companies in the markets of their
rivals.

As Adam Smith, the father of economics, pointed out in
the eighteenth century, businessmen have an instinctive
preference for curtailing competition rather than for intensifying it. Cartels may be found anywhere, and at any time,
and they still exist today. But in the inter-war period conditions were particularly ripe for their development on an
international scale. Industrialists were worried about excess
capacity. In many industries they had expanded their factories during the war only to find that after an initial boom
the level of post-war demand was lower than they required.
With the onset of the Great Depression the problem of over-
capacity grew worse. At the same time the number of large
companies involved in most industries was quite small owing
to the rise of great monoliths incorporating many smaller
concerns that had taken place through the industrial concentration of the preceding decades. It was obviously much
easier for the British Imperial Chemical Industries (ICI),
the German IG Farben, and the U.S. Du Pont and Allied
Chemical to reach understandings with each other than it
would have been for the plethora of British, German, and

U.S. chemical concerns that had been absorbed into those giants.

To the men who ran the monoliths the concentration of a particular industry within one country was frequently regarded as merely the first step towards an agreement with similar concerns abroad. The founders of ICI (established in 1926) certainly took this view. A Du Pont official recorded for his company's confidential files the following account of a conversation with ICI's chairman Sir Harry (later Lord) McGowan: 'Sir Harry . . . went on to give me a general picture of what he and Sir Alfred Mond (another of ICI's founders) had in mind in the matter of international agreements . . . Sir Harry explained that the formation of ICI is only the first step in a comprehensive scheme which he has in mind to rationalize the chemical manufacture of the world. The details of such a scheme are not worked out, not even in Sir Harry's own mind, but the broad picture includes working arrangements between three groups – the IG in Germany, Imperial Chemical Industries in the British Empire, and Du Ponts and Allied Chemical and Dye in America. The next step in the scheme is an arrangement of some sort between the Germans and the British.' *

The first international cartels were formed well before 1914. One of the earliest documented examples is in the aluminium industry in which the U.S. Alcoa and the Swiss AIAG reached an agreement in 1896. In 1901 this was expanded to include three other producers. Also before the war the Nobel Dynamite Trust, which at that time had subsidiaries in Britain and Germany, the German Vereinigte Koln-Rottweiler Pulverfabriken and Du Pont formed an explosives cartel to divide world markets between them. However it was not until after 1918 that the cartels became really widespread. At one time or another they were to be found in practically every major industry.

Sometimes their internal arrangements were so extensive

* *Cartels in Action* by George W. Stocking and Myron W. Watkins (The Twentieth Century Fund).

and the degree of cooperation demanded from their members so far-reaching that, on paper, the scope of their activities looks much the same as that of an international company with subsidiaries in several different countries. But the modern international company is a highly coordinated, disciplined, and integrated form of organization. The cartels, by contrast, tended to break down under stress, and the members often failed to fulfil their obligations to each other.

In the first steel cartel, established in 1926, the main steel-producing companies of Germany, Luxembourg, Belgium, the Saar, and France, undertook, in effect, to pool their interests. It was agreed that each country should be allotted production and export quotas, and that those members who exceeded their limits should be fined. To contemporaries the formation of the cartel seemed an event of great historical significance. A representative of the U.S. Department of Commerce in London said: 'The conclusion of the European steel agreement has been hailed by some of its sponsors as the greatest recent economic development and the first step towards the formation of an "Economic United States of Europe".' *

These high hopes were quickly shattered. The Germans were suffering from an enormous over-capacity, and exceeded their export quotas from the start. In the first year of the cartel their fines amounted to the equivalent of $10m., which was ninety-five per cent of the total penalties incurred by all the members. This situation could not endure, and by mid-1931 the cartel had collapsed.

A second arrangement was started in 1933 to which the British, Americans, Czechs, Poles, and Austrians in due course adhered as well as the original members. A central management group consisting of representatives from each country was set up, and another representative committee dealt with the export and sale of the various products (bars, rods, structural shapes, and the like). The exports of each country were determined centrally, and all export sales

* *Cartels in Action.*

were made through the central organization. Distributors in the importing countries were licensed and guaranteed both a fixed profit margin, and a share of their local market. This cartel was more successful than its predecessor. Prices rose throughout the duration of its life. But this was at least partly due to the revival of business conditions in general, and to the fact that the German rearmament programme meant that the German companies no longer had to fight for exports.

The oil cartel was officially formed in 1928 when Shell, Anglo-Persian (now British Petroleum), and Standard Oil (New Jersey), the three largest oil companies in international trade, agreed to combine their non-U.S. interests, and to share each other's facilities. In various markets this offer was extended to other companies, and usually accepted, even by the Russian export agency. The cartel members agreed to charge common prices, and not to steal each other's customers. At one time they even agreed to coordinate their advertising, and to submit their individual plans to a joint committee. These commitments undoubtedly inhibited competition, and helped maintain prices at a higher level than would otherwise have been the case. But it is significant that the rules were broken so often that four separate agreements had to be signed. Even in Sweden, where there was a relatively small market, few companies, and unusually close cooperation, Shell estimated that the cartel never achieved more than fifty or sixty per cent effectiveness.

The less ambitious cartels fared no better. In 1927 Courtaulds, and the leading rayon producers in Germany, Italy, Holland, Switzerland, France, and Belgium reached an agreement for limiting exports to the U.S. in order to maintain prices there. Within months it was broken. When the Depression began in 1929–30 the rayon companies put forward ambitious plans for exchanging information on all their activities and setting sales quotas. But as soon as business began to revive in 1933 these were forgotten.

In all industries the desire of management to increase sales at the expense of the other companies always remained stronger than the desire to cooperate when it actually came to the point of having to choose between securing a contract and making a sacrifice for the common good. It also proved impossible to devise rules to which the members of the cartel would adhere in bad times as well as in good, and which could be enforced at law.*

Another weakness of the cartels was that companies were not sufficiently tightly organized for the central management always to know what its subsidiaries were doing. In 1936 my father, Dr Georg Tugendhat, and Dr Franz Kind started an independent refining company in Britain called Manchester Oil Refinery. This was contrary to the interests of the cartel, and a leading figure in Shell warned them that they would not be able to secure supplies. However, without much difficulty they found an American broker, who dealt in crude oil on a wholesale basis, and he provided them with cargoes purchased from the Shell subsidiary in the U.S. The major companies also tried to prevent Manchester Oil Refinery from selling its output in Britain, and this problem was circumvented when the Belgian subsidiary of Gulf Oil, another cartel member, agreed to buy it.†

For all their deficiencies the cartels were a step in the evolution of today's multinational companies. They gave industrialists a training in international cooperation. They also gave them an understanding of national differences, and of the need to modify business practices to take these into account. Instead of thinking primarily in terms of supplying their home markets, and exporting surpluses, they became accustomed to approaching the problems of their industries on a world basis. These lessons were to prove extremely useful in the changed conditions of the post-war world, especially to the Americans.

* For further details see Appendix.
† For full details of the pre-war international oil cartel see *Oil: The Biggest Business* by Christopher Tugendhat (Eyre and Spottiswoode).

2. The American Invasion

The period since the end of the Second World War has seen a complete transformation from the situation prevailing between the wars. It has been marked by an explosive expansion in international direct investment, which for much of the time has been rising at twice the rate of the world gross national product. The international company with subsidiaries in many countries is no longer a rarity; it is well on the way to becoming the characteristic industrial organization of the age.

The Americans are mainly responsible for the change. Between 1946 and 1969 the book value of their foreign direct investments rose from $7,200m. to $70,763m. As a result U.S. companies now account for an estimated sixty per cent to sixty-five per cent of all foreign direct investment. The balance between European interests in the U.S. and U.S. interests in Europe has been completely upset. Until 1956 European companies' holdings in the U.S. exceeded those of U.S. companies in Europe. In 1957 the Americans went ahead when the value of their European direct investments reached $4,151m. compared with European investments in the U.S. of $3,753m. Since then Europe has been left far behind. At the end of 1969 the book value of the U.S. stake in Europe was $21,554m., while that of Europe in the U.S. was only $8,510m.*

Few U.S. companies can claim the same depth of experience or range of interests as the largest and the longest established European international companies. For all their talk of multinationalism, and despite such remarks as one by

*Department of Commerce.

the President of Dow Chemical Europe, that Dow is 'a global company whose headquarters happen to be in Midland, Michigan,'* they are usually firmly American in ownership, management, and the outlook of their executives. The great majority are still dependent primarily on the U.S. market, and it is rare to find non-Americans in senior positions at headquarters. None the less they have been the principal agents in the creation of a new international business structure in which European and other companies will have to live for as far ahead as can be seen. It is a structure in which large companies must think in world terms.

The revolutionary improvement in communications of every sort has done much to make this possible. With the aid of the jet aeroplane and modern telecommunications the head office of an international company can coordinate and control the activities of its foreign subsidiaries to a degree that would previously have been unthinkable. It is necessary to give only two examples to illustrate this point. Ford has linked its engineering centres in Britain and Germany to Detroit by telephone cable so that the designers in those countries can use the head office computer facilities; while IBM has over three hundred international communications centres through which more than ten thousand teletyped messages pass every day. A critical limitation on the growth of human organizations is the ability of the centre to control and coordinate the extremities. During the last twenty-five years the abilities of international companies in this respect have been extended enormously. It is difficult to over-estimate the importance of this development in contributing to their growth.†

*Herbert Doan, as quoted in *Time*, 29 December 1967.

† Professor Raymond Vernon has pointed out ('Economic Sovereignty at Bay', *Foreign Affairs*, October 1968) that between 1953 and 1965 the arrivals and departures of international travellers in North America and Europe grew at the rate of about ten per cent a year. Over this period U.S. direct investment in other advanced countries rose at the same rate. He suggests that there is a direct relationship between these two figures.

The world itself has changed as dramatically as its communications. Throughout the post-war era political and economic conditions have, in contrast with the inter-war years, favoured the growth of international direct investment and international companies. World trade has increased steadily from year to year, and, despite occasional alarms and recessions, there have been no major setbacks comparable with the Great Depression. In every industrialized country, and in many others as well, the standard of living has risen rapidly. In these circumstances companies have felt encouraged to undertake new investments, and to seek to open up new markets instead of worrying about how to protect their existing interests.

At the same time the economies of the non-Communist countries have been brought much closer together than in the inter-war years so that it has become much easier to expand abroad. Through the General Agreement on Tariffs and Trade (GATT) nations have accepted a common set of principles to govern their international trade instead of negotiating mutually exclusive trading agreements with each other. Despite frequent backsliding they have also been consistently dedicated to removing tariff and other non-tariff barriers to trade. These two factors opened the way to the establishment of inter-related plants in different countries, whereas under the old system it was only practical to establish foreign plants to serve their own local national markets. The trend towards inter-related plants has been considerably helped by the formation of the European Economic Community and the European Free Trade Area within which companies can operate on a continental scale formerly possible only in the U.S. It is not only the opportunities for international direct investment that have improved since the war. The attitude of governments towards foreign-owned companies has also changed. The old aim of industrial self-sufficiency has been largely forgotten. Central governments and local authorities are now obsessed with the need to achieve a high level of industrial investment and a low level of unemployment. Ever since 1945 they have been competing with each other in their efforts to persuade international companies to help them.

From the outset U.S.-owned companies were better placed than others to take advantage of the post-war changes. In the early years most of their rivals were either completely or partially destroyed. The world was crying out for American goods, and dependent on American financial aid. Although Europe began to recover very quickly, U.S. companies continued to enjoy immense advantages until at least the early 1960s. In many industries they were able to seize the leading positions, and they still set the tone in which much of international business takes place.

For many years European governments were so short of foreign exchange that it was very difficult for European companies to invest abroad at all. They had to seek permission from their parent governments, and support their applications with a wealth of evidence to show that the proposed investment would promote exports from the parent country. Even then it was difficult to secure. In its 1954 annual report the German chemical company, Hoechst, expressed the view that, 'Experience has shown that the success of the export drive has become dependent to an increasing extent on the support of local manufacturing plants controlled by the company.' Yet when Bayer, another of the German chemical giants, wanted to invest in the U.S. it could not transfer funds direct from Germany, but had to raise the money in Switzerland. It was only with great difficulty that it managed to persuade the Bundesbank to allow it to provide a guarantee of repayment.

Only Britain was able to make much headway. In the U.S., the Commonwealth, and the Middle East in particular, it began with a substantial existing base. By retaining profits where they were earned rather than repatriating them to Britain the companies concerned were able to expand. But British companies too faced huge problems in persuading the authorities to allow new operations to be established in Europe or elsewhere for which money had to be raised at home.

Not until 1958 did most European currencies become convertible again, and it was only in about 1960 that it became apparent that the rest of the world's shortage of dollars had come to an end. Since then foreign investment has become much easier, but most governments continue to restrain capital outflows for balance of payments reasons. This is true to some extent even within the Common Market, although the Treaty of Rome laid down that there should be free capital movements between members.

U.S. companies were not only free to invest abroad when others were not, they were positively encouraged to do so. The U.S. Government hoped that a flow of company investment funds would reduce the level of official loans and grants needed to launch Europe's economic recovery. It exhorted companies to go overseas, and took practical steps to help them by negotiating double taxation agreements with a large number of governments, and by guaranteeing their investments against restraints on the repatriation of profits. The European governments, for their part, welcomed the U.S. investor as an invaluable helper in the task of rebuilding their war-shattered economies. Some established offices in the U.S. in order to attract American companies to their countries, and most offered financial inducements and tax incentives of various sorts. The import controls operated by most governments provided a further inducement to the more daring U.S. companies since a company which built a local plant in a country with import controls could capture a larger share of the market than one that relied on shipments from the U.S.

At first progress was slow. Companies were happy to invest in Canada, which was near, politically stable, and prosperous. But Europe was another matter. The Soviet threat, political instability, and closer government regulation of economic and industrial affairs than was customary in North America combined to deter many companies from crossing the Atlantic. It needed time for businessmen to accept that Europe's recovery was firmly based, and its growth potential worth taking risks for. For many years Britain attracted most attention. There were several reasons for this. U.S. assets there had emerged relatively unscathed from the war, its politics were more stable than the continent's, the lack of a language barrier made it easier for American executives to find their way around, and an investment in Britain provided the additional bonus of access to Commonwealth markets on preferential terms. So Britain secured more U.S. direct investment than the six Common Market countries combined, and it was not until 1963 that it lost its overall lead.

The formation of the European Economic Community, or Common Market, in 1957 had a decisive impact on the attitude of U.S. companies towards investing in Europe. Between 1957 and 1962 the value of their holdings more than doubled, and between 1962 and 1967 they did so again. At the same time the emphasis switched from Britain to the Six. U.S. companies saw that if the hopes of the signatories to the Treaty of Rome were fulfilled another continental market similar in scope to the U.S. would be created. They would be able to use there all the techniques for large-scale production and distribution which they had developed at home. They saw too that its success would have the double effect of enlarging the market for the individual producer within the Community, while discriminating against U.S. exports in favour of sales from Community plants. It therefore became more attractive to locate a plant in the Community than it ever had been to put one in an individual member country. The formation of the Community also convinced many American businessmen that Europe would combine political stability with economic expansion. They assumed that it was the first step on the road to a united Europe. The European Free Trade Area (EFTA) was regarded as another move in the same direction, and welcome in itself inasmuch as it created another large trading area for manufactured goods. If Britain had joined the Common Market in the early 1960s it would have remained the most favoured location for U.S. investment, but as hopes that this was imminent declined so the weight of U.S. investment shifted towards the continent. Another reason was, of course, Britain's disappointing economic performance compared with that of its neighbours.

Europeans were also excited about the formation of the EEC, and believed that it would lead to much closer economic and industrial cooperation between the members. But they were acutely aware of the problems that had to be overcome, and they continued, as they do now, to think primarily in national terms. Americans, by contrast, immediately began to think in terms of 'the European consumer', and 'the European market'. A report* prepared by the American Management Association provides a typical example of this approach. It declared that 'The European consumer ... has deep-rooted traditions and displays a degree of distrust toward new equipment and techniques,' and that 'another "notable" characteristic is the European's general distrust of the written word'. It asked, 'What, generally speaking, is the European's motivation?' To Europeans themselves, accustomed to thinking of national frontiers as representing cultural as well as political divides, this sort of generalization appears absurd. It can also lead to gross misjudgements of how an individual market is likely to react to a product that has already been tested in another. None the less it has helped U.S. companies to think big about Europe in a way that Europeans have found impossible. This, in turn, has enabled them to see and take advantage of opportunities that European companies either failed to see, or were afraid to go for.

Most of the U.S. investments in the 1940s and 1950s and the greater part of those in the 1960s were made by the larger companies. This is not really surprising. Some of them, such

* American Management Association report number 18, entitled *The European Common Market*, New York, 1958.

as Standard Oil (New Jersey), better known as Esso, General Motors, and Ford had been well established in Europe before the war. They were the first to see the new opportunities that were opening up, and other large companies were not far behind. Smaller companies were slower to react, and when they wanted to they found it harder to arrange the necessary finance than their bigger rivals.

Other considerations must also be taken into account. In 1965 the economist Stephen Hymer drew attention* to the relationship between oligopolistic market structures in the U.S. and the foreign investment activities of U.S. companies. He pointed out that forty-four per cent of the principal U.S. foreign investors came from industries where four companies supply three-quarters of the total sales, although those industries accounted for only eight per cent of the value of U.S. industrial output. At the same time only one of the seventy-two firms classified as major foreign investors came from an industry where the four largest companies supplied less than a quarter of the total sales.

In an oligopolistic market it becomes increasingly difficult for the leading companies to capture a larger share of the total sales. Each additional percentage point in a company's share of the market becomes more expensive to secure than the one before. The easiest way to grow is through the acquisition of rival concerns. But if the rivals are all about the same size this is frequently impossible. Even when it is practical it is very expensive. Moreover the Department of Justice has, since the war, become progressively more reluctant to allow mergers or takeovers by large companies of each other that would reduce competition. Consequently foreign expansion has offered companies in oligopolistic industries the best prospects for further growth.

* 'Direct Foreign Investment and International Oligopoly' by Stephen Hymer, June 1965 (mimeographed).

For a further discussion of this point see 'American Direct Investments in the Common Market' by Bela Balassa. (*Banco Nazionale del Lavoro Quarterly Review*, June 1966.)

The Department of Justice has also done much to encourage competition in foreign markets. Between the wars U.S. companies, often through their Canadian and other subsidiaries, played a prominent role in the international cartels. During the late 1930s and 1940s the U.S. Government hardened its attitude and policies against this sort of activity. The anti-trust laws were tightened up, and government agencies took steps to publicize cartel arrangements in such a way as to make it very difficult for them to be re-formed. In the case of oil, for instance, the Federal Trade Commission published a document in 1952 called the International Petroleum Cartel, which showed with a wealth of detail how the international oil companies had contrived to maintain high prices and to reduce competition before the war and afterwards.

The Department of Justice made full use of its powers and the opportunities they provided to attack a variety of arrangements that smacked of cartelism. One of the earlier cases concerned titanium pigment, the manufacture of which was based on three independent inventions. National Lead and Du Pont each had certain rights with respect to these inventions, and had used these rights to divide world markets between them. In the case of United States v. National Lead Company, the company was forced to divest itself of interests in four foreign titanium companies, and both National Lead and Du Pont were directed to grant non-exclusive licences to any interested party, U.S. or foreign.

In the case of United States v. Aluminium Company of America (Alcoa) the shareholders and directors of Alcoa were forced to divest themselves of the fifty-one per cent stake they held in the Canadian Aluminium Limited after the court had decided that the Canadian company's involvement in the pre-war aluminium cartel had affected the U.S. import trade. As a result of the case of United States v. Imperial Chemical Industries that company and Du Pont were forced to break up a joint company in Canada, and to dissolve a long-standing agreement for exchanging patents and technical information and allocating markets. These cases and several others were decided between 1945 and 1952. They showed that no company, large or small, U.S. or otherwise, could become involved in a cartel without running the risk of falling foul of the Department of Justice. So for a U.S. company that wanted to operate on an international scale there was no longer any chance of avoiding the enormous cost involved in foreign investment by forming a cosy alliance with foreign competitors.

The big companies who led the way after the war are still by far the most important U.S. investors in Europe. Indeed it comes as something of a shock to discover how few of them control how much. It was estimated in 1967 that forty per cent of all U.S. direct investments in France, West Germany, and Britain belonged to Standard Oil (New Jersey), General Motors, and Ford. Altogether two-thirds of the total existing U.S. investment in Western Europe in that year was held by twenty companies.* Another study, conducted in 1969, showed that in the U.K. alone forty per cent of the total U.S. stake was held by five companies, and another forty per cent by twenty-five companies.†

In future the overwhelming preponderance of this small group of giants will diminish as more and more U.S. companies go overseas. Between July 1960 and December 1966, according to one survey,‡ 2,507 U.S. manufacturing companies established about 3,000 new overseas manufacturing facilities and expanded about 1,000 old ones. In 1968 the Department of Commerce stated that 3,300 companies, not all of which are engaged in manufacturing, were reporting to its Office of Foreign Direct Investments. Many of these

* *Transatlantic Investments* by Christopher Layton, Second Edition, January 1968 (The Atlantic Institute).

† *The Role of American Investment in the British Economy* by John H. Dunning. PEP Broadsheet 507, February 1969.

‡ *New Foreign Business Activities of US Firms*, Thirteenth report by Booz, Allen and Hamilton.

are quite small, and their investments tiny. But there is a clear trend towards an ever-increasing internationalization of U.S. industry.

During the 1950s and even more in the 1960s Europe's growth potential was attracting a growing number of U.S. companies. This was particularly true of those industries regarded as characteristically American, such as cars, consumer durables, sophisticated plant and machinery, oil, and chemicals. When the post-war boom in the U.S. had worn itself out and the local markets for these products seemed to be nearing saturation point, it became harder to achieve impressive increases in sales, wages were rising, and profits difficult to find. Europe seemed to provide a way out of the impasse. It was rapidly acquiring U.S.-type tastes, and the demand for goods that U.S. companies could satisfy was insatiable. Between 1950 and 1965 production of motor vehicles in the U.S. rose by 39 per cent compared with nearly 500 per cent in the rest of the non-Communist world, while telephone sales rose by about 100 per cent in the U.S. and 200 per cent outside, to give only two examples.

The first step was to export goods from the U.S., and the next to invest in the countries where they were being sold. The arguments in favour of undertaking the investment instead of relying on sales from home have been well explained by John J. Powers, President and Chief Executive of Chas. Pfizer & Co., a leading chemical and pharmaceutical concern. 'To compete effectively for a good share of any major market,' he argues, 'requires direct investment in the marketplace in the form of sales offices and warehouses and, at least, packaging and assembly plants, if not basic production units. It is just not possible for a mere exporter to become a major long-term factor in a market in this second half of the twentieth century.' * This view is held by executives in many companies. They are convinced that local

* 'The Multinational Company.' A speech by John Powers to the semi-annual meeting and midyear conference of the Manufacturing Chemists' Association, New York, 27 November 1967.

55

plant gives the customers more confidence in a company's long-term ability to provide a service, as distinct from its ability to fulfil a short-term need. It also enables a company to take advantage of a sudden change in the level of demand or in the type of product required by its customers more quickly than a rival whose supply lines extend back to the U.S. In the opinion of most U.S. industrialists, the choice facing a company that has established a position in a foreign market is not between building a local plant or not doing so. It is between building or accepting a slower growth rate than its rivals with such plants, and possibly the complete loss of the market. The dilemma has been neatly expressed by an official of Du Pont: 'Should we choose not to set up a plant ourselves, the void would be filled by a domestic competitor. Hence we have the alternatives of losing business either to a domestic producer or to ourselves. We prefer the latter.' *

Sometimes a local plant is essential if a company is to establish itself at all. In many less developed countries governments insist on a local plant as a condition of entry to the market, or impose such stiff tariffs that local production becomes essential. In industrialized countries governments often pursue the same aim with more subtlety. They demand that buyers whom they can directly influence, such as their own departments, the post office, the armed services, and the public utilities, should buy their equipment only from companies with local plants. They may also make it clear that if a company wants something from the government it had better help the balance of payments by replacing the imports it is bringing into the country by local production. A classic example of this policy in action occurred in Britain in 1964 when the government was allocating licences for the North Sea search for oil and natural gas. These were much sought after by the international oil companies. When the government declared that preference would be given to those

*'Investments in the Common Market' by Bela Balassa. (*The Banco Nazionale del Lavoro Quarterly Review*, June 1966.)

companies which could show the greatest contribution to the country's fuel economy, several announced that they would build refineries so that they could import crude oil instead of the more expensive products that had been refined elsewhere.

Quite apart from pressures of this sort, and the desire to be in a position to take advantage of whatever opportunities may arise, U.S. companies have had sound financial incentives to invest in Europe. At first in the 1950s the rate of return that could be earned on investments in Europe was much higher than in the U.S. It was this prospect which helped to overcome the initial reluctance of many companies to establish themselves in an unknown territory. Wage rates and production costs are still generally lower in Europe than in the U.S., but the boom-time profits have disappeared. The effect of competition on prices has seen to that. However even in those instances where the rate of return on investments in the U.S. and Europe is the same, the company which has established a market position in Europe, or the one wanting to do so, must still invest there. For if it relied on a U.S. plant the combination of tariffs and transport costs would bite deep into its profits.

Once a company has begun to invest in one European country continued growth draws it into establishing plants in several others. This is partly because it sees new ways of taking advantage of the particular strong points of various countries, such as, for instance, the port facilities in Holland and the availability of labour and the investment incentives in Scotland. Another factor is the desire to show the governments of the countries where they sell that they are making a contribution to the local economy through the provision of jobs, the payment of taxes and the building of local plants rather than relying on imports from neighbouring countries. Finally there is the desire not to appear too big in any one place. From long experience in Latin America U.S. companies know that the larger a company is in relation to the local economy the more exposed it becomes to political pressures and nationalistic resentments.

Once the leading companies in an industry have started to invest successfully abroad, great pressure builds up on the second and third rank companies to do the same. There is an element of fashion in this, which should not be disregarded. It can be seen in the way company presidents like to boast about their companies having become multinational. But there are practical reasons as well. As one executive put it: 'Our competitors were going overseas, and we were afraid that they would get a headstart in a potentially rich market, or would acquire a cheap source of supply for possible re-import into the U.S., thus threatening our market position'.* There is a strong feeling in corporate, as in other, circles that if you are doing the same as the crowd and it turns out to be wrong you cannot be blamed, whereas if you stand out against the prevailing trend and you are wrong you will have no defence. In short, once the leaders in an industry start to move overseas, the rest begin to think not so much of the risks inherent in following as of those they will run by not doing so.

Some of the later comers have missed the large rewards of the forerunners and run into a good deal of trouble. In France General Electric lost $47m. in the first forty-two months after taking over the ailing Machines Bull in 1964 in an effort to challenge IBM's position in the European computer market. In 1968 Chrysler's foreign operations provided less than one-eighth of its pre-tax profits, although they accounted for a quarter of its total production and a fifth of its total sales. In Italy Raytheon had its subsidiary's plant in Sicily taken over by the government after it had threatened to close down, and was forced to file a suit for bankruptcy on its behalf.

During the 1970s U.S. companies are unlikely to maintain their phenomenal expansion of the last few years in Europe. The annual increase in U.S. investment abroad reached a peak in 1965, and has been declining since. This is partly

*'The Rewarding Strategies of Multinationals' by Sanford Rose, *Fortune*, 15 September 1968.

because of the restraints imposed by the U.S. Government. But in any case the time has come to pause for breath. The big companies have established a firm base, the Europeans themselves have become much more competitive, and the overall rate of return on U.S. manufacturing investments fell consistently during the years from 1964 to 1967 when it went below ten per cent.

However, even if the pace of the advance is slower the invasion will continue. Most of the influences that set it off are still present, and some are stronger than ever.

The anti-trust division of the Department of Justice is intensifying its activity. In 1969 it declared that it will probably attack any merger involving the top two hundred companies in the country. It will also usually challenge any proposed merger between a company with twenty-five per cent or more of a local market, and a potential entrant into that market. In addition companies are to a greater extent than in the past being forced to divest themselves of subsidiaries acquired several years previously in order to increase competition. It was no coincidence that General Foods Corporation's 1969 attempt to take over the British Rowntree came soon after it had been forced to dispose of its SOS household products subsidiary in the U.S.

Europe is no longer crying out for U.S. investment to rebuild its ruined cities and factories. But European governments are more than ever anxious to develop their depressed areas. The inducements offered to companies to help with this task become more attractive each year, and provinces and towns compete with each other to persuade companies to come into their regions. This was true even of France under de Gaulle. When Fairchild opened a new plant in southern France in 1966, the company said that government and local officials had 'moved heaven and earth to provide us with facilities'.* When Motorola expressed an interest in establishing a European plant the town of Toulouse immediately sent a representative out to the company's head-

* *France Actuelle*, 14 December 1966.

quarters in Arizona, and when company officials arrived in the town they were accorded a civic reception. In Belgium U.S. investment is so important that as soon as the U.S. Government announced its mandatory restrictions on overseas investment in 1968 the Belgian Government started work on a scheme to help U.S. companies find the money they might need for new projects and expansion in Belgium from local and European sources.

The newcomers to Europe and those companies which try to expand primarily through takeovers rather than the development of their existing operations will come from a number of different categories.

Some will be relatively small companies, which live by providing goods and services to larger concerns. A typical example is Eaton Yale and Towne, which manufactures components for the motor industry among other things. Explaining why his company came to Europe, its president, E. M. de Windt, said: 'Originally it was quite simply because our major automotive customers rather strongly suggested that we establish manufacturing facilities in the various countries where they proposed to build trucks and cars, in order to supply them with the same components that they were accustomed to obtaining from us in Detroit – but made by local labour from local materials.' From this beginning it was a logical progression for Eaton Yale and Towne to look for customers among the European car manufacturers, and the company's international activities acquired a life of their own. They 'are now expanding rapidly under their own steam', says de Windt. 'No longer are they considered the "ugly stepsisters" who used to be a constant source of irritation at the domestic plants with their neverending requests for drawings, specifications, and technical assistance.'* Many other companies have been virtually

* 'The role of the multinational company in the world marketplace.' Remarks by E. M. de Windt during a European tour, 1969.

The overseas expansion of U.S. banks, advertising agencies, and law firms can to a great extent be explained in the same way. But their activities are outside the scope of this book.

pushed abroad by their customers in the same way as Eaton Yale and Towne, and more will follow.

Another group will consist of companies exploiting new products or products that have been improved to such an extent that they are regarded as new. European companies are less inventive than the Americans, and, what is more important, they are slower to apply the fruits of scientific research to commercial ends. There are, of course, numerous exceptions to this generalization, but the statistics leave no doubt that a technological gap exists between Europe and the U.S. Some of the most thorough research on this subject has been carried out by the Organization for Economic Cooperation and Development (OECD), which published its results in 1968. These show that U.S.-based companies had the highest rate of 'original innovation' over the previous fifteen to twenty years. 'Of 140 innovations examined,' said the report,* 'they have originated approximately sixty per cent.' This proportion is not wildly out of line with the size of the U.S. economy in relation to that of the other OECD countries combined. But the record of the Americans at commercially exploiting scientific and technological breakthroughs is vastly superior to that of the Europeans. When Professor Joseph Ben-David of the Hebrew University, Jerusalem, conducted a survey† of major industrial innovations, he found that of the inventions behind them, ten had been initiated by Britain, France, and Germany, and nineteen by the U.S. But only seven had been converted into final product innovations by the three European countries as against twenty-two by the U.S.

It is not only in high technology that the U.S. leads. The country provides the largest, richest, and most competitive market in the world for goods of almost every sort. Consequently it is the place where most new products are

---

* *OECD Observer*, April 1968.

† 'Fundamental Research and the Universities.' Some comments on international differences by Joseph Ben-David, OECD, Paris, 1968.

launched, be they enzyme detergents, micro-circuits, copy-
ing machines, or contraceptive pills.

How the book value of U.S. companies' investments in Europe has risen

| | | ($m) | |
Year	Europe Total	EEC Total	UK Total
1950	1·733	637	847
1951	1·979	742	961
1952	2·145	810	1·038
1953	2·369	908	1·131
1954	2·639	1·009	1·257
1955	3·004	1·161	1·426
1956	3·520	1·399	1·612
1957	4·151	1·680	1·899
1958	4·573	1·908	2·058
1959	5·323	2·208	2·475
1960	6·681	2·644	3·194
1961	7·742	3·104	3·523
1962	8·930	3·722	3·805
1963	10·340	4·490	4·172
1964	12·109	5·426	4·457
1965	13·985	6·304	5·123
1966	16·209	7·584	5·657
1967	17·882	8·405	6·101
1968	19·407	9·012	6·694
1969	21·651	10·255	7·190
1970	24·471	11·695	8·015

Source: U.S. Department of Commerce.

At the other extreme from the technological and new
product 'whizz kids' are those companies with long established products, which find that it is cheaper to manufacture
overseas in countries with lower wage and other costs than
the U.S. One such company is Singer, which now sells its
customers approximately three sewing machines produced
abroad for every two produced in the U.S. In 1969 an

executive of a U.S. engineering company considering the takeover of a British concern said that some products could be made in Britain and delivered to the U.S. at three-quarters of the cost of making them in the U.S. itself. The main reason why most U.S. companies have expanded abroad is their desire to <u>capture foreign markets</u>; but in some industries the time may be approaching when companies go abroad in order to establish low cost facilities with which to <u>supply the American market.</u>

Finally it must not be forgotten that one of the most common reasons why one company decides to take over another is the belief that it could do better than the existing management. Better in this context means quite simply transforming a loss into a profit, or a small profit into a larger one. Some of the best European companies have managements that are as good as the best that can be found in the U.S. But the general level in the U.S. is higher. For as long as this remains true U.S. companies will see opportunities for earning money in companies where Europeans are losing it.

3. Europe's Riposte

Whenever Europeans express concern about the rapid rate at which American-owned companies are buying up their industry the standard American answer is that European companies should invest more in the U.S. They argue that for European, or other, governments to place obstacles in the way of the continued expansion of U.S. industrial growth in their countries would be contrary to the interests of both sides, but that if international investment could become more of a two-way traffic all would gain. President Nixon himself argues this case, summoning history to his support. 'As far back as 1791,' he says, 'Alexander Hamilton, our first Secretary of the Treasury, taught us the value of investment from abroad. "Instead of being viewed as a rival", he said, "it ought to be considered as a most valuable auxiliary, conducing to put in motion a greater quantity of productive labor, and a greater portion of useful enterprise, than could exist without it". So by encouraging businessmen from other lands to invest in the United States, we do not establish a new policy. We renew an old invitation. And we continue to follow Hamilton's sound counsel as we say "welcome" and "Invest in the U.S.A.".'*

From Hamilton's death in a duel in 1801 until the outbreak of the First World War foreign money, like foreign immigrants, poured into the U.S. Both were equally vital to the opening up of the West and to the success of the American industrial revolution, which began before the Civil War and gathered momentum after it. But whereas the proportion of British to other immigrants declined

* *Invest in the U.S.A.* (The Department of Commerce , 1969.)

steadily, London remained the principal source of funds. In 1913, the last full year of peace, the value of British investments in the U.S. amounted to £754·6 m. By comparison the German total of £181·9 m. in the U.S. and Canada combined, and the French total of £79·3m. in the U.S., Canada, and Australia combined pale into insignificance.*

Most of these funds were provided by financial institutions, such as banks, and individuals who purchased the stocks and shares of U.S. companies and the bonds issued by the federal and state governments. They were what is known as portfolio investments† undertaken for the purpose of financial gain. They did not involve the direct ownership of physical assets, and the control and management of the companies in question remained firmly in American hands. The U.S. itself was unable to generate sufficient savings to satisfy the enormous capital requirements of its burgeoning industry, and so looked to foreign investors to fill the gap. Although a number of leading European companies, such as the British Courtaulds and Lever Brothers, the Anglo-Dutch Shell, the German Bayer, and the Swiss Hoffmann La Roche, among a host of others, established thriving U.S. subsidiaries, the value of their direct investments in plant, machinery and business facilities was only a fraction of the portfolio investments provided by individuals, banks and investment trusts. For all its reliance on foreign capital, the U.S. retained the ownership and control of the great majority of its major industrial enterprises in the hands of its own citizens.

The pattern established before 1914 remains substantially true today. In rough terms two-thirds of the European investment in the U.S. is composed of purchases by financial

* *The Problem of International Investment.* A report by a Study Group of members of the Royal Institute of International Affairs. (Oxford University Press, 1937.)

† For an explanation of the differences between direct and portfolio investment see the footnote on pages 30–31.

institutions and individuals of the stocks and shares of American owned companies and the bonds issued by the federal and state governments. Only a third is represented by the assets of the subsidiaries of European companies. In global terms the value of European investments in the U.S. is not much smaller than that of the Americans in Europe. But the pattern of the U.S. investments is quite different. Three-quarters of it is accounted for by the assets of the subsidiaries of U.S. companies as against a quarter under the portfolio heading. A striking illustration of the relative sizes of the international activities of U.S. companies on the one hand and companies from other countries on the other is provided by the provisional figures for 1969. During that year overseas expenditure by U.S.-owned companies on new plant and equipment is estimated to have been $12,000m. At the end of the year the total stake held by foreign companies in the U.S. is estimated to have reached that same figure. In other words U.S. companies annually spend abroad as much as the total value of foreign companies' investments in the U.S.

When the U.S. balance of payments was strong, its reserves apparently unlimited, and its dollar untouched by any hint of possible devaluation, the government could face the massive outflow of capital by U.S. companies with equanimity. In today's conditions that is no longer possible. Under President Johnson the government was forced to introduce a number of measures to stem the tide of U.S. investment overseas. But in the words of Johnson Garrett, the Industrial Development Attaché for Europe, 'we do not like restrictive approaches in this field any more than we do on the trade side. We would much prefer to try to build up the Europe-to-U.S. direct investment flow'.*

The U.S. Government wants to encourage foreigners to invest in America not only to offset some of the resentment

* 'Foreign Direct Investment in the United States.' A speech by Garrett to the International Trade Committee of the American Chamber of Commerce in France, 22 November 1966.

against the growth of U.S. companies abroad. It also wants
their money to help its balance of payments. In 1962 the
first official programme for this purpose was launched, and
in 1966 a special office was established in the U.S. Em-
bassy in Paris under Mr Garrett to encourage European
companies to invest in the U.S. Since then the campaign
has been intensified, and several state governments have
opened offices of their own in European capitals.

The U.S. effort to attract foreign industry has coincided
with a growing desire by European companies to invest in
the U.S. In the last few years their interests have expanded
so rapidly that in August 1969 *Business Week* told its readers,
'that after years of watching American companies cover the
world with their investments . . . foreign businessmen are
beginning to turn the tables.'* Jacques G. Maisonrouge,
the Frenchman who is president of IBM's World Trade
Corporation, holds the same opinion. 'The pendulum,' he
says, 'is now swinging the other way.'† It still has a long
way to go before reaching an equilibrium; between 1966
and 1968 the book value of U.S. investments in Europe
rose twice as fast as those of European companies in the U.S.
None the less European companies have recently been making a far bigger impact on the U.S. industrial scene than
ever before.

While the well-established subsidiaries, such as those belonging to Shell, Lever Brothers, British-American Tobacco
and SKF, have been extending their activities, newcomers
have broken in through takeovers, joint ventures, and,
occasionally, the setting up of entirely new enterprises.
Some of the most impressive challenges have come in industries where the Americans have been advancing most
rapidly in Europe. In chemicals, for instance, the German
big three – Hoechst, Bayer, and BASF, whose earlier
investments were expropriated during the war – have

* 16 August 1969.
† 'The Evolution of International Business.' A speech to the American
Bankers' Association, Miami, Florida, 15 May 1968.

The book value of foreign companies' investments in the U.S. in 1970 ($m)

TOTAL	13·209
Canada	3·112
United Kingdom	4·110
Other Europe	5·405
Belgium and Luxembourg	338
France	294
Germany	675
Italy	100
Netherlands	2·121
Sweden	208
Switzerland	1·550
Other countries	119
Japan	233
Latin America	228
Other countries	121

Source: Department of Commerce.

consolidated a bridgehead and are now growing rapidly, following the example of Du Pont and Union Carbide in Europe. In synthetic fibres Courtaulds has gone some way to rebuild the position it lost through the forced sale of its subsidiary, the American Viscose Corporation, in 1941.* In aluminium the French Pechiney is creating substantial production facilities, and in office machinery, a field long dominated by the Americans, the Italian Olivetti has spent over $100m. putting the Underwood typewriter company back on its feet since taking control in 1959.

However the most striking event so far has been the arrival of British Petroleum. In 1968 it played an important part in the discovery of the vast north Alaskan oilfields, which seem likely to double the existing level of U.S. oil reserves, and in 1969 it was involved in two massive mergers. First it paid $400m. for a chain of petrol stations, two

* This was insisted upon by the Americans before they would provide Britain with lend-lease.

refineries, and a stake in some pipelines, which belonged to Sinclair Oil, and which had to be sold under pressure from the anti-trust division of the Department of Justice, when that company was taken over by Atlantic Richfield. Then it merged its subsidiary, BP Oil Corporation, with Standard Oil (Ohio), a company founded by John D. Rockefeller and once the heart of his empire. Although the terms of this deal are extremely complicated, they provide BP with eventual control.

While the BP–Standard merger was being considered by the anti-trust division, two more major European initiatives took place. BASF took over Wyandotte Chemicals, and the Dutch KZO* acquired International Salt, the country's second largest salt company. The BP–Standard merger was the largest ever to involve a foreign and domestic company in the US., and BASF's purchase of Wyandotte was the biggest direct takeover of a U.S. company by a foreigner in American history.

The size of these deals and their implications served to create an impression that a new era was beginning in the industrial relations between the U.S. and Europe. Taken together they provide convincing proof that Europeans can do in the U.S. what Americans have long been doing in Europe.

British Petroleum showed that within the space of a few months a foreigner could move from nowhere into the big league of a major industry. KZO made the same point in a less important sector of the economy. The significance of BASF's acquisition of Wyandotte was different, and perhaps even greater. Wyandotte, an international company in its own right, was losing money, and its management had clearly failed. When BASF stepped in with a cash offer and firm plans for future expansion it was hailed by managers, workers, and shareholders alike as a saviour. This is a role which U.S. companies frequently play in Europe; it was a

*It has since merged with AKU, another Dutch company, to form AKZO.

novel experience for Americans to see a European company play it in their country.

It would be easy to over-estimate the real effects of British Petroleum, BASF, and KZO. Europeans have been running large companies in the U.S. since the nineteenth century, and Olivetti began the rehabilitation of Underwood a decade before BASF started with Wyandotte. But because European companies in the period since 1945 have been unable to match in the U.S. the grand strategies pursued by U.S. companies in Europe, it was widely assumed that transatlantic investment must always be largely a one-way traffic. A combination of events, each in itself in some way notable, is frequently necessary before a widely held assumption can be called into question. This is what British Petroleum, BASF, and KZO provided.

The rapid growth of European investment in the U.S. in recent years is the result of many factors. But the most basic is simply that the necessary money is now more generally available than before. Until the late 1950s Europe suffered from an acute shortage of long-term capital which ruled out ambitious overseas investment programmes, especially in the U.S., a country with which most European nations were running a permanent and substantial trade deficit. Companies with existing operations, who could plough back profits or raise money locally, could continue to expand. But it was difficult for others to make a start. European governments were above all anxious to encourage exports to the U.S., and before a company could secure the foreign exchange to finance a direct investment, it had to convince its government that the investment would lead to a sharp short-term increase in exports. Although capital movements are still not entirely free, and governments are apt to impose curbs at short notice, the situation is infinitely easier than it was even a few years ago. Moreover many companies now have operations outside their own country generating profits, and they can seek funds through the international Euro-currency markets that are not subject to government control, and which only came into existence within the last decade.

The attractions of investing in the U.S. are enormous. It is the largest market in the world, and its citizens have, on average, more individual purchasing power than anybody else in the world. In 1968 its gross national product was over $880,000m. compared with $380,000m. for the European Economic Community countries combined, and $191,000m. for the members of the European Free Trade Area. Thus the U.S. has a substantially larger economy than the EEC and EFTA put together. The prosperity of the Americans can be shown by assessing their gross national product on a *per capita* basis and comparing* it with those of other areas. It works out at $4,380 for every man, woman, and child in the country. The equivalent figure for the EEC is $2,040, and for EFTA $1,920. The only places that come within hailing distance of the U.S. are Sweden with a gross national product per head of $3,230, and Canada with $3,010. The rate of growth is slower in the U.S. than in many other markets, but its size is so great and its people so rich that even a small share of it yields a larger turnover than would a dominant position in many other countries, as the experience of the French company Air Liquide demonstrates. In 1969 it acquired three U.S. industrial gas concerns. In 1970 it disclosed† that its four per cent share of the U.S. market in industrial gases will add about fifteen per cent to its revenues and may result in a profit increase of nearly twenty per cent. Most companies do not achieve such dramatic results as Air Liquide, but the hope of doing so persuades many managements to invest in the U.S.

*These figures provide only a rough and ready basis for comparison. As anyone who has worked in the U.S. knows, the internal purchasing power of the dollar is less than its exchange rate against foreign currencies may suggest. Moreover personal spending habits and the demands made on the private individual's income vary from one country to another.

† *Wall Street Journal,* 10 February 1970.

The argument that 'to compete effectively for a good share of any major market requires a direct investment in the market place', which U.S. companies use to justify their investment overseas, applies even more strongly to other companies wishing to build up a position in the U.S. There are one or two well-known exceptions to this rule, such as Volkswagen. But in general it is true to say that long-term success in the U.S. depends on having a local production base.

Because of the Buy American policy U.S. government agencies and subsidized universities, which together constitute an enormous market, are required by law to give preference to goods made in the U.S. rather than imports. Many Americans would prefer to do this anyway. 'It is a question of psychology,' explains Jean Morel, export manager of the French Intertechnique, which makes scientific instruments and has opened a plant in New Jersey instead of relying on shipments from France. 'A lot of our customers,' he says, 'might doubt that Frenchmen are capable of making advanced electronic equipment.'* This is quite a common view among European businessmen and often cited as a reason for establishing a plant in the U.S.

Another is that a local plant is vital if a company is to provide the standard of service demanded by American customers. 'We often have to deliver stocks by air freight – something we couldn't do from Europe,'* said an executive of Artos Machinen, a German manufacturer of textile processing equipment, when asked why his company had opened a factory in North Carolina. A local plant, of course, also gives customers confidence in a foreign company's commitment to the market, and in its ability to maintain supplies, regardless of what happens in its home country. Yet another consideration is that it enables a company to keep pace with the constantly altering pattern of demand. More than half the items to be found in U.S. supermarkets have been introduced in the last ten years, and similar

* *Business Week*, 16 August 1969.

sweeping changes are to be found in many other sectors of the economy.

As well as being the largest, the U.S. is the most sophisticated market in the world. Its companies are accustomed to a faster rate of economic, technical, and social change than those of any other country. A company with a subsidiary in the U.S. is able to learn the latest techniques of management, production, marketing, and financial control at the same time as its American competitors. As a result it becomes better equipped to fight the Americans and everyone else in other markets than would be the case if it did not have a position in the U.S.

Professor Raymond Vernon argues that when European governments try to protect their industries from the American challenge by giving national producers a privileged position and guaranteed sales in their home market, they find themselves 'satisfying next year's demand with last year's technology'. He maintains that the best way for Europeans to match the innovation and aggression of the leading U.S. companies 'is by exposing themselves more widely to the challenges and opportunities of the U.S. economy. A casual exposure such as occurs through normal export efforts may not be enough. It may be necessary to establish an operating subsidiary in the United States in order to recognise the opportunities for industrial innovation that the market affords.'*

This view is shared by several European companies that have achieved success in the U.S. According to Roberto Olivetti, 'the experience of Olivetti Underwood is a source of strength for us, and it conditions our responses in many ways. It keeps us modern and aggressive.' He finds that when the managers of Olivetti Underwood in New York visit the parent company's headquarters at Ivrea in northern Italy they give the impression that they are the ones who know about the real hard world, and that the people in

* 'An Outsider's View of the Technological Gaps'. Report by Raymond Vernon, published in the *OECD Observer*, April 1968.

Ivrea are in some ways sheltered and provincial. 'And you know,' he says, 'they just may be right.'*

H. G. Lazell, the former chairman of Beechams, the toiletries and pharmaceutical group that includes Brylcreem and Macleans toothpaste among its products, was convinced after the war that if the company was to prosper in the rest of the world it had to have a U.S. subsidiary. 'I recognized,' he says, 'that in this country (Britain), and in the markets we were competing in, the Americans were very strong, and I recognized early on that if we didn't attempt to match them we would be pushed out. I don't think that if you are a world-wide business you can neglect the American market – it affects you in so many other areas of the world if you do. You are going to be in competition with U.S. companies all over the world. I thought the best way to learn to match them was to compete with them on their own ground.'†

Beechams has shown itself well able to do this. Eight years after its post-war re-launch in the U.S. in 1951 Brylcreem was the best selling American hairdressing lotion, and it is still the leading white cream on the market. Macleans has become a major factor in the toothpaste market with factory sales three times larger than in Britain, and the company has also built up a position in pharmaceuticals. In 1968 the Western Hemisphere (which means mainly the U.S. although it includes Canada and Australasia) accounted for over twenty-eight per cent of Beecham's sales. But the company has earned far more than just money from the U.S. It has acquired a wealth of experience that has enabled it to compete more successfully in other markets than would otherwise have been the case.

Looking back on his business career Lazell is unstinting in his acknowledgement of the value of his American ex-

* 'Olivetti's Crisis of Identity' by Walter Guzzardi Jr. *Fortune*, July 1967.

† 'The Years with Beechams' by H. G. Lazell. *Management Today*, November 1968.

perience. In a memoir published soon after he had announced his decision to retire, he wrote: 'The main lesson I learnt from the U.S. was the thoroughness with which Americans went about their marketing processes. I learnt this as much from looking at what our competitors did to meet our challenge as from what we had to do ourselves. . . . In America I was brought into contact with market research and consumer research. We use these techniques over here, but not so thoroughly or so seriously as the Americans . . . I learnt over there that it wasn't the job of the top man merely to sit at his desk, it was also his job to get out into the market . . . The lessons we learnt from our American experience have been applied here.'*

Great as are the potential gains to be derived from investing in the U.S., there are also problems to be overcome. The most crucial is the lack of self-confidence that many European companies have in their ability to compete in the U.S. This attitude is exemplified by a reply given to the Atlantic Council's study group on American business in Europe when the members asked a European concern why it did not counter U.S. opposition in its home market by investing in the U.S. 'We could not compete,' they were told. 'We are not big enough. We do not have the people, management, money, or even awareness of the market.'† This is an understandable reaction. The vast bulk of U.S. investment in Europe has been carried out by the largest companies – some two-thirds is in the hands of only twenty concerns – and much of it is in the most technologically advanced industries. Europeans have been exposed to competition from some of the largest and best companies in the U.S., and have come to the conclusion that the rest of American industry is the same.

It is indeed dominated by large companies, and these are

---

* 'The Years with Beechams' by H. G. Lazell. *Management Today*, November 1968.

† 'Building a Bigger Atlantic Community Market' by Gene E. Bradley. *Harvard Business Review*, May–June 1966.

becoming steadily more powerful at the expense of their smaller competitors. The Federal Trade Commission reported in November 1969 that in 1968 the two hundred largest manufacturing corporations controlled almost two-thirds of all manufacturing industry assets, a proportion equal to the share held by the thousand largest corporations in 1941. As the report pointed out, this increase in power came at a time when the actual volume of industrial assets was itself growing rapidly. Even the largest European companies are often dwarfed by their U.S. counterparts. In 1969 there were twenty-three U.S. companies with sales of $3,000m. a year or more, but only six in Europe – Shell, Unilever, Philips, Volkswagen, British Petroleum, and Imperial Chemical Industries. Volkswagen is the largest company in Germany yet its sales would put it no higher than seventeenth in the U.S., while Renault, the largest company in France, would be in the fortieth position. This does not mean that European companies cannot compete in the U.S. But, as Olivetti has shown with Underwood and BASF with Wyandotte, it does mean that they have to have plenty of self-confidence.

The size and sophistication of the U.S. market make it a particularly difficult and expensive one to break into. When U.S. companies expand into Europe they are usually large in relation both to the national market they are moving into, and to the companies already in the field. The new subsidiary of an American concern may itself be small, but behind it stand all the financial and management resources of the parent company. During the initial build up period these can be deployed in its support whenever necessary, and if it takes rather longer and costs rather more than had originally been expected to secure a satisfactory position the parent can afford the mistake. By contrast a European company breaking into the U.S. tends to be small in relation both to the market, and to the existing competition. It is also generally accustomed to a less competitive atmosphere, and a less rapid rate of technological and product change.

So a decision to establish a U.S. subsidiary represents a far greater challenge and risk to a European company than the decision to invest in Europe means to an American. If the European miscalculates on the time and cost needed to establish its subsidiary on a profitable footing, the losses can be crippling. When Professor Jack N. Behrman conducted his survey into the rise of the multinational enterprise, several European companies 'in both the technologically advanced and consumer-oriented industries argued that to enter the U.S. market would require $100m. of capital over a few years'.* This is not a tremendous investment by U.S. standards, but for most European companies it is very substantial. As a result, Behrman found, a number had concluded that they could not commit so much to a single venture since a miscalculation would jeopardize the well-being of the parent company elsewhere in the world.

Even some companies which have made a success of their U.S. affiliates are daunted when they recall the sums of money that were needed. Signor Sergio Pizzoni-Ardemani of Olivetti Underwood has said that 'If anybody had told the Olivetti management in 1959 that they were out for an investment of $100m. in the United States, they probably would not have gone ahead. They were not thinking in those terms. But having started with $8m. and then realizing that more and more was needed, the management went ahead gradually increasing its commitment. In the end it had a tremendous investment, much bigger than originally expected. But it also found itself in the position of having seized opportunities of proportions originally unsuspected too.'†

* 'Some Patterns in the Rise of the Multinational Enterprise' by Jack N. Behrman. Research Paper 18. (Graduate School of Business, University of North Carolina.)

† 'Direct investment in the U.S. yields more than balance sheet shows' by Sergio Pizzoni-Ardemani. *American Banker*, 26 May 1967.

To some managements the story of Olivetti Underwood is an inspiration and convinces them that they too can compete in the U.S.; to others it is a hideous warning of the dangers of biting off more than one can chew. Only companies that are convinced they have the resources and skills to undertake a U.S. operation can accept the inevitable risks. For others the best course is to rely on exports, or on a licensing agreement with a U.S. company.

Some European companies have by themselves built up successful U.S. operations from scratch, but because of the cost and problems associated with breaking into the market most foreigners prefer to seek local partners rather than go it alone. The foreigner supplies the product, manufacturing skill or whatever it may be plus some of the money, while the American helps with the financing and provides the local management. This is in direct contrast with the usual practice of U.S. companies expanding into Europe, who usually finance the whole operation themselves, and, in the early years at least, rely on American managers to run it. The difference in approach reflects the advantages in terms of managerial talent and financial resources that U.S. industry has over its European counterpart.

Behrman mentions one anonymous European company which had $100m. to invest in the U.S., but found that even this sum was not enough to enable it to go into all the products of its line. It therefore teamed up with several other companies, which provided raw material supplies, new technology, a management pool or a marketing organization. This company entered these joint ventures, despite the fact that it usually seeks one hundred per cent ownership of its foreign affiliates, because it felt it had no other choice. Some European companies with joint ventures in the U.S. regard them as temporary expedients while they prepare to branch out on their own; others see them as permanent arrangements. But whatever their attitude most European companies would not dare to establish manufacturing subsidiaries in the U.S. entirely on their own account. The choice is between some form of local partnership or nothing at all.

This frequently brings them into potential or actual conflict with U.S. anti-trust law as interpreted by the anti-trust division of the Department of Justice. The purpose of this law, which has been developed in a number of statutes, is to maintain free competition in U.S. industry and markets. The anti-trust division challenges, through legal action, all mergers which it considers would jeopardize this purpose. It also takes legal action to force companies to hive off some of their existing subsidiaries, or break up partnerships and joint ventures, if it believes them to be contrary to the principles of the law. In the context of American history, which shows that the main internal threat to the government has come from the very large corporations, and in view of the tremendous concentration of the country's manufacturing industry in the post-war era, it is understandable that the division should pursue a vigorous policy. In its time it has attacked or circumscribed virtually every major U.S. company.

However, its activities bear particularly hard upon foreign concerns. This is not a matter of deliberate policy. Indeed there is some evidence to suggest that foreign companies sometimes escape more lightly than Americans. It is partly because partnerships and joint ventures are vital to foreigners if they are to operate in the U.S. at all, and partly because of the uncertainties of U.S. anti-trust theory and practice.

The uncertainties are of several kinds. To begin with, to use the words of a leading U.S. expert, 'there is today no coherent enforcement policy at the anti-trust division which can be discerned by the outside observer. Businessmen interested in combination mergers or joint ventures must engage in what is little more than a lottery. It is well known that the anti-trust division does not have sufficient funds or personnel resources to apply the laws equally to all combinations of this kind . . . Many mergers like those

79

attacked went scot-free.'* Those words were written in 1965, but they are just as true today.

Another problem arises from the fact that the division not only challenges mergers which may eliminate existing competition, but also those which may eliminate potential competition. Richard W. McLaren, the assistant attorney-general in charge of the anti-trust division, has explained what this means: 'Suppose company A is a large producer of widgets in the Western United States. And suppose company B is seriously considering entry into the western widget market by establishing its own plant in that area; it has the resources and incentive to do so. Company B would then be a potential entrant into that market. If company B, instead of building its own plant, proceeded to acquire company A, that potential competition would be eliminated.'† McLaren went on to say that the application of this rule 'was not easy.' That is an understatement. For a foreign company to convince the anti-trust division that it will not enter the U.S. unless it can form a joint venture or partnership is extremely difficult. The bare facts and figures of a company's situation can be interpreted in any number of ways. In the last resort everything must depend on the presentation of its case, and on the personal judgement of the responsible official at the division, or if a case is brought, the personal judgement of the judge who hears it.

More serious than both these points is the fact that a company engaged in a merger or joint venture never knows when it is safe. The anti-trust division may do nothing to prevent the original agreement between two companies to establish an operation, and then many years later decide to pounce. Its attitude was expressed in 1966 by assistant

---

* Gerhard A. Gesell, *The Anti-trust Bulletin*, 1965, pages 34–5.

† 'International Investment and the U.S. anti-trust laws'. An address by Richard W. McLaren, assistant attorney-general anti-trust division, before the European Institutional Investor Conference, Savoy Hotel, London, 1 December 1969.

attorney-general Zimmermann who told the Senate sub-committee on anti-trust that 'merger cases never close.'

This is no idle threat, as the German Bayer chemical company has discovered. In 1954 it established a joint venture with the U.S. Monsanto called Mobay for the production and sale of isocyanates and other products used in the manufacture of polyurethane. At the time the venture seemed of little importance, and did not attract much attention. By 1962 Mobay had secured fifty per cent of the U.S. market in these products, and this brought it to the attention of the anti-trust division. A prolonged legal wrangle ensued. Eventually in 1967 the two companies were forced to separate, and following a Consent Decree Monsanto sold out its share. The partnership had worked harmoniously in the interests of both parents, and the intervention of the anti-trust division caused great resentment at Bayer.

Notwithstanding the numerous problems involved, the growth of foreign direct investment in the U.S. will continue. The size and prosperity of the market, and the tremendous opportunities it provides for acquiring practical experience of the most advanced techniques in every sort of business activity will see to that. Although the difficulties will remain, the example of companies that overcome them and go on to earn large profits will encourage others to take the plunge.

But the chances of European investment in the U.S. ever again approaching the scale of U.S. investment in Europe is remote. For as long as the U.S. remains the largest, richest, and most inventive economy in the world, its companies will continue to hold and provide the lion's share of all international direct investment.

4. The European Merger Boom

The rapid expansion of international companies during the 1960s, and the growth of large integrated markets in the European Economic Community and the European Free Trade Area, has had a cumulative effect and provoked a merger boom of unprecedented dimensions. Throughout Europe large and small companies alike are coming together in attempts to take advantage of the new opportunities and to create defensive formations to withstand the new competitors. A small, though highly publicized, percentage of the mergers involve contested takeover bids, but the vast majority are carried through on an amicable basis. In Britain it is estimated that almost ninety per cent are agreed between the participants,* and in Europe as a whole the proportion is almost certainly higher. Mergers are only one aspect of the industrial concentration that is taking place. Companies may also form joint subsidiaries and cooperate in numerous other ways in order to achieve some of the advantages of a merger while retaining their independence and separate identities.

The advantages are readily apparent. Throughout the post-war era the scale of almost every aspect of industrial activity has increased substantially. If a company is to generate the funds required to finance the enormous research and investment programmes required in large-scale, capital intensive, and internationally organized industries, it must be built on a substantial basis. The examples of IBM spending $5,000m. on the development of its 360-

*I am indebted to David Hargreaves, Division Director – Acquisitions and Mergers, of PA Management Consultants, for this estimate.

The family trees of three mergers

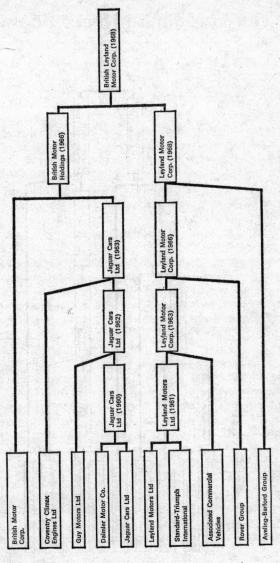

1. British Leyland Motor Corporation

2. International Computers Ltd

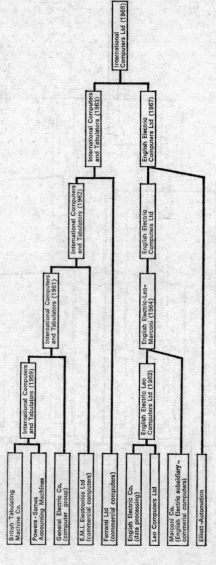

British Tabulating Machine Co.

Powers - Samas Accounting Machines

International Computers and Tabulators (1959)

General Electric Co. (computer group)

E.M.I. Electronics Ltd (commercial computers)

International Computers and Tabulators (1961)

Ferranti Ltd (commercial computers)

International Computers and Tabulators (1962)

International Computers and Tabulators (1963)

International Computers Ltd (1968)

English Electric Co. (data processing)

English Electric Leo Computers Ltd (1963)

Leo Computers Ltd

English Electric-Leo-Marconi (1964)

Marconi Co. (English Electric subsidiary – commercial computers)

English Electric Computers Ltd

English Electric Computers Ltd (1967)

Elliott-Automation

3. The French Electrical Industry

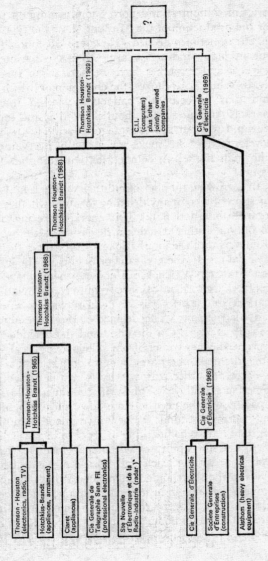

series of computer, and Ford $50m. simply on tooling up
for the production of the Mustang show the type of money
that is sometimes needed. These are exceptional projects,
but in many industries large groups with international
markets and resources have been dazzling their smaller
rivals. When Lord Stokes, the chairman of British Leyland,
said that 'a company cannot survive in international
markets without size, without marketing and service out-
lets, and without the advantages of scale for research and
development,'* he spoke for virtually every industrialist
who finds himself in competition with international companies.

In a growing number of industries there is no longer any
question of a company deciding for itself whether or not to
compete internationally. If its markets are invaded it has
no option. Either it fights a defensive battle on its home
ground against the internationals, or it carries the fight into
their camps. In the great majority of cases the latter is the
best strategy. Whichever is chosen, mergers are likely to
result. Large resources are required to invade foreign
markets, and a merger is the quickest way in which a company can expand. The defence of the home market also
leads to mergers. On the one hand the defenders want to
prevent the newcomers from taking over local concerns,
while the newcomers are trying to do just that.

There are other reasons why companies have come together in recent years, and will continue to do so. Over-
capacity and the need to close down surplus plants is one,
and shortage of funds for new investment is another. The
desire to reduce competition in order to increase profits is a
third, and the ability of one management to earn larger
profits on existing assets and therefore to pay better dividends to the shareholders than the existing management is
a fourth. In some industries competition from international
companies and the internationalization of competition constitute the merger boom's main fuel. These factors have also

* *Fortune*, 15 September 1968.

encouraged governments to support many mergers on the grounds that the new combine will be able to compete more effectively in international markets than its component parts. Indeed governments sometimes give the impression that they regard it almost as a matter of prestige that the largest locally owned company in a particular industry should be at least the same size as comparable foreign concerns.

The most dramatic manifestation of the merger boom occurred in Britain in 1967 and 1968. During those two years more than 5,000 British companies were involved in corporate marriages of one sort or another. Nearly seventy of the country's top one hundred companies entered the bidding, or were bid for, and more than a quarter of the companies registered at the beginning of 1967 with a value of £10m. or more were taken over. A sum in excess of £6,100m. was offered for the equity of those companies that lost their identity.* Quite apart from all this, the steel industry was nationalized in 1967, which resulted in the formation of what was then the world's second largest steel company, the British Steel Corporation.† This was done partly on grounds of Socialist dogma, but partly too because it was believed that a unified British steel industry provided the best hope for competing in international markets.

The events of 1967–8 were the culmination of almost a decade of industrial concentration, which transformed the face of British industry. When the British Leyland Motor Corporation was formed in 1968 following the merger of British Motor Holdings and Leyland Motor it included ten companies that in 1960 had been independent. Similarly the formation of International Computers Limited as the largest computer company outside the U.S. was the result of a series of mergers spread over ten years and involving a total of nine companies or divisions of companies. Until

* These figures are derived from *Management and Merger Activity* by Gerald D. Newbould (Guthstead, 1970).

† A small private sector remains dealing mainly with special steels.

1967 Britain had three major electrical engineering concerns – the General Electric Company, Associated Electrical Industries, and English Electric. By the end of 1968 General Electric, which is no relation to the U.S. company of that name, had absorbed the other two.

The concentration of industry enjoyed the active encouragement of the government. In December 1966 the Labour administration established the Industrial Reorganization Corporation in order to create an industrial structure 'which will enable us to make effective use in years ahead of our resources of skill, management, and capital.'[*] It became extremely active. As one commentator put it in March 1970: 'The IRC has spent the last three years loping through one industry after another, shotgun in hand, pushing sometimes reluctant, sometimes eager, companies to the altar.'[†] As well as the government's moral support, the IRC was given the authority to draw up to £150m. of public money with which to lubricate the deals it wished to push through. Its influence was felt in practically every sector, although its most spectacular interventions were in the largest mergers. In electrical engineering it backed Sir Arnold Weinstock of the General Electric Company as the man likely to carry through the reorganization and contraction of the industry's capacity most efficiently, and helped him gain control of Associated Electrical Industries and English Electric. In motors it selected Lord Stokes, and consistently used its influence on behalf of his Leyland company. The IRC was not always successful, as for instance when its proposed three-way boiler merger between International Combustion, John Thompson and Clarke Chapman came unstuck. But its financial resources gave it enormous leverage. When George Kent and the Rank Organization were bidding against

[*] The Industrial Reorganization Corporation. White Paper, Command 2889.
[†] 'Europe's Love Affair with Bigness' by Philip Siekman. *Fortune*, March 1970.

each other for Cambridge Instruments the I R C decided that George Kent better represented British national interests, and provided the company with the money needed to carry the day.

Many mergers took place in which the I R C played no part, but its influence extended far beyond its own immediate activities. Its mere existence, and the fact that its policies were known to enjoy official blessing, acted as a catalyst throughout industry, and so intensified the merger mania of the period.

By the beginning of 1970, however, doubts about the wisdom of the I R C's approach were beginning to be widely expressed. It was felt that its policy of creating enormous companies, sometimes incorporating virtually the whole of the British-owned sector of an industry, was going too far. Fears of the dangers inherent in monopoly situations started to reassert themselves, and as the problems involved in massive mergers became more widely appreciated the opinion spread that a more gradual and organic form of industrial growth might be preferable. With the return of a Conservative government the I R C found its freedom of action progressively curtailed, and in October 1970 its abolition was announced.

While the I R C approach was losing support in Britain, it was gaining adherents in France. In March 1970 the Government announced the formation of the Institut de Dévelopement Industriel, commonly called the I D I. It was given access to 1,000m. francs (200m. francs in the first year), and the task of converting medium-sized companies into bigger units that would be more competitive in world markets.

Even before the establishment of the I D I, the Government was acting as an unofficial marriage broker in an effort to speed up the pace of change. In 1968 about 2,200 corporate marriages of various sorts took place, and in 1969 a further 1,800. During the decade as a whole the structure of the country's industry was dramatically altered. In steel

Usinor and Wendel-Sidelor accumulated two-thirds of
the total crude production. In the electrical and electronics
industries companies responsible for forty-five per cent of
all sales were absorbed into the Compagnie Générale
d'Électricité and Thomson Houston-Hotchkiss Brandt. As
these two already cooperate in a number of ways, most
notably through their joint ownership of the Compagnie
Internationale pour l'Informatique, France's entry for the
international computer industry, further moves seem quite
possible. In motors the state-owned Renault and the private
enterprise Peugeot cooperate to the point where they
collaborate on research and purchasing, and own a joint
engine factory near Lille. Elsewhere St Gobain, which has
made glass since the reign of Louis XIV, and Pont-à-
Mousson, which specializes in steel pipe and other heavy
industrial equipment, have come together. In September
1970 plans for an even larger merger were announced by
Pechiney and Ugine Kuhlmann. By any standards this will
be a major European industrial event. Pechiney is Europe's
leading aluminium company and has large copper refining interests, while Ugine Kuhlmann leads in the stain-
less steel and steel alloy fields besides being the world's
second largest producer of ferro-chromium. When the deal
has been completed the new company will be among the
largest in the world outside the U.S.

In France contested takeover battles on the British and
American pattern are rare. There is also a tolerant approach towards inter-company understandings and equity
cross holdings. Consequently much industrial reorganization takes place through the hiving off by one company of
certain activities to another in exchange for shares, and
through collaboration agreements. This makes it difficult
for the outsider to evaluate the implications of many of
the changes that take place, but their long-term significance is none the less considerable. In 1970 it was estimated*
that three giants, Pont-à-Mousson–St Gobain, Rhône

Guardian, 27 January 1970.

Poulenc, and Pechiney together already employed one in every forty Frenchmen. For a country which still has a substantial peasant population this represents a considerable degree of industrial concentration.

In Germany merger mania has been less apparent than in France or Britain. This is partly because the country's economy has been the most consistently successful in Europe since it recovered from the worst of the post-war devastation. German industry, therefore, has not been under the same pressures to reorganize as its counterparts in France and Britain.

There are other reasons as well. Successive governments have favoured competition in the sense that there should be several different companies operating in every market. At the same time there is a certain cosiness about German industry that softens the effects of this system. Much of the economy is controlled by the big three banks, the Deutsche Bank, the Dresdener Bank, and the Commerzbank. These owe their position to the fact that they offer a far wider range of services than banks in Britain and the U.S. They lend to industrial companies, which in those countries would be more likely to raise money through the issue of shares or loan stock; they run investment trusts; they do the work of stockbrokers; they run large portfolios on their own behalf and for clients; and they manage new issues of shares. Their directors are to be found on the boards of every sort of company, and their influence is felt throughout industry. Until a few years ago a single banker might be a director of twenty or thirty companies, but a law was passed limiting each man to ten. Another feature of the German industrial scene is that the country has a strong tradition of companies working together through cooperative agreements and understandings, rather than swallowing each other up.

Thus the rise of the General Electric Company in Britain is paralleled in Germany by the increasing cooperation between the two electrical giants, Siemens and AEG-

Telefunken. In 1969 they formed two joint subsidiaries, Kraftwerk Union for power generating equipment, and Trafo-Union for transformers. They also joined forces for the construction of a sodium cooled fast breeder reactor, developed by Siemens. Similarly in steel Thyssenhuette and Mannesmann work closely together. In 1969 they unveiled a far-reaching plan, which involved handing over their tube-making capacity to a joint subsidiary two-thirds controlled by Mannesmann, while Mannesmann's rolled steel plant passed into the control of Thyssenhuette.

Even in motors, where Germany produces about twice as many cars as Britain, there are signs of increasing cooperation. In 1969 Volkswagen took over NSU so that there are now only three German-owned concerns left, the mighty Volkswagen itself, Daimler-Benz (which makes Mercedes), and the relatively tiny but highly successful BMW,* which resisted a takeover from Daimler-Benz in 1959. A merger between Volkswagen and Daimler-Benz in the near future is highly improbable. But it is significant that the two companies have a jointly owned subsidiary known as the Deutsche Automobil Gesellschaft.

Through this company they pool certain results of their research and development. Should either one day find itself in serious trouble the link could provide the basis of a merger. If that does not happen it is still likely to lead to greater mutual understanding and more limited competition than would otherwise be the case. In the truck end of the business the pattern is very similar. As a result of acquisitions and takeovers there are here too only three German-owned concerns, Daimler-Benz, MAN, and Klockner-Humboldt-Deutz. The first two have a joint affiliate to handle their interests in the making of jet engines. This is only a limited link, though it could turn out to be important if the turbine propulsion of land vehicles ever becomes a commercial proposition, but it shows the way the companies' minds are moving.

*Its official, though rarely used, name is Bayerische Motoren Werke.

When an industry is faced with really intractable problems and the need to adjust to new and unfavourable conditions, the Germans can merge with the best, and the government is quite prepared to act as marriage broker. The rapidly declining coal industry provides a good illustration. Twenty-five mining companies have been brought together in a single unit called Ruhrkohle, which accounts for over ninety per cent of the total Ruhr output.

If Germany is the country where the government has held most aloof from direct involvement in industry, Italy is the one where interventionist policies have been carried furthest. The most famous names in Italian industry, Fiat, Pirelli, and Olivetti are in private hands, and each dominates its own sector of the economy. But the state holding company, Istituto per la Ricostruzione Industriale, IRI for short, controls an enormous area of commercial, financial, and industrial activity. Altogether it owns about 140 companies. These include Alfa Romeo, Alitalia, the major steel concerns, telephone, telegraph and broadcasting companies, several banks, and a host of other enterprises. Its industrial companies are estimated to account for some fifteen per cent of the country's total industrial output.

IRI was set up by Mussolini during the Great Depression as the centrepiece of the government's efforts to counter the effects of the collapse of a number of banks. Since then it has grown, like Topsy, with the post-war expansion of the Italian economy. Its chairman, Dr Giuseppe Petrilli, has described the process as one of 'empirical evolution' with the state wanting to maintain its role as 'guarantor of the public interest', without compromising the workings of a 'market economy'.*

In many respects IRI subsidiaries operate exactly like other commercial enterprises. Many have shares that are traded on the stock exchanges, and they can raise money direct from the public. Their executives are powerful men with minds and policies of their own. It would be impos-

* *Men and Money* by Paul Ferris (Hutchinson).

sible for IRI to exercise tight and detailed control over such a diverse and independent collection of satrapies. None the less the component parts of its empire lack the sovereignty of genuinely independent concerns, and IRI can intervene to override the wishes of their management. It can merge or break up units, and it can dictate non-commercial policies, such as, for instance, investment in the development areas of the south.

Another bastion of state power is Ente Nazionale Idrocarburi (ENI), which operates in oil and natural gas, both within Italy and outside. It is separate from IRI, but the two sometimes cooperate. The most notable example of this was in 1968 when they launched a takeover bid for Montecatini Edison, Europe's second largest chemical company, in order to place it under ENI's control.

The combination of the state concerns plus the enormous private empires of Fiat, Pirelli, and Olivetti means that the most important sectors of Italian industry are exceptionally highly concentrated. Decisions affecting the greater part of the country's productive capacity can be taken by a very few men acting together, if they happen to agree on a common objective.

It is however dangerous, and often misleading, to compare this situation with what has been happening in Britain, France, or Germany. In those countries companies and governments, in their different ways and to differing degrees, are trying to reorganize an industrial structure inherited from the past. Italy, by contrast, does not have a long industrial history. Most of its industrial revolution has occurred since the war, and within a structure that was already controlled by the government and a small number of private companies.

Among the smaller European countries too, straightforward national comparisons are misleading. But a pattern can be discerned. In Switzerland the two chemical and pharmaceutical giants, CIBA and Geigy, have come together. In Holland the two biggest chemical companies,

AKU and KZO, have merged, while in Sweden 2,000 mergers affecting a fifth of the industrial labour force occurred during the 1960s. Although each government and each company reacts individually to the problems confronting it, the trend towards industrial concentration and companies of ever-increasing size is clear throughout Europe.

During the 1970s the events of the last few years are likely to come in for a good deal of criticism. There is already widespread disappointment in the rather poor performance of some of the recently created giants, and as the gap between their promise and fulfilment grows so will the doubts about the desirability of their formation. Fashions, whether in clothes, ideas, or industrial organization, usually tend to go to extremes, and the merger boom is no exception. In the 1960s many industries in European countries were divided into too many small units unable to compete effectively on the world stage. The formation of larger units capable of financing massive research and investment programmes was needed, and in some sectors still is. But in the pursuit of size it was forgotten that mergers generate difficulties of their own, and that large companies present their managers with problems of control, coordination, and administration that take time to solve.

Mergers are highly complicated undertakings, and most fail to live up to the hopes of their initiators. In 1967 John Kitching, in an article* in the *Harvard Business Review*, estimated that only about one in four U.S. mergers succeed. He noted exaggerated estimates of production economies, critical incompatibilities in selling and distribution techniques, and, above all, contradictory objectives among senior management as being the main reasons why the pay-off from putting together what appeared to be complementary assets often fell below expectations. His estimate may be on the optimistic side. In 1969 David Har-

*'Why do mergers miscarry?', by John Kitching. *Harvard Business Review*, November–December 1967.

greaves of PA Management Consultants suggested that in Britain the success rate is one in nine.*

At first sight it seems strange that so many mergers should fail to achieve the classic objective of two plus two equals five. After all a merger only takes place if the bidder believes he can make a better use of the assets of the company concerned than the existing management, or if both participants agree that their combined forces would be stronger than if they remained apart.

The root cause of the problem is that the potential gains are always large and obvious, while the difficulties to be overcome are comparatively small so that their sheer number and complexity tend to be overlooked. Just as Gulliver was held down by a multiplicity of Lilliputian ropes, so can a merger misfire because the extent of the difficulties is unrealized. This analogy is not exaggerated. The U.S. expert, Forrest D. Wallace, estimates that even a modest amount of integration between two companies may involve 2,000 changes and 10,000 major non-routine decisions. When the Pennsylvania and New York Central railroads came together the critical path programme used to consolidate their equipment maintenance functions alone had four hundred separate steps. David Hargreaves produced a list of fourteen points,† which in turn generate a mass of decisions, that have to be considered during a merger. These are:

(1) Personality problems at senior level.
(2) The launch of a new product.
(3) Reorganization of the sales force.
(4) Making new systems work.
(5) The research and development programme.
(6) The salary structure.
(7) Major redundancies.

*'Establishing and Implementing Your Acquisition Programme'. Speech to conference organized by Corporate Seminars Inc. on Acquiring, Merging, and Selling. Brussels, 9 December 1969.

† Corporate Seminars conference.

(8) How to reduce the number of product lines, while maintaining turnover.

(9) Getting the sales and production divisions to harmonize their activities.

(10) Concentrating production in two instead of three factories.

(11) Securing union cooperation.

(12) Pension arrangements.

(13) The manner in which the published accounts are presented.

(14) The company letterhead.

In most companies a serious consideration of most of these points occurs only once every few years, otherwise senior management would never have time to carry on the day-to-day running of the company. During a merger action must be taken simultaneously on all fourteen fronts.

Many of the decisions are painful, and difficult choices must be made between the conflicting demands of the two parties to the merger. The most important management task in the period immediately after the formal agreement to come together is the creation of a new corporate loyalty strong enough to enable the individuals concerned to carry through the necessary changes. The two original companies all too easily retain their former identities, fight for their own interests, and, in the end, fail to carry through the union at the operational level. The most recent example of a large merger failing because the two managements involved refused to work together as one is that between the Pennsylvania and New York Central railroads. Within just over two years of their union the new joint company, the Pennsylvania Central with assets of almost $7,000m., was forced to file for bankruptcy. The failures of the British Motor Corporation, formed by Austin and Morris in 1952, and of Montecatini Edison in Italy have the same explanation.

Europe, and especially Britain, has an unfortunate habit

of adopting American fashions just as they are beginning to be called into question in the U.S. This is as true of business and industry as it is of pop songs and television programmes. In the U.S. it was for long regarded as axiomatic that, as in so many other aspects of American life, to be biggest meant to be best. Best in turn was taken to refer both to profitability and efficiency.

Recently, however, doubts have set in. They are exemplified by an article by Fred Wittnebert,* the vice-president in charge of technical development at the Parker Pen Company. It is based on two charts, reproduced opposite, which show that 'whether judged by the criterion of return on sales or that of return on equity, large corporations have suffered a declining profit performance since 1960, while smaller companies have enjoyed improving results'. So far as the comparative rates of return on sales are concerned, the larger companies were still well ahead of the field at the end of 1969, although their advantage was less than it used to be. But on the basis of the rate of return on stockholder's equity, the small companies with assets of less than $1m. had taken a clear lead.†

Obviously tables such as these do not tell the full story. Some large companies have done magnificently on both counts, and some small ones have fared very badly. But the overall picture confirms Wittnebert's conclusion that 'contrary to popular opinion, big business is no longer much more profitable than small business; since 1960 it has been fast losing its margin of superiority, and has in fact already fallen behind small business in some respects'. The latest *Fortune* figures provide further confirmation of this thesis. They show that in 1969 the top five-hundred industrial corporations in the U.S. increased their sales by no more

* 'Bigness versus profitability' by Fred R. Wittnebert. *Harvard Business Review*, January–February 1970.

† Since going to press Mr Wittnebert has kindly sent me the figures for the first half of 1970. These show a deviation from the trend in the first quarter, but a significant return to it in the second.

Declining profit superiority of large manufacturing corporations in the U.S.

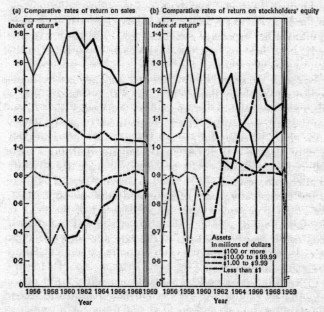

(a) Comparative rates of return on sales   (b) Comparative rates of return on stockholders' equity

* Profits/sales for size category divided by profits/sales for all categories.

† Profits/equity for size category divided by profits/equity for all categories.

Sources: Data for the years 1955 through 1967 is from the *Statistical Abstract of the United States* (Washington, D.C., U.S. Government Printing Office, 1955 through 1967); data for the year 1968 is from the *Quarterly Financial Report for Manufacturing Corporations* (Washington, D.C., Federal Trade Commission and Securities Exchange Commission, 1968). *Source:* Wittnebert.

than the average for all U.S. manufacturing concerns. Moreover, within the top five hundred the first fifty, which account for almost half the group's total sales, performed particularly badly. Whereas the group's average sales growth was 9.7 per cent, the sales of the first fifty went up by only 6.5 per cent.

Comparisons between U.S. and European business experience are never easy because, apart from Britain, European standards of disclosure are so much lower than those of the U.S. The best available yardstick is provided by the French business magazine, *L'Expansion,* which publishes annual profitability studies for leading British and community companies comparing their rates of return on capital with sales. This is a rough-and-ready measure, and it would be unfair to judge a company solely on the basis of one year's figures. None the less it is notable that no particular relationship between size and profitability can be found. In 1968, the latest year for which the statistics are available at the time of writing, there was not a single industrial category in which the largest company was also the most profitable. In several the giants were to be found near the bottom of the table of those listed. In chemicals, for instance, Montecatini Edison was the second largest, and the least profitable, while Imperial Chemical Industries was outdistanced by the German trio of Hoechst, Bayer, and BASF, all of which are smaller. In electrical equipment Philips was the second largest and the second most unprofitable, and in food and liquor Unilever was the largest and least profitable.*

A point that emerges clearly from both the U.S. and European statistics is that it is often the smaller companies with a strong entrepreneurial spirit that turn in the best performances. More often than not they also have a narrow product line, or some special service to provide. They know their market, they can move quickly, and their managers have a deep personal commitment to increasing profitability since their own personal incomes are closely tied to their company's earnings.

However, the most successful and dynamic small com-

*The Fortune Directory of the 500 largest industrial corporations. *Fortune,* May 1970.

pany frequently does not remain small for long. It gets rich quickly by exploiting an original idea or new invention, or by finding a gap in the market. But after this halcyon period it finds itself in a new and more difficult position. It may wither and die, as other companies seek to emulate it and competition increases or as the original money spinner becomes obsolescent. Alternatively, if it continues to prosper it will either be taken over by a larger group or grow large itself.

There will always be room in an advanced industrialized economy for the small dynamic company. Indeed in many areas they will be the pioneers of new techniques and the inventors of new products and processes. But the increasing scale and cost of virtually every form of industrial activity means that large companies must be responsible for a large and growing proportion of the western world's industry. The lesson to be drawn from the success of the small companies is not that large companies should be broken up. It is that they should learn how to provide the conditions and incentives that will enable them to do better.

A major reason why small companies do better than large ones is the accelerating pace of change. This applies to products, processes, materials, markets, channels of distribution, sources of supply, transportation, and everything else. It is harder for a large company to respond to change as quickly as a small one since any alteration of established practices usually requires decisions by a considerable number of people, usually organized into a complicated series of committees. Moreover the speed at which the changes now take place means that management know-how and experience quickly becomes obsolete, thereby creating a need for 'younger managers who have learned more recently, can relearn more quickly, and can adapt more easily than their seniors'.* Large companies, like civil services, tend to have well established promotion ladders and management development programmes de-

*Wittnebert.

signed to bring the best men to the top sometime in their forties, or even early fifties. The opportunities for young men to do interesting jobs, shoulder responsibility, and earn enough money to accumulate capital may be very limited. This in turn has a deadening effect on their initiative and ability, and leads some of the ablest and most dynamic to join small companies where the prospects are often much better.

Large companies realize this and are looking for ways of injecting entrepreneurial spirit into their operations and giving greater responsibilities, independence, and opportunities to younger men. 'Venture management' is the jargon term currently used. The idea is to put a relatively young man in charge of a new venture, give him a high degree of autonomy as well as the right to draw on central financial and technical services, and to reward him accordingly. Those who do well make a double jump up the corporate salary and promotion ladder, while those who do not either go back into the ruck or have to leave altogether. As Kelsey Van Musschenbroek has pointed out, 'it is significant that companies like Du Pont and Monsanto, which have gone farthest along the road of presenting venture management as a new concept, are also those with indifferent profit records'.*

As the troubles of the jumbo jets, the oil supertankers, and the massive new electricity generating sets after their introduction to commercial operation show, the economies of scale, and other advantages of large units that are so obvious on paper, do not always materialize in practice. Unforeseen troubles appear, and men have to get used to operating in a new and different environment. When something goes wrong the effects of the error are proportionately greater than with a smaller unit. The same applies to large companies, especially those which result from the throwing together of two organizations rather than through organic

* 'Organization man or entrepreneur' by Kelsey van Musschenbroek. *Financial Times*, 1 July 1970.

growth spread over a number of years. During the 1970s a good deal will be heard of the need for ensuring that the theoretical advantages of large companies are secured in practice.

5. Trans-European Doubts

In the early 1960s it was hoped that industrial concentration would take place within the context of the movement towards greater European political and economic union. Companies from different European countries were supposed to come together as equals to form a new species of transnational European company that would unite its executives and workers in a common industrial purpose. It was also believed that the existence of the European Economic Community would lead to greater cooperation and closer links between companies from member countries than between those companies and outsiders.

In the event most of the hopes and theories of those days have been confounded. Industrial concentration has turned out to have very little connection with the movement towards European unity, and the existence of the EEC has had a quite different impact on corporate behaviour in this field than was expected. The most important mergers and takeovers have taken place within frontiers, as described in the last chapter, not across them. Where cross-frontier mergers and takeovers have occurred they have mostly been between community companies on the one hand, and non-community companies on the other. The same applies to more limited forms of cooperation, such as the creation of shared subsidiaries and reciprocal shareholdings.

The most comprehensive statistics concerning mergers and takeovers involving community companies were published in the European Commission's 'Colonna Report'* on industrial policy in 1970. They were the result

*'Industrial Policy in the Community.' A memorandum by the European Commission.

The merger, takeover and partnership activities of selected categories of community companies

COOPERATION – MINORITY HOLDINGS
RECIPROCAL HOLDINGS
COMMON SUBSIDIARIES
COMMON PARENT COMPANIES

MERGERS – TAKEOVERS
(or controlling minority)

Year	Between undertakings in the same Country	Between Common Market undertakings	Between Member Country and Third Country undertakings	Same Member Country	Different Member Countries	By a Member Country in a third Country	By a Third Country in a Member Country
1961	100	104	362	131	19	26	102
1962	141	114	343	162	11	21	85
1963	55	61	228	157	28	9	82
1964	132	123	335	172	34	18	110
1965	177	140	364	228	17	20	70
1966	205	112	289	221	31	20	93
1967	166	104	292	253	32	36	115
1968	231	160	387	272	35	29	106
1969*	145	83	197	265	50	36	57
Total	1352	1001	2797	1861	257	215	820

Source: OPERA MUNDI: data published in the Colonna Report.
*1969 figures cover only the first six months.

of a census carried out on behalf of the commission by Opera Mundi, and covered fifteen sectors or subsectors of manufacturing industry, 'which seemed to be most significant.'

They showed that between 1961 and the first half of 1969 inclusive, 1,861 mergers and takeovers* took place within individual member countries, and only 257 between companies from different community countries. During the same period non-community companies made 820 acquisitions of community companies, while community companies in their turn made only 215 acquisitions outside the Common Market. In the case of more limited forms of co-operation, there were 1,352 deals between companies in the same community country, 1,001 between community companies of different nationality, and 2,797 between community companies and those from outside. No breakdown is given between Americans and the rest among the non-community concerns, but in view of the massive increase in U.S. investment in the Common Market during the period they obviously constitute the great majority.

The ideal of marriages between companies of equal stature to create transnational European companies has been only rarely achieved. Within the community there are a mere two examples. The first, in 1964, involved two photographic concerns, the German Agfa, and the Belgian Gevaert. The second, in 1969, brought together two minor aircraft companies, the German Vereinigte Flugtechnische Werke (VFW) and the Dutch Fokker. Both are small beer compared with the proposed union between the British Dunlop and the Italian Pirelli announced in 1970. Together these two form the world's second largest tyre and rubber company with total sales approaching £1,000m. a year and production facilities in every continent. Significantly the negotiations between the two companies began

*The words merger, takeover, and acquisition refer to controlling minority shareholdings as well as to majority shareholdings and outright purchases.

before the final round of talks about British entry into the Common Market, and Dunlop–Pirelli was designed to continue, whatever happened to the British application.*

So much fuss has surrounded these three corporate marriages that it is sometimes thought they represent something entirely new in European history. They have been hailed as the forerunners of a new industrial age in which Europeans will sink their national differences to cooperate in a common cause. In these circumstances it is well to remember that all three unions are dwarfed by those enormous and venerable Anglo-Dutch twins, the Royal Dutch Shell Group, formed in 1907, and Unilever, established in 1929.

The failure of European industry to progress further and faster towards transnational cooperation is one of the chief disappointments of the European movement. The sense of failure has been heightened within the European Economic Community by the extent to which companies in community countries have sought to cooperate with, or allowed themselves to be taken over by Americans and other non-members.

Much of the disappointment stems from a misunderstanding of European industrial realities. All corporate mergers, takeovers, and partnerships involve a host of problems. Companies, like countries and individuals, have differing aims and interests. It is never easy to reconcile them so that the potential advantages are achieved. Even when the companies concerned are of the same nationality the failure rate is high. When different nationalities are involved the problems are multiplied several times.

This applies as much to deals involving U.S.-owned companies as to any others. But U.S. companies in Europe enjoy two advantages. Those that expand abroad are almost invariably among the most technologically advanced in

* The decision to merge was announced in March 1970, at which time it was stated that the companies intended their plans to take effect at the beginning of 1971.

their particular industry, and able to command substantial financial resources. Consequently they have a great deal to offer a potential partner, or the shareholders of a company they wish to take over or purchase a stake in. For the reasons described in chapter 2 they have been, and remain, anxious to strengthen their positions in European markets, and have used these advantages to the full. For their part European companies have welcomed the opportunities for improving their competitiveness provided by a link with a U.S. company, while shareholders have jumped at the chance to make large capital gains by selling out to U.S. companies. This is the case even when a government frowns on a deal, but it is not prepared to block it, as the Texaco takeover of the German oil company DEA a few years ago shows.

When a community company offers similar advantages to a potential partner, or to shareholders in another European country, it succeeds as well as the Americans. But such situations occur comparatively rarely. With few exceptions community companies do not have as much to offer, either technically or financially, to other Europeans as the leading Americans, which limits the scope for partnerships and co-operative agreements. Moreover, community companies have neither the incentive nor the means to embark on a large-scale programme of cross-frontier mergers and take-overs in Europe. They are already part of the Common Market that the American companies wish to break into. It is therefore relatively simple for them to expand into other member countries through direct sales from home. In the case of steel, for instance, which is an industry organized very largely on the basis of national units, trade between community countries has risen about twice as fast as their production. In these circumstances it is preferable for a company to build up subsidiaries of its own gradually rather than to plunge into mergers and takeovers on the American pattern. At the same time it is difficult for them to raise the money necessary for big takeovers beyond their own frontiers. This may seem odd in the light of the number of mergers taking place within national frontiers. But a domestic takeover can be implemented to a great extent through an exchange of shares, whereas a foreign one requires a large element of straight cash payment.

In view of the small number of takeovers and partnerships involving community companies of different nationality, it is hardly surprising that there have been so few mergers between equals. Such mergers are always among the most hazardous business operations to carry through successfully. The principal object of a corporate union of any sort is to increase the profitability, competitiveness, and efficiency of the combined enterprise so that the whole is greater than the sum of the parts. This usually involves pooling resources, cutting out duplicated activities, closing down redundant plants, and reducing the number of staff at all levels. When one company takes over another there is no doubt about who is the master. If the management of the company that has carried through the takeover has the strength of character, the experience, and the plans it can impose its will. In the last resort it need not pay too much attention to the feelings of the executives of the company that has been acquired. In a merger between equals the normal problems are rendered far more difficult because there is no undisputed master, and the interests of both sides to the marriage must at least appear to receive equal treatment.

The injection of nationalist feelings adds a further complication. The normal jealousies, rivalries, and suspicions of bad faith are increased, and it becomes harder than ever for a single undisputed decision-maker commanding the obedience and respect of all to merge. In international organizations, such as the European Commission, the North Atlantic Treaty Organization, and the United Nations agencies, it is the practice to ensure that each member state gets its fair share of the plum jobs; nationality in short takes priority over ability. In a transnational merger it is difficult to avoid the same thing happening on a modified scale. Nationality as well as ability must be taken into account in making senior appointments, which leads to a tendency to duplicate rather than to reduce staff. Agfa–Gevaert, for instance, had to appoint two marketing directors at one stage because the Germans did not want a Belgian controlling marketing in Germany. The closure of plants also becomes more difficult because the government and trade unions in each country are anxious to ensure that the people for whom they are responsible should not lose their jobs in order to help factories abroad. In ordinary mergers men can be offered alternative employment in the expanding factories if their own are closed down. In a transnational merger this is likely to be impractical. 'For every move towards rationalization an explanation is demanded,' says Dr Albert Beken, a Belgian director of Agfa–Gevaert. 'This makes it difficult to reap the rewards of efficiency.'*

The attitudes of governments and their demands for assurances about how the merged company will function play a major part in the discussions leading up to a proposed transnational merger, and can indeed deter the companies concerned from going ahead. Large companies and industries that are closely linked with a country's defence effort, and one way or another many are, cannot be considered in a purely commercial context. For strategic and foreign policy reasons governments are reluctant to see them pass out of the exclusive control of their own nationals, just as they do not like to commit all their armed forces to an international command. Their feelings tend to be especially strong on this count when the company involved in the proposed merger is the only nationally-owned representative in a particular industry.

There are other matters too which arouse their concern. Large companies are substantial employers of labour, and the impact of their orders is felt throughout the economy.

* *The Times*, 30 June 1969.

Governments are anxious to ensure that their work, expansion programmes, and orders are not diverted to foreign countries. This is a danger inherent in the operations of all international companies, but governments are in a much stronger position to demand assurances while merger discussions are in progress than when they are dealing with an established enterprise.

Although a merger between equals is not the same as a takeover, the results are in many ways similar. The merged company will have to take account of other national interests to a greater extent than if it was on its own. A merger must also mean that the decision centre will, at the very least, be partially removed from both countries involved if two headquarters are set up, and completely removed from one if there is a single headquarters. In the eyes of government and public opinion this may be regarded as a blow to national prestige. In fact, the Colonna Report suggests that the movement of a decision centre is 'a psychological problem, which is probably the most difficult obstacle to be overcome in respect of multinational mergers within the Community'.

There have been several examples of how strongly governments feel in these matters. In France a determined, though ultimately unsuccessful, official effort was made to prevent the Italian Fiat from gaining effective control of Citroen, despite the desire of Michelin, Citroen's owners, that the deal should go through. In Germany the Government was more successful when it prevented the Compagnie Française des Pétroles from securing a thirty-two per cent stake in the Gelsenberg oil company. In Britain the Industrial Reorganization Corporation stymied the plans of the Swedish SKF to increase its already substantial share of the ball bearing industry.

None of these examples concerns a straightforward merger between equals, but nor were they straightforward takeovers in which the junior company stood to lose all its identity. They fall somewhere in between. But whatever the proposed form of association between the companies had been, it is difficult to believe that official attitudes would have been very different. In all three cases the governments made it quite clear that they were primarily motivated by nationalism, and the desire to maintain exclusive control of the companies in the hands of their own citizens. Moreover, it is significant that the French and German actions were taken against companies from within the Common Market, while the British took theirs against a company from a fellow member of the European Free Trade Area. In short, this is a field in which the reality of international cooperation is quite different from the theory.

Quite apart from nationalism, in both its official and personal manifestations, there are a number of technical problems that render it extremely difficult for two companies of different nationality to merge as equals. In an ordinary takeover involving two companies one purchases the shares of the other, either by agreement or not. The company taken over may disappear as a corporate entity. If it continues to exist, it does so as a subsidiary with all or most of its shares in the hands of the company that bid for it. In a merger between equals the situation is more complicated.

Neither side is prepared to sell out to the other, or to give the appearance of having done so. A new arrangement must be devised. Basically there are three alternatives. A new company may be created in which both sink their assets and identities, and in which their respective shareholders are accorded positions of equality; or a new system of jointly owned subsidiaries may be established; or the two companies link their activities to such an extent that they operate as one. Any of these or a combination of them may be used.

The creation of a new company raises so many difficulties that it has never been tried. The most obvious is that it would have to be incorporated under the laws of one or other of the countries concerned, or in some third country.

This would involve dissolving the company to be moved and reconstituting it in a new form in its new home. In most countries taxes would have to be paid at both stages of the operation, and in all the permission of the government would be required. In France, Belgium, and Luxembourg such a move would require the unanimous assent of the shareholders, which would, in practice, be impossible to secure. Even where unanimity is not required it is difficult to imagine shareholders accepting such a move easily. In most countries they are prepared to hold some of their capital in foreign shares, but in all the great majority prefer that most of it should be in domestic shares, and in many countries the big institutional investors, such as insurance companies and pension funds, are obliged by law to follow this policy. This is not simply a matter of narrow nationalism. Differences in tax rates and systems, and exchange control regulations, create a number of practical problems for both shareholders and companies.

Other problems would also arise. One is that in some countries the institutions hold a much greater proportion of the shares of large companies than in others. In Germany, for instance, the banks are particularly powerful. Consequently a company merging with a German concern might find that one of the big banks became by far the largest shareholder in the merged concern. This would not only pose operational difficulties, it would also make it very difficult to devise a deal that would simultaneously meet the requirements of a small group of large shareholders on the one hand, and a large group of small shareholders, as would be the case with a British company, on the other. Another problem under this heading is the preference of shareholders in different countries for different types of security. The British, for example, prefer equities, although the Belgians like fixed interest stocks; and while, within a single country, mergers and takeovers can be carried through by an exchange of securities with a relatively small cash element, in a transnational merger this becomes desperately complicated with the different interests of the two sets of shareholders.

The two founding fathers of transnational mergers, Shell and Unilever, each chose different ways of putting their plans into effect. Shell is based on the joint subsidiary principle, while Unilever works through linking the activities of its British and Dutch ends so that the two function as one.

The Royal Dutch Shell Group, to give it its full name, is in reality a family of companies sixty per cent owned by the Royal Dutch and forty per cent by the British Shell Transport and Trading. All assets, interests, and dividends on the one hand, and all taxes and expenditures on the other are divided between them on a 60/40 basis so that the balance between their respective shareholders is always maintained. The group itself begins with two holding companies, each owned 60/40 by the parents. One is called Shell Petroleum NV and has its headquarters in Holland, while the other is Shell Petroleum Limited based in Britain. They are responsible for the disposition of the group's capital, its investment policy, the return on capital, and the related appraisal of results. The focal point of the whole organization and the ultimate seat of authority is the Committee of Managing Directors, which consists of the managing directors of Shell Petroleum Limited, and the members of the Presidium of Shell Petroleum NV. The committee's views and instructions are implemented by four service companies, which are responsible for controlling, coordinating, and advising (the word the group likes best) the operating companies throughout the world.

Unilever is a straightforward 50/50 union between Unilever Limited in London and Unilever NV in Rotterdam. Either one or the other owns all the capital in most of the subsidiaries, and a majority or a large part of it in the rest. The two parents are separate companies, but so closely linked that they work as one. Each director is on the boards of both, and at the top there is a Special Com-

The Shell group of companies

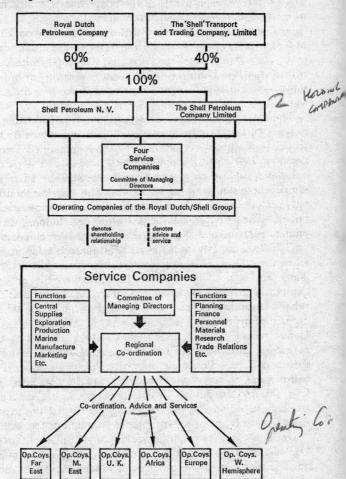

The Multinationals

mittee of three men to which the board has delegated most of its functions, and which takes virtually all the decisions that matter. At present it consists of Dr Ernest Woodroofe, the chairman of Limited, Harold Hartog, the chairman of NV, and David Orr, the vice-chairman of Limited. Beneath them come a number of product group coordinators and regional committees that control, coordinate, and advise the operating companies. All these groups are completely integrated between the two parents. In addition the parents are linked by a number of agreements, the most important of which provides for the payment of equal dividends to their shareholders.

Agfa–Gevaert has drawn on both the Shell and Unilever precedents, though more on Shell's. The marriage contract between the German Agfa, which is 91.5 per cent owned by Bayer and 8.5 per cent by Boehringer & Söhne, and the Belgian Gevaert, which has numerous shareholders, is based on two jointly-owned operating subsidiaries. The

Agfa-Gevaert's marriage contract

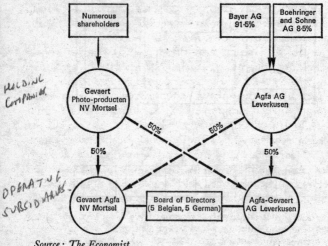

Source: The Economist

parents are simply holding companies. The real work is
done by the subsidiaries, Agfa-Gevaert in Germany, and
Gevaert Agfa in Belgium, each of which is owned 50/50 by
the two parents. Theoretically the subsidiaries have separate
boards, but in practice the same five Belgians and five
Germans sit on both. From there on down the operation
of the two companies are integrated in varying degrees with
joint committees on production, research, planning, administration, sales, and so forth. Profits are pooled, and
divided equally between the parents.

The union between Dunlop and Pirelli came into effect
on 1 January 1971 although the two companies did not
complete their exchange of interests until 30 June 1971.*

The details of the marriage are complicated by the fact
that Pirelli is itself a dyarchy with parent companies in
Italy – Pirelli SpA – and Switzerland – Société Internationale Pirelli SA. But the essential point is that it is a
marriage between equals. Dunlop acquires a 49 per cent
interest in Pirelli's operations in Italy and the other countries of the European Economic Community and 40 per
cent elsewhere in exchange for transferring to Pirelli
equivalent interests in its own operations. The result is the
corporate structure shown overleaf.

The former Dunlop and Pirelli parent companies are
now holding companies, and all the operating companies
are owned by them in the agreed proportions. Dunlop and
Pirelli each have the right to be represented on the boards of
the jointly-owned companies, but the management responsibility for them rests on the partner having the higher
percentage shareholding. The key group in the new arrangement is the Central Coordinating Committee, which determines the partnership's policies towards research and
development, production, and investment, and issues instructions to the individual operating companies. Dunlop

*Certain activities of both companies have been kept out of the
merger, and continue to be owned separately by their original parents.
They are not significant enough to alter the concept of the union.

and Pirelli each have four members on this committee, and it is shared alternately by Sir Reay Geddes of Dunlop and Signor Leopoldo Pirelli, with Sir Reay taking the first year.

The VFW–Fokker arrangements are more simple, and fall short of a full merger in the technical sense. The two groups have set up a joint management company called Zentral Gesellschaft in which they hold equal shares to coordinate their activities. It is based in Düsseldorf, and has three Dutch and three German directors.

The examples of Shell, Unilever, Agfa–Gevaert, VFW–Fokker, and Dunlop–Pirelli show that if companies of

The Dunlop-Pirelli union

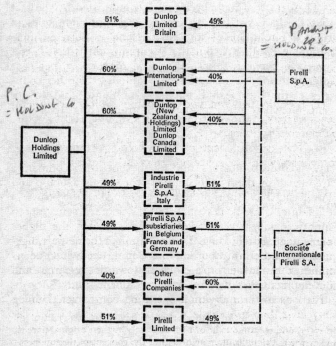

118

different nationality want to merge they can. It is not necessary for their home countries to join the Common Market, or for the companies concerned to receive any special legal, tax, or other privileges. The mergers can be fitted into the normal existing framework so long as the companies themselves have the will to make their agreements work.

There is, however, a strong body of opinion which contends that a uniform European company statute is necessary. The statute has become something of a symbol of European unity, and its absence is widely used as an explanation for the failure of European industry to move further and faster towards transnational mergers. Consequently the European Commission's announcement in the summer of 1970 that it had adopted a draft statute that would be submitted to the Council of Ministers was warmly welcomed. In the first instance the statute will, if accepted, be open to joint stock companies engaged in three types of venture:

(1) Mergers between two companies which have their headquarters in different member states, but wish to combine across frontiers.

(2) The establishment of joint holding companies by companies with their headquarters in different member states.

(3) The establishment of joint subsidiaries by companies with their headquarters in different member states.

The community-based subsidiaries of non-community companies, such as BP Germany or General Motors Belgium, qualify to take advantage of the statute, and there is a minimum capital requirement of $500,000 for mergers and holding companies, and $250,000 for subsidiaries.

The object is not to supplant the existing national company laws, but to provide a new legal framework within which companies could more easily initiate transnational operations. At present national company laws vary widely so that the rights, and duties, of corporate bodies also differ. So too do the responsibilities, privileges, and obligations of boards of directors, and shareholders. To bring the national codes into line with each other will be a massive task. Though the commission is working on a long-term harmonization programme, it wants to provide a new statute to enable companies to be incorporated under terms that would be equally acceptable in all member countries. The statute is designed to run in parallel with the existing national statutes.

A company incorporated under the community statute would be registered at the community's Court of Justice and come under that body's judicial control in a number of respects. But it would not be a supra-national body in the true sense of that word. It would have to follow the tax regime of the country in which it elected to place its headquarters, and whatever legal obligations might be imposed on corporate bodies by the local government. Lawyers foresee considerable trouble in distinguishing between questions that should be decided in the national courts according to national law, and those that should go to the European Court. They consider that national courts may not always be prepared to allow references to the European Court or to accept its rulings in cases where the statute is unclear and issues of national law are involved.

There is no doubt that a decision by member countries to accept a new community statute would have an important psychological impact. It would turn industrialists' minds towards the possibilities of European cooperation and mergers, and encourage them to seek ways round the obstacles that remain. But it would be only the first step on a very long road. The others include common tax laws and rates, common accountancy and auditing procedures, and a common code of stock exchange regulations. These are highly technical matters, but none the less crucial to a company's *modus operandi* and to the public's confidence in it. It is inconceivable that a community statute could become a device for enabling companies to arrange their affairs in such a way as to take advantage of the least demanding tax systems, accountancy practices, and stock exchange regulations to be found in the member countries. If it did, the governments would be forced to withdraw their support, but long before that the investing public would refuse to buy the shares or take up the bonds of the companies involved. They would prefer the protection provided by more familiar institutions set up under their own national laws.

The development of a complete legal, financial, accounting, and investment framework within which transnational European companies could evolve and operate as easily as national companies will take a long time. A long time will however also be required before companies are ready to embark with confidence on the enormous organizational and administrative problems inherent in cross-frontier mergers.

Part Two:

How Multinational Business
Works Today

6. Planning in a Multinational Company

A characteristic feature of multinational companies is that their subsidiaries operate under the discipline and framework of a common global strategy, and common global control. The head office is their brain and nerve centre. It evolves the corporate strategy, decides where new investment should be located, allocates export markets and research programmes to the various subsidiaries, and determines the prices that should be charged in inter-affiliate exchanges. The relationship between the head office of a multinational company and its national subsidiaries is similar to that of the supreme headquarters of an army with its subordinate commands in the field. Brigadiers and battalion commanders are powerful and important men. Much is left to their discretion and initiative. Their advice is sought by the general and taken into account when the plan of campaign is drawn up. If their spirit or judgement fails the army will be undone. But the limits of their authority are set at headquarters, and can be increased or diminished as the general decides. They take their decisions and formulate their plans within the context of his strategy, and in the knowledge that he can sack or promote them as he wishes. The same applies in a multinational company.

A multinational is no different from any other company in this respect. All companies are judged by their overall performance. The component parts cannot be regarded in isolation. They must be assessed in the light of their contribution to the profits and objectives of the company as a whole. In some cases the top management may decide to delegate considerable powers to the subsidiaries, and in others to centralize as much as possible. But in any event the subsidiaries are supposed to put the wider interests of the company as a whole above their own, and the managers know that their own future and promotion prospects depend on the good opinion of the top men at head office.

This raises important issues of principle in the relationship between multinational companies and governments. Governments regard themselves as the guardians of the national interest, and are held responsible for the conduct of national economic affairs by the electorate. They are therefore anxious to ensure that companies operating within their frontiers pursue policies which harmonize with their objectives. The local subsidiary of a multinational naturally tries to meet the wishes of the government, and may be prepared to undertake a number of ventures of dubious commercial validity in an effort to secure its good will. But this does not alter the fact that it has an overriding extra-territorial commitment to its parent company.

The parent secures this commitment through a variety of means. But it exercises its most constant influence on its subsidiaries through its control of the overall company structure and the planning function, which between them determine the flow of investment funds. Company structures and planning procedures vary widely depending on management style, the nature of the industry, and a host of other factors. No company could be described as typical. However, the Canadian Alcan Aluminium provides as good an illustration as any of how a leading multinational works in these respects.

Alcan makes and sells nearly half the aluminium that moves across frontiers in the non-Communist world. Unlike its U.S. rivals it cannot rely on a large home market, and always has to think and plan in global terms. It has a long and impressive list of directors and officers, but the key men are the five members of the Group Executive Committee: the president, Nathanael V. Davis, and four executive vice-

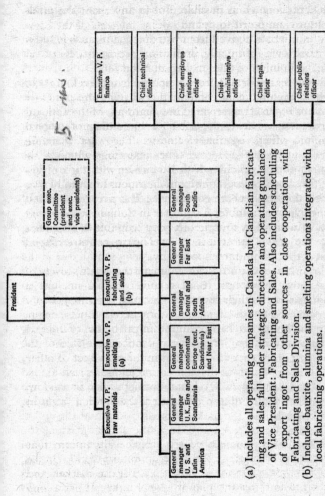

5 Abs

(a) Includes all operating companies in Canada but Canadian fabricating and sales fall under strategic direction and operating guidance of Vice President: Fabricating and Sales. Also includes scheduling of export ingot from other sources – in close cooperation with Fabricating and Sales Division.

(b) Includes bauxite, alumina and smelting operations integrated with local fabricating operations.

Alcan Aluminium Limited group organization chart

presidents, one each in charge of finance, raw materials, smelting, and fabricating and sales.

Aluminium is derived from bauxite, a substance found in the earth's crust, which looks like red sandstone. It consists of an aluminium oxide, called alumina, and iron oxide.* The raw materials division is responsible for the first stages in the company's chain of activities. It finds and mines the bauxite, which is then refined into alumina. Most of Alcan's bauxite reserves are in the Caribbean, and the production of alumina, which resembles a fine white powder, generally takes place near the mine. The next stage involves the reduction of the alumina into aluminium metal ingots in a smelter. The process requires an enormous amount of electricity, and smelters are normally cited in areas with plenty of cheap power. Most of Alcan's are in Canada and Norway, both of which have numerous rivers capable of sustaining large-scale hydro-electric facilities. The two countries supply most of the aluminium imported by Alcan subsidiaries in the main consumer countries, although in recent years several of these subsidiaries have built relatively small smelters to produce some of their own requirements. The final stage is the conversion of the ingot into fabricated products ranging from cooking foil to cables, and from car bodies to building materials. This manufacturing operation, the sale of the products, and most of the smelters in the consumer countries are all in the hands of the fabricating and sales division led by David M. Culver. To quote from the company's own internal account † of its organization, the division 'assumes, to a large degree, the make-or-break position at the end of the mine-to-market chain'. It is the largest part of the company, and responsible for the bulk of its international

---

*Four tons of bauxite are needed to produce two tons of alumina, which in turn yields one ton of aluminium. About 18,000 kilowatt hours of electricity are required to smelt a ton of aluminium. This is the equivalent of a two-bar electric fire switched on for more than a year.

†*Compass*, Vol. XI, Number 10, December 1967. *Compass* is the company house magazine.

interests. It has sales offices, resident representatives, or agents in more than a hundred countries.

In common with many other multinationals, Alcan organizes its global interests on a regional basis. The various national subsidiaries in the fabricating and sales division are grouped together in areas, each with its own general manager. The heads of the national subsidiaries report to the general managers, who in turn report to David Culver at the head office in Montreal. Each area is supposed to be largely self-sufficient, which means that the subsidiaries within it trade extensively with each other, but not much with their sister companies in other areas, apart from importing their raw materials. Some plants are built to serve single national markets, while others are designed with a whole area in mind. A typical example of the latter is the rolling mill at Norf in Germany, which supplies the entire continental European area.

Significantly, Alcan's areas are not based on the politico-economic divisions drawn up by governments. There is a single general manager for Britain, Ireland, and Scandinavia, although Ireland is not part of the European Free Trade Area, and another for Europe and the Near East, whose empire includes the Common Market plus such EFTA members as Switzerland, Austria and Portugal. The main considerations are the location of Alcan's interests, its lines of communication and transportation, and the necessity of ensuring that each area is not too large for a single general manager to control.

The annual planning cycle begins in late spring or early summer with the aim of drawing up a fairly detailed plan for the coming year, and rougher outlines for those beyond. The raw materials and smelting divisions are told by the Executive Committee to assume a certain level of production and sales, and to plan accordingly. The fabricating and sales division approaches the problem from the other end. David Culver asks his managers what they think they can do. They in turn ask the national subsidiaries. Each subsidiary makes its own plan. These are welded into larger area plans, which are sent to the head office in Montreal. There they are consolidated into an overall division plan for submission to the Executive Committee at a meeting which usually takes place in the last week of July.

Salesmen are congenital optimists, and the fabricating and sales division's plan invariably calls for more money and metal than the group can provide. Accordingly the Executive Committee's task is to match the capabilities of the raw materials and smelting divisions to the requirement of fabricating and sales. At this point the finance division has an important role to play. It conducts a review of changes in production rates and major capital investment projects on the one hand, and the transfer prices charged in exchanges between the various parts of the company on the other, in order to ensure that the group as a whole is making a profit. The result of all this discussion is that agreement is usually reached on a plan somewhere between that originally put forward by fabricating and sales and those of the two producer divisions.

In the event of a dispute between the executive vice-presidents, the arbiter is Nathanael V. Davis who, as president, carries the 'ultimate responsibility for all group activities.' He takes the final decisions involved in 'selecting that combination of investments in raw material, smelting, and fabricating capacity that will earn the greatest return on the group's capital and managerial resources.'* His task, like that of any head of an international company, is to survey the world impartially, and to decide which course of action is in Alcan's best interests. All other considerations must be subordinate to that.

After the Executive Committee meeting the three divisions know what their programmes are, and what target rates of return on investment and capital employed they must strive to achieve. They themselves, under their own executive vice-presidents, must decide which

* *Compass*, Vol. XI, Number 10, December 1967.

of their projects to keep, which to trim, and which to drop.

As soon as the Executive Committee's deliberations are over, the fabricating and sales division's area general managers assemble in Montreal. They have already been told how their original plan fared, and it is up to them, under David Culver's chairmanship, to put together a new one within the prescribed limits. Each general manager is naturally anxious to defend as much of his own proposals as possible, and the debate can be fierce and tough as each tries to show why he can secure the best rate of return, move the most metal, or in some other way best serve the interests of the Alcan group.

When the order of priorities has at last been worked out, they return home to call meetings of the heads of the companies within their areas. The same procedure is repeated until eventually every national subsidiary knows where it stands in the company's plan. Each has its own particular set of aims, and its own target rate of return. These vary from country to country to take account of the different competitive and other pressures in the various markets. It is for the local executives themselves to decide how to fulfil the objectives they have been set. The crucial point is that these objectives, which dictate the parameters within which the national companies must work, have been set from the centre with the wider interests of the group as the first consideration.

The plan is not a solid unchangeable structure. If it was, Alcan would be unable to react to circumstances. As situations change so can projects be added to or subtracted from the agreed programme.

An example of an important addition coming into the plan in mid-year occurred in early 1967 when John Elton, the general manager for Britain, Ireland and Scandinavia, told Montreal that the British Government was becoming anxious to establish a large local aluminium smelting industry. The government's attitude owed much to a proposal put forward by Rio Tinto-Zinc, a British-owned international metals group that wanted to break into the British aluminium market following its discovery of enormous bauxite reserves in Australia. Alcan, the leading aluminium company in Britain, had no desire to undertake a smelter project of its own at that time, although it had been considering the possibility of building one sometime in the future. However Rio Tinto-Zinc's initiative could not be ignored. British Aluminium, the second largest company in the market, and the smaller Swiss-owned Star Aluminium both began working on ideas for smelters of their own, and it was clear to Elton that unless Alcan did the same its position in Britain would be threatened. So he asked Montreal for permission to go ahead. Culver put the proposal to the Executive Committee. Nobody much liked it. A British smelter would disrupt the group's investment plans, and the flow of metal from the big smelters in Canada and Norway which supplied the British subsidiary. But the committee was convinced that if Britain created a smelting industry, and Alcan was not part of it, the company would inevitably lose its leading position in the market. Accordingly, Elton was given permission to try to get one of the projects envisaged by the British Government for Alcan, and he succeeded.

No company likes to lose a dominant position in a market, and all are keen to maintain good relations with the governments of the countries where they operate. But the crucial point in the authorization of a new project is that it should be in the overall interest of the group as a whole. This can only be measured in financial terms. It may be that a company will decide to go ahead with a project that does not fulfil its customary financial criteria. There may be many reasons for this, such as the need to protect an existing investment, or a belief that one day the project will provide an opening through which the company will be able to take advantage of great opportunities. But at least it wants to know the cost so that it can decide whether the potential benefits are worth the price.

At Alcan all major projects, whether entirely new, such as

the British smelter, or already allowed for in the forward plans, have to receive an individual appropriation from Montreal. If the project is already in the plan it is marked 'specified', and the process is normally fairly straightforward. If it is unforeseen it is designated 'unspecified', and the examination will be more rigorous. But in both cases, in the fabricating and sales division, the sequence of events is the same. The first step is an examination by the division's development committee, which sends a recommendation to David Culver. Both he and the executive vice-president in charge of finance, John Hale, must then approve it. If the project is particularly costly or significant it would also go up to the full Executive Committee, and at any stage a higher authority can overrule a lower.

In addition to setting the subsidiaries' rates of return and approving the financial appropriations for their major projects, Montreal has one other important means of financial control at its disposal. This is its control over the distribution and price of the raw materials used by the subsidiaries. All the ingot and alumina produced within the group, and supplied to the national subsidiaries in the fabricating and sales division, is sold through a central pool run by head office. The subsidiaries are charged for whatever they buy at a price set by Montreal.

Within the parameters established by head office Alcan's managers have considerable freedom of action to run their own affairs. The company's senior executives emphasize that they do not want yes-men. Unless the area and national managers are dynamic individuals willing to fight for sales to customers and for all they can get at internal planning sessions with equal vigour the system would break down. At the point of sale, and at the point at which the information is collected and forecasts made on which the central planning decisions are largely based, the company's success depends on the men who run the subsidiaries. But just as a military unit cannot operate without supplies of food and ammunition, so the subsidiary of a multinational company cannot survive without money. In the words of Nathanael V. Davis: 'We sure have it on financial control.'

The company where the principle of financial control has perhaps been taken furthest is the U.S.-based International Telephone and Telegraph, or ITT as it is usually called.* ITT is the world's largest conglomerate with world-wide interests ranging from telecommunications to Sheraton Hotels and Avis Rent-a-Car. It is run by Harold Geneen, who has acquired a legendary reputation as manager. Between 1959, when he took over as chief executive, and 1969 the company's sales increased from $766m. to $5,475m., and it made over two hundred takeovers. His whole life is the company. Richard Griebel, a former ITT executive who is now president of Lehigh Valley Industries, has been quoted as saying: 'Three things should be written on Hal Geneen's tombstone – earnings per share, fifteen per cent growth, and size'.

The company claims that its planning and controls system is the most sophisticated in the world. The men who run the subsidiaries have considerable freedom of action to propose policies for their companies, and to run them as they think fit, so long as everything is going well, but their lives revolve round Geneen. Every month ITT's top European managers meet under his chairmanship in Brussels. He is accompanied by about forty people from the head office in New York, and a number of more junior managers and specialists are invited, either to learn or to provide facts and advice.

The meetings last between four and ten hours with occasional breaks for sandwiches and nothing stronger than beer to drink. They 'are conducted as a teach-in', says Ken Corfield, managing director of a British subsidiary Standard

*I am much indebted to David Palmer, Management Editor of the *Financial Times*, for this section on ITT. A fuller account of the company's methods was published by him under the title 'What it's like to work for Geneen', in the *Financial Times* on 11 September 1970. I have drawn heavily upon it.

Telephones and Cables. They begin with the financial results for the previous month, arranged by individual company, product line, and group. Then come reports from the European treasurer and manufacturing staff set out on the same lines. All the figures and other information are measured by two yardsticks – the annual budget, set every September for the year beginning 1 January, and the monthly forecast made each month for the following month. Corfield says Geneen can interpret the figures instantaneously, and pick out the weaknesses or potential weaknesses in every operation. 'If things are going wrong, he will ask – "What actions are you taking to put these right?" And if the actions you report do not seem adequate, a task force is set up consisting of members of the European and American staff who come and make a report on what you are doing.'

Geneen also chairs quarterly meetings of 'Strategy and Action boards' for each of ITT's major product lines where the same methods are employed. Altogether he is estimated to run about thirty-five a year in Brussels and about 130 in the rest of the world. There is no aspect of the company's activities that escapes his scrutiny, and he coordinates its affairs throughout the world with the aim of improving the earnings per share of the parent company and maintaining its rate of growth.

Only an exceptional man could work like Geneen, and there is much speculation as to whether his system of personal control could survive his retirement or death. Be that as it may, his example shows the extent to which an international company can be directed from the centre in pursuit of the centre's interests. ITT is subjected to many different pressures, and must take account of many different national interests, but its operations transcend frontiers to the same extent as those of General Eisenhower when the armies under his supreme command advanced across Europe in 1944 and 1945.

7. The Companies and World Trade

The most dramatic manifestation of the influence of international companies on the conduct of national economic policy is the share of world trade now accounted for by the movement of goods between their subsidiaries in different countries. Statistics on this subject are more than usually scarce, and for most countries completely unobtainable. But those that are available show that the internal transactions of international companies have become of crucial importance to the balance of payments of Britain and the U.S.

In an analysis * of British trade in 1966, the only year for which this particular exercise has been carried out, the Board of Trade found that twenty-two per cent of Britain's exports in value terms were accounted for by 'transactions between related concerns'. This means a sale by a branch of an international company, whether British or foreign-owned, in Britain to an affiliate abroad. A shipment by Ford of Britain to Ford of Belgium, or by Imperial Chemical Industries in Britain to Imperial Chemical Industries in Germany, are typical examples. The Board of Trade's research showed that a striking feature of the activities of U.S.-controlled companies in Britain is that their principal trading partners overseas are their sister companies. In 1966 fifty-six per cent of their total exports went to affiliates, while other foreign-owned companies sent thirty-five per cent of their exports to affiliates, and British-owned international groups twenty-seven per cent of their exports to overseas subsidiaries. No statistics have so far been published concerning the proportion of Britain's imports resulting from similar

* *Board of Trade Journal*, 16 August 1968.

internal transactions within international companies. But the proportion is likely to be at least as high as in the case of exports.

The only remotely comparable information is published in the U.S., and it too is badly out of date. The Department of Commerce has calculated * that in 1964 sales by U.S.-based international companies to their affiliates abroad accounted for about twenty-five per cent of all U.S. exports. In 1969 the department published † additional figures for 1965 covering the activities of 320 companies with combined exports amounting to $8,500m. These showed that the companies channelled more than half their overseas sales through their affiliates. Not only would the figures themselves now be very much larger, but in view of the rapid expansion of U.S. investment overseas since the mid-1960s it can be assumed that the importance of internal transactions to the U.S. balance of payments has further increased.

Most other countries do not publish similar statistics on the composition of their foreign trade. But it is reasonable to assume that in several smaller European nations international companies play an even larger role than in Britain and the U.S. Professor Jack N. Behrman suggests ‡ that in one year the two-way exchanges between the Ford plants in Belgium and Germany constituted about a sixth of Belgium's total exports and imports.

Companies are usually very careful not to draw attention to the implications of their multinational production by openly threatening to take reprisals against a government whose policies they do not like. But sometimes the mask drops. In 1969 when the British Government was considering the recommendations of the Sainsbury Committee, which it had appointed to advise on the reorganization of

* *Survey of Current Business*, November 1965.

† *Survey of Current Business*, May 1969.

‡ 'Some Patterns in the Rise of the Multinational Enterprise' by Professor Jack N. Behrman. Research Paper 18 (Graduate School of Business, University of North Carolina, 1969).

the pharmaceutical industry, Justin Dart, the chairman and president of the U.S. Rexall Drug and Chemical Company, issued a significant warning.* He pointed out that two-thirds of the British pharmaceutical industry was American controlled, and that American companies were responsible for about £50m. of the industry's favourable trade balance of £77m. 'These exports,' he said, 'could go forward from Canada, the U.S., Australia, or the continent ... If the climate here (in Britain) becomes too unfavourable for American-based companies to develop exports, then inevitably they are bound to re-locate at least a portion of such operations.'

The position of multinational companies makes nonsense of conventional theories of international trade as taught in classical economics, where it is assumed that international trade is the result of bargaining between independent traders in different countries with a willing buyer in one doing a deal with a willing seller in another on the basis of such commercial criteria as price, quality, and date of delivery. The ability of governments to intervene by tying markets in one country to producers in another, or by cutting trading links altogether for political purposes, is recognized. But the role of companies with production facilities and markets all over the world is not generally appreciated. An international company is simultaneously both buyer and seller. Its plants in different countries can be linked so that they cooperate in the production of a single product. Although separated by many hundreds or even thousands of miles, they may be as much a part of the same production chain as two assembly lines housed in separate buildings in the same factory. The patterns of their trade are set not through a series of bargains struck by free or impersonal competition but by the management's decision on where to locate its plants, and what the task of each affiliate should be.

IBM is a case in point. Outside the U.S. it does not manu-

* *Financial Times*, 10 April 1969.

facture a complete 360-series computer in any single country. Its subsidiaries in Britain, France, Germany, Italy, and elsewhere each concentrate on producing various components and pieces of equipment, which are eventually brought together for final assembly. A typical 360 may include components from as many as four or five countries.

Tractors provide another example of how a modern international business can work in practice. Ford has three main plants – at Basildon in England, at Antwerp in Belgium, and at Highland Park, a suburb of Detroit in the U.S. Antwerp makes all the transmissions for Highland Park and Basildon, while Basildon makes the hydraulics and engines for the other two. Both Basildon and Antwerp import the selectospeed gear system from Highland Park, and Basildon supplies engines to Highland Park for the giant tractors used on the North American prairies. The 1964 annual report of the U.S. International Harvester declared that the company's French and German subsidiaries had combined to bring into production a new Common Market line of tractors. The German subsidiary was given the responsibility for the diesel engines, sheet metal components, and engineering work, while the French was entrusted with the transmissions and final drive assemblies. The Canadian Massey-Ferguson is equally transnational in scope. It can make tractors in the U.S. for sale in Canada that contain British-made engines, French transmissions, and Mexican axles.

The motor industry is also moving towards a considerable degree of internationalization. The extent to which Ford's European interests are already interwoven was shown during a month-long strike at the company's British plants in the early part of 1969. Within a week of its outbreak Belgian Ford had to lay off 2,000 men, and the production lines at German Ford's Cologne factory were disrupted. When the men returned to work Ford of Britain had lost production worth $89m., while the company's continental plants had lost $26.4m. It was especially unfortunate for Ford that the strike coincided with the launch of the Capri.

The Multinationals

Hailed as the first ever European car, the Capri was jointly designed by the British and German subsidiaries under the guidance of Ford of Europe, which coordinates the company's European interests, and is produced simultaneously in both countries. When the flow of parts from Britain dried up, the German output had to be cut temporarily by twenty-five per cent before alternative supplies could be secured from other sources.

Despite this blow Ford is moving rapidly towards organizing its interests on trans-European rather than national lines. The Escort small car, which originated from Ford of Britain, is already being assembled in Belgium from largely British parts for sale in Germany, and within two years Ford's entire car and truck range is expected to be common to the British and German subsidiaries. As the existing engines reach the end of their life they too will be replaced by common units. The cars and engines may sometimes differ slightly in order to achieve a national identity, or to meet a particular national preference, but their component parts will be duplicated as far as possible. Often they will come from the same factory, such as the company's transmission plant, currently under construction, near Bordeaux in France, which is being designed to supply Ford's needs throughout Europe.

The links between the Ford production facilities in Europe and North America are also being tightened. The Pinto, launched in 1970 as the company's challenger in the North American small car market, shows the shape of things to come. It is being manufactured in New Jersey and Missouri in the U.S. and Ontario in Canada, but most of its engines and transmissions come from Britain. Altogether Ford of Britain provides about one-sixth of the value of each car.

Significantly Ford of Germany will also be able to provide the same components so that if the British factories are hit by strikes or their shipments are disrupted for some other reason, there will be an alternative source of supply. Ford, like most other large groups, invariably tries to establish a reserve capacity of this sort in order to minimize the dangers of making its plants dependent on each other.

All companies engaged in mass production industries have to balance the advantages to be gained from going for the lowest unit costs with the need to ensure that they cannot be held to ransom by a single government or trade union. On purely economic grounds the best policy in most such industries would now be to concentrate the production of each component in a single factory in order to achieve the dramatic cost reductions that can be obtained from long production runs. But the economic advantages of this policy must be weighed against the dangers of strikes and other disruptions. Consequently companies usually try to maintain at least one alternative source of supply for each component. A second line of defence is computerized stock control so that stocks are maintained at a level which takes account of the degree of disruption normally expected. A third is to ensure that, where practical, production lines are sufficiently flexible to be able to switch from one model or component to another with a minimum of delay.

Computers, agricultural machinery, and motors are examples of industries which achieve their economies of scale through the manufacture of components and parts in several different countries so that the finished product is the culmination of an international cooperative effort. There are several others in the same position or moving towards it. But there are also those where a similar result may be achieved in a different fashion. Each subsidiary is given the task of manufacturing a particular product or range, and relies on its sister companies for the rest of the product line. Once again companies rarely put all their eggs in one basket for fear of strikes and other breakdowns in supply lines. But the basic principle is that each subsidiary should achieve the maximum economies of scale through concentrating on a limited and clearly defined task.

The Dutch Philips Lamp and the Italian Olivetti are

examples of this approach. They have adopted it only in the last few years. When they first expanded abroad before the war each national subsidiary manufactured a variety of products. But with the formation of the Common Market and the European Free Trade Area, the steady decline in world tariffs, and the rapid advance of mass production techniques, specialization has become the principal objective. It is one that cannot be achieved overnight; plants have to be closed, men retrained, and retailers reconciled to receiving their supplies from abroad. It is doubtful whether complete specialization with one or two factories accounting for each of all the major products would ever be practical.

Nonetheless, both companies have already made a good deal of progress. Philips has concentrated the manufacture of flat irons and mixers in Holland, electric fan heaters in Scotland, and cassette tape recorders in Austria. Italy, where the company has a controlling interest in Ignis, is its main source of refrigerators. Olivetti produces all its portable typewriters in Spain, and most of its manual machines in Scotland. But its aim is to have two plants for each product. Thus electric typewriters are made in Italy and the U.S., calculators in Italy and Mexico, and adding machines in Italy and Argentina, to take three examples.

Besides deciding how and where its products should be manufactured, the top management of an international company determines where they should be sold. Its subsidiaries are not free to choose their own export markets, or to compete for them with each other. General Motors sends Vauxhalls from its British subsidiary to Canada, and reserves the U.S. for Opels, which it usually brings in from Belgium rather than Germany. Ford used to import British Cortinas into the U.S. rather than German Taunuses until it started to produce the Pinto, when British Ford was given the engine contract to make up for the lost Cortina sales. There is no question of the British, German, or domestic U.S. managements disobeying the instructions from headquarters, nor can they do anything more than complain if the role they are given in the company's world-wide strategy is not to their liking. As the managing director of one of General Motors' European affiliates once explained: 'GM assigns us a plot of ground, and then judges us by what we grow on it'.* The same could be said of any other international company.

The plots of ground that these companies can assign are already substantial, and will grow very much larger. On the basis of present trends it seems quite possible that by 1980 forty per cent of Britain's manufactured exports could be provided by U.S.-controlled companies, and a further ten per cent by other foreign-owned concerns. Most of the rest will be accounted for by British companies with international interests. Britain is second only to the U.S. as a home base for international companies. Most other countries will rely on foreign-controlled companies for a much larger proportion of their exports. But the important point is not the nationality or the location of the headquarters of the companies. It is that a very high proportion of world trade will be in the hands of companies controlling subsidiaries in many countries.

During the 1970s three aspects of this situation are likely to cause increasing concern to governments. In the first place governments will worry that their national interests are being sacrificed in favour of another's. Second, they will be anxious to secure a reasonable share of an expanding company's new investment, and, third, they will be concerned over the effects of a company having to cut back its interests.

The issue of conflicts of national interests has already arisen in an acute form over the U.S. Government's restrictions on trade with Communist China. There are numerous examples of the foreign subsidiaries of U.S. companies refusing to accept export orders from China, which the local governments would have liked to accept, for fear of contravening these restrictions. Sometimes non-American com-

* *Stock Exchange Journal*, December 1968.

panies with extensive U.S. interests have also preferred to reject Chinese orders for fear of what the U.S. Government might do. The Canadian Alcan Aluminium, for instance, admitted in 1959 that 'it had declined a possible $1m. sale to Communist China because it feared an adverse political reaction in the United States. A spokesman for the company said from Montreal that while U.S. legal factors were not involved in Alcan's decision U.S. political factors were '.* The company was at the time under-producing in Canada, and the Canadian Government would have liked the Chinese deal to go through, but the company put U.S. feelings first 'rather than jeopardise its U.S. markets'.* The U.S. attitude towards trade with China has softened since 1959, but companies may be forced into having to make similar choices between the wishes and interests of two governments whenever intense international disputes arise. In the nature of things the wishes of the government of the country on which the company is most dependent are likely to prevail.

The securing of a reasonable share of an expanding company's new investment and export markets is a less clear-cut matter. The motor industry provides an example. Neither Britain nor Germany can reasonably complain about the records of Ford and General Motors in their respective countries. Both companies have spent a great deal of money purchasing local raw materials and components, continually expanded their plants, and achieved impressive export records. None the less the British and German Governments and trade unions must be worried at the pace at which the companies are expanding their assembly plants in Belgium, and the rate at which Belgian exports are increasing. What is good for General Motors cannot simultaneously be equally good for Britain, Germany, Belgium, and all the other countries where the company operates. And what is good for any one of them may very easily be bad for another.

The worst, though rarest, of the three major problems arising out of the international companies' position in world

* *Globe and Mail*, 22 January 1959.

trade concerns the effects of a large and important company
having to cut back its interests. The more a company ration-
alizes its interests and makes its plants dependent on
each other, the less viable each of its national subsidiaries
would be if they had to live on their own. If IBM went
bankrupt the governments of the countries where it operates
would find themselves left with the responsibility for providing employment for many thousands of men working in
plants that were designed to be links in a production chain
rather than self-contained entities. Cut off from the other
links they would be industrial white elephants. It is in the
highest degree improbable that IBM will go bankrupt, but
the same cannot be said for all large international companies. A few years ago it seemed to many that when a company reached a certain size it could never go to the wall; a
view that was encouraged by Professor J. K. Galbraith's
book *The New Industrial State*.* The bankruptcy of the
Pennsylvania Central Railroad, a major domestic U.S. company, in 1970 shattered that illusion, and created widespread
concern about many other corporate giants. One of the most
suspect was Chrysler, which occupies a key position in the
French and British motor industries as well as the American.
Within a few days of the Penn Central announcement
Chrysler decided to issue a highly unusual statement † to the
Press about its position and prospects in order to allay the
investment community's fears.

It is almost certainly too much to hope that the world can
survive the 1970s without at least one major multinational
going bankrupt or being forced to withdraw from its international commitments. When that happens it will be the
governments of the countries where its plants are situated
that will have to pick up the pieces, and look after the men
who are thrown out of work.

*Published by Hamish Hamilton.
†See *Wall Street Journal*, 24 June 1970.

8. How SKF Evens Out the Trade Cycle

One of the best examples of how a modern multinational company regulates its international trade is provided by the Swedish Aktiebolaget Svenska Kullagerfabriken, usually known simply as S K F. In terms of its position in a world industry S K F is the most powerful company in Europe. It is the world's largest manufacturer of ball and roller bearings, and accounts for about a quarter of the non-Communist world's supplies. It is about twice the size of its nearest rival, the U.S. Timken, and three times as big as its nearest European rival, the German F A G.

Bearings have none of the glamour of computers or aerospace, and their manufacture rarely engages political or nationalistic feelings.* None the less they are indispensable. They are a vital component in practically every manufactured product with moving parts. A diesel locomotive contains forty-five, a car twenty, and a bicycle or an operating table twelve each. S K F plays an important role in the economies of most advanced countries, and many others as well. Even in the U.S., where it holds only about twelve per cent of the markets, its technology is so highly regarded that government agencies employ it on basic research for the space and defence programmes, notwithstanding Sweden's political neutrality.

With nearly eighty per cent of its production and about ninety-five per cent of its sales outside Sweden, S K F takes

*S K F did however arouse precisely these feelings in Britain in 1968 and 1969 when it tried to increase its share of the market through the proposed takeover of a British company. The move was stymied by the I R C. See Chapter 5.

its multinationalism very seriously. In 1966 the managing director, Folke Lindskog, decided that it was no longer practical to retain Swedish as the company's internal language. So, despite the fact that SKF is Sweden's largest industrial concern and in some ways almost a national institution, like ICI in Great Britain or Volkswagen in Germany, he replaced it with English. Now all documents have to be prepared in English, and internal communications within the group are conducted in that language. It has become a business *lingua franca*, like Latin in the medieval Church. When non-Swedes are promoted beyond their local national company to another affiliate or to head office they are required to speak English, and do not have to know any Swedish, although some knowledge of the language is obviously a social advantage for anybody who has to live in the company's home city of Gothenburg.

Because bearings are so vital to those who use them SKF has always believed in establishing factories near its main customers. It was founded in 1907 by Dr Sven Wingquist, a textile engineer who invented the self-aligning ball bearing. He felt that if the company tried to supply its foreign markets from Sweden it would not be able to guarantee deliveries, and would therefore be vulnerable to local rivals. In 1910 he opened his first overseas plant in Britain, and by the end of the First World War, which shattered most links between the combatant nations, SKF had established others in France, the U.S., and Germany. Today the SKF group manufactures in fifteen countries, and has sales companies in 120 countries.

Many international companies like to maintain the fiction that each of their subsidiaries operates as if it was an independent concern, despite the self-evident absurdity of such a proposition. SKF is not so hypocritical. Lindskog argues frankly that in industries where profits depend on high-volume production lines working as near full capacity as possible, international companies enjoy substantial advantages over those whose activities are geared specifically to

The relationship between SKF's turnover and various Gross National Products

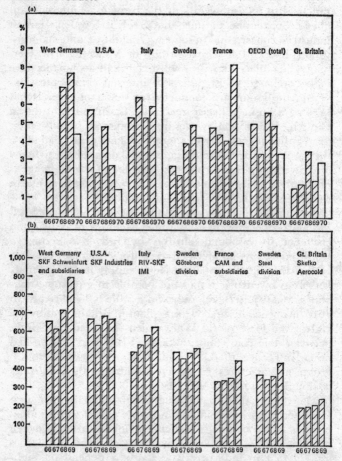

(a) *Increase in Gross National Product 1966–1969 and OECD forecast for 1970 by percentage*
(b) *Turnover comparison between the larger SKF Companies 1966–1969 in million Kroner*

meet the demands of a particular economy. They can also serve the needs of the countries where they operate more effectively. SKF contends that its aim is to maintain an even growth for all the companies in the group. Accordingly it does not expand its facilities in one country if there is spare capacity in another. It shares out the available work between its affiliates by switching export orders from one to the other.

SKF likes to illustrate this point by reference to its Italian affiliate RIV, of which it gained control in 1964 and 1965. When SKF engineers arrived at the RIV headquarters in Turin in 1964, the company was almost completely dependent on the Italian market, and had based its expansion plans on an over-optimistic assessment of the rate at which demand would rise. It was suffering from such overcapacity that it was in danger of collapse. So SKF kept it going by feeding it export orders worth over 50m. Swedish kroner. Then when Italian demand revived RIV was able to revert to concentrating on satisfying the local demand, and the export orders were cut off.

This sort of situation is far from unusual. In 1966 and 1967 the SKF factories in Germany found themselves short of work, and orders were re-directed there from other companies in the group. In 1968, however, German demand rose to the point where they could no longer meet it unaided, and so they turned to their partners in Italy, France, and Britain for supplies. As a senior executive explained with conscious under-statement: 'These orders together with others from several different sources within the SKF group helped the French SKF factories considerably after the events of May 1968.'

The details of the terms on which inter-affiliate deals take place are a closely guarded secret in all companies, national and international, and SKF is no exception. But they are based on two principles. The first is that the group tries to maintain a high level of capacity utilization among all its members so that international purchases are directed to those that need them, and not necessarily to the plants with the lowest costs. The other is that sister companies should not take advantage of each other's problems to drive the sort of hard bargain they would look for in an arm's-length deal with an outsider, but should share whatever sacrifices and benefits may be involved. This boils down to a cost-plus formula, though the extent of the crucial plus can vary from deal to deal.

The company derives several advantages from this system. The demand for bearings in any country is closely linked to the performance of the economy as a whole, which means that sales can fluctuate quite sharply. But except in a world depression it is rare for sales to decline simultaneously everywhere. There are usually some countries where they are rising and others where they are falling. So by sharing the workload among its affiliates SKF does not have to lay off men in one place, while hiring them, in competition with other employers, in another. It can also plan the likely rate of return on its investments in various countries with more certainty than would otherwise be the case by ensuring that they always operate above a certain minimum level of capacity. Another advantage of the system is that the company is saved from a wasteful duplication of facilities.

By coordinating the activities of its affiliates SKF protects them from the worst effects of the trade cycle. They do not have to increase their labour forces in one year only to cut them back in the next. They do not have to expand quickly to meet a sudden upsurge in demand only to find that they have either over-estimated its strength and are left with surplus capacity, or that they have been too cautious and are losing orders they cannot fill to competitors. They can move steadily forwards. This form of international co-operation with sister companies in different countries helping each other to overcome the fluctuations of the trade cycle represents, in an industrial context, the sort of relationship between nations that governments have long been striving to achieve in the political and defence spheres. In politics and defence conflicting national ambitions constantly create problems. But in industry, which attracts less public attention and is less emotive, enormous progress has been made. SKF is only one company among many.

Governments have been slow to grasp the implications of what is happening. When companies coordinate their activities on an international scale the individual affiliates necessarily become far less responsive both to government policy and to other influences within their own country. Thus if Britain devalues it does not follow that the local SKF factories will suddenly be able to export more bearings at a more competitive price to the continent at the expense of their French, German, and Italian sister companies. The interests and prospects of the British SKF will have to be weighed against those of the other affiliates at head office. Similarly, if French costs are increased as a result of strikes and other civil disorders the exports of the French SKF factories do not necessarily decline in line with their loss of competitiveness. They may even increase.

In a modern internationally coordinated company the key point at which long-term national interests are decided is the allocation of new investment.* Once plant and machinery have been installed in a particular country a company naturally wants to make as much use of it as possible. It also wants to remain on good terms with the local government by running its operations in a responsible fashion, paying taxes and duties, and observing local customs in labour relations. But this does not mean that it will necessarily be prepared to increase its investment. On the one hand it may decide that a country's long-term prospects are such that it ought to become a base for large-scale exports. On the other it may come to the conclusion that the best policy is to use exports only as a last resort when domestic orders are hard to find. This may be because the currency is over-valued, the trade unions irresponsible, the taxes high, or a combination of these and other reasons.

* For a full account of how international companies assess investment climates and decide where to put their new plants, see Chapter 12.

When international companies say they try to maintain a high level of work in all their subsidiaries this is usually true, but only half the story. The other and more important half concerns the rate at which their existing facilities are being enlarged in relation to their activities as a whole.

In the past all the major SKF manufacturing companies produced a full range of bearings. So each specific type was produced in several different factories. Now the company is 'trying to transform itself from being a collection of factories into a fully integrated corporation'. The aim, which is common to many international groups, is to cut out duplication as far as possible.

Especially in an industry that is vital on both economic and strategic grounds it is impossible ever to eliminate duplication entirely. If SKF decided to concentrate all its manufacture of aircraft bearings in, say, Sweden or Germany, it could hardly expect other governments to allow their airforces to remain dependent on it. The company must also maintain the ability to produce all the main types of bearing in its principal manufacturing centres as an insurance against strikes and other interruptions to supplies. It would be intolerable if the German motor industry, for instance, could be brought to a complete halt because of a strike in Britain or France, and the inability of the German SKF factories to fill the breach. Despite these limitations, however, there is plenty of scope for rationalization, particularly inside the Common Market and the European Free Trade Area. These two groups may duplicate each other's ranges, but within each one the company would like its affiliates to be complementary and inter-dependent rather than self-contained entities.

9. IBM's International Integration

Another aspect of the same problem is presented by IBM's research programme. Not since the nineteenth-century heyday of John D. Rockefeller's Standard Oil has a company achieved such an overwhelming position in a world industry of major strategic and economic importance as IBM.* It accounts for over seventy per cent of the general purpose digital computer market in the U.S., and has produced at least half of all the computers now installed in Western Europe. Its share of the non-Communist world market is between sixty-five and seventy per cent, and Britain is the only substantial country where it is not the market leader. A computer company depends more than most on research and development for its success, and IBM employs people from all over the world in these activities. As one of its executives once told me, 'People sometimes feel we are exploiting their country's brains and talents in the same way as a mining company exploits its natural resources.'

IBM is unusually sensitive to the issues raised by its dominant position. So instead of concentrating its research and development in the U.S. and thereby encouraging a massive 'brain drain' of researchers from the rest of the world to its domestic laboratories, it tries to help the countries where it operates to participate in its technological advance through work done in local laboratories. At present the company maintains seven in Europe and nineteen in the U.S., and new ideas and inventions can originate in any of the countries concerned.

*In some less critical industries, such as sewing machines with Singer, and banknotes with De La Rue, there are other companies holding comparable positions.

How IBM dominates the European computer scene

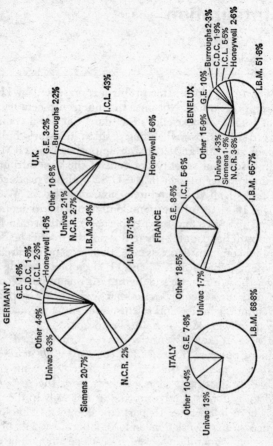

GERMANY

G.E. 1·6%
C.D.C. 1·5%
I.C.L. 2·3%
Honeywell 1·6%
Other 4·9%
Univac 8·3%
I.B.M. 57·1%
Siemens 20·7%
N.C.R. 2%

U.K.

G.E. 3·2%
Burroughs 22%
Other 10·8%
Univac 2·1%
N.C.R. 2·7%
I.B.M. 30·4%
I.C.L. 43%
Honeywell 5·6%

FRANCE

G.E. 8·5%
I.C.L. 5·6%
Univac 4·3%
Siemens 1·9%
N.C.R. 3·8%
Other 18·5%
I.B.M. 65·7%

BENELUX

G.E. 10%
Burroughs 2·3%
C.D.C. 1·9%
I.C.L. 5·5%
Honeywell 2·6%
Other 15·9%
I.B.M. 51·8%

ITALY

G.E. 7·8%
Other 10·4%
Univac 13%
I.B.M. 68·8%

Source: *Fortune*, 15 August 1969.

There is no doubt that IBM makes a tremendous contribution to the countries where its laboratories are located. It enables their men and women to play a part in the world's most advanced computer programme. In some cases, such as Sweden and Austria, the alternative to sharing in IBM's programme would be no large-scale computer research at all. Even in Britain, Germany, France, and Holland, where the governments are trying to encourage indigenous computer companies, IBM enormously enhances the range of opportunities open to scientists and technologists in this field. All the evidence suggests that the scope for doing more advanced work than at home and the superior facilities available in the U.S. are more important causes of the brain drain than the high level of American salaries. By allowing its subsidiaries to participate in research as well as to manufacture and sell IBM helps to encourage talented people to remain in the countries where they were born and educated.

But there is a political price to pay for the scientific and social benefits. All IBM's subsidiaries are controlled and coordinated from its headquarters in the U.S. The corollary of sharing in its research programme is acceptance both of its objectives, and of the particular role allotted by headquarters. The various IBM laboratories in different countries and their research programmes are inextricably bound together. Each makes sense only in the context of the whole. They could no more live apart from each other than a man's arm could sustain a separate existence from his body. To talk of nationalization or the subordination of a laboratory's work to national ends is quite simply impractical.

The only completely self-sufficient, or potentially self-sufficient, country in the IBM network is the U.S. It has two of the company's three fundamental research laboratories, which are responsible for providing the scientific basis for new technologies and new ways of using computers. Their work is concerned with basic research into the physical sciences, mathematics, computer organization, new approaches to programming, and advanced applications of computers. The U.S. also has seventeen laboratories devoted to computer development. Their task is to turn the ideas and concepts of the fundamental researchers into practical computer systems for the production divisions to manufacture. In Europe there is one fundamental research laboratory at Zurich, and six development laboratories in Germany, Austria, Britain, Sweden, France, and Holland respectively.

This is not an unreasonable division. Besides being its home country, the U.S. accounts for over three-quarters of the company's gross income. Because the market is so large IBM can produce all the components needed for a computer. Elsewhere this would be unprofitable as the individual national markets are too small to support a full operation while enabling the company to achieve the long production runs necessary for maximum profitability. So each country specializes in a particular range of components, and the completed computers are an amalgam of parts from several different countries. If each of the main national subsidiaries is also to engage in research this function must be broken down in the same way. The company could have chosen the alternative of concentrating production and research outside the U.S. in one or two countries, but this would have been less desirable than the present policy for those which would then have had to rely exclusively on imports, instead of only partly so.

The laboratory sites are chosen for a variety of reasons, and IBM are not anxious to suggest an order of priorities. One is the educational level, particularly in technical and scientific subjects, of the local population. It is much easier to recruit staff with the necessary qualifications and skills in, say, Germany or Britain, than in Spain or Greece. This applies not just to the people who undertake the really complicated tasks and the advanced research, of whom only a relatively small number are available to a single company in any country, but also to those who carry out the more mundane and routine functions. At the company's British laboratory at Hursley Park near Winchester, for instance, the ordinary computer operators are recruited largely from among local girls with 'O' and 'A' levels in mathematics and related subjects.

The performance of the local manufacturing and sales affiliate is another consideration. IBM likes to have close links between its manufacturing and sales arms. So the more successful the local salesmen the more the local research and manufacturing facilities stand to gain. This gives the laboratories in France and Germany, where IBM is very strong, an advantage over their counterparts in Britain, where the company is in the unfamiliar position of holding a smaller share of the market than a local competitor, International Computers Limited. But the arrangement works both ways, and if a laboratory makes an important advance in a field not covered by the local manufacturing affiliate, the affiliate may still be allowed to take over production of the result. Thus when the British laboratory developed a new sort of disc file for the System 3 computer, the company decided that it should be manufactured in Britain instead of Germany, which normally has the responsibility for this product line.

The vexed question of politics enters into the decision as well. A laboratory is one of the most effective ways in which a company can identify itself with a country, and secure the approval of the local government. By building one it can show that it is willing to contribute something to the country as well as to make profits there. But it is difficult to know whether IBM, or any other international company, for that matter, responds better to harsh or gentle treatment from the authorities. One of IBM's biggest European research facilities was built up at La Gaude near Nice in France during the period when de Gaulle was in power, and there was greater official hostility to foreign companies than anywhere else in Europe. Italy has nothing remotely similar, although IBM manufactures there, and has the same sixty-five to seventy per cent share of the market as in France.

Each laboratory has its own special area of work and

responsibility. IBM believes that 'it probably has the broadest product line of any single company in terms of the required research and development'. The company therefore tries to break down the enormous range into a number of manageable areas, and to create what it calls 'a critical mass of people who can specialize in particular product areas'. As J. S. (Bunny) Stanton, the British laboratory manager, explains: 'It becomes a skill in itself to evolve printers, telecommunications, central processors, or whatever, and then map out a development plan.'

The laboratory missions, as IBM describes them, are very clearly defined. The company aims to avoid competition both between individual foreign laboratories, and between those laboratories and the U.S. But there is a good deal of overlap with laboratories following similar lines of research with slightly different emphases. Thus Hursley Park, the company's largest laboratory outside the U.S., and the German laboratory at Böblingen near Stuttgart are both engaged in work on central process units, with the Germans working on a size smaller than the British.

On any given product or component there is usually a U.S. and an overseas laboratory working along the same lines. The company is therefore never entirely dependent on foreigners, although the laboratories do try to dovetail their missions. In the case of the medium-sized central process units Hursley is working in conjunction with a U.S. laboratory, while the Nordic laboratory near Stockholm and San José in California are cooperating in the development of new terminal equipment and computer control systems.

The U.S. parent company pays for the research carried out on its behalf, which accounts for much of each laboratory's programme. The various IBM marketing companies then pay royalties on the revenue derived by them from the laboratory's work. There is also a certain amount of subcontracting between IBM subsidiaries in different countries, and just over twenty-five per cent of Hursley's funds now come from non-U.S. sources. In addition each laboratory can sponsor some ideas of its own, and the local research chief in each country has some spare funds available for this purpose.

However before an idea can be developed to the point where substantial sums of money are required it has to be cleared with the parent company. When that happens it does not necessarily follow that the subsequent work will take place in the laboratory where the idea originated. This may be because the local research chief himself feels that the project would unbalance his existing programme, or the parent company may decide that its fits better into the expertise and programme of another laboratory.

There is, of course, competition between the laboratories for different projects. They can argue that they are the best qualified, or that they have the best record for whatever undertaking is in question. But the allocation of missions is firmly in the hands of the IBM headquarters in the U.S. The orders are transmitted through the appropriate regional headquarters, but nothing alters this reality. The allocations are made partly on the basis of a laboratory's previous record, and partly on its availability of resources, both technical and financial. The company claims that with these criteria it is usually pretty obvious which laboratory should be given which task. The decision to give Hursley the primary responsibility for the development of the PL/1 computer programme language is used as an illustration. The company says that the development of the concept and the outline of its specification in the U.S. coincided with the development of the appropriate skills at Hursley.

The political implications of IBM's position for the countries where it operates are tremendous. In the past nations have always regarded advanced technological research as a top secret matter. This had been equally true of projects handled directly by government agencies and those carried out by private companies. Computers are a branch of this sort of research and vital on strategic as well as economic and industrial grounds. Yet all the countries which rely on

IBM are dependent on each other in this field. The company headquarters knows everything that is going on, and coordinates all the programmes. Apart from the U.S., they can have no secrets. Indeed their inter-dependence means that their effectiveness depends on a free exchange of information.

10. The Problems of Financial Transfers

The most frequent source of dispute and conflict between multinational companies and governments is the companies' ability to move enormous sums of money between their affiliates in different countries. Prince Guido Colonna di Paliano, the former commissioner in charge of industry in the European Economic Community, estimated* in 1970 that the liquid assets in the hands of U.S. companies and banks with international operations amounted to $30,000m.–$35,000m., or to three times the size of the U.S. Government's reserves. 'Yet,' to use his own words, 'it is an amount which flows in giant waves from one country to another,'* along with the considerable additional amounts belonging to non-American international enterprises. The scale and course of these tidal waves can be influenced by governments, acting alone and in concert, but are beyond their power to control. The movement of funds within multinational groups, when several are following the same policy, can threaten, and sometimes destroy, national policies with regard to currency exchange rates, balance of payments, and the availability of credit.

The multinational companies have not deliberately set out to challenge governments. Nor is there anything sinister about the manner in which the funds are transferred. They are conducting normal business operations – providing funds for new investment, repatriating profits, and controlling the exchange of goods between subsidiaries. Among the ways in which the money moves are dividend, royalty, and interest payments; loans, and other capital transfers; and payments for goods, services, and know-how.

* *Wall Street Journal*, 17 February 1970.

It is the fact that these activities transcend national frontiers that creates special problems for governments. If they took place within a single economy, they could be followed, subjected to controls, and made liable for publication in a systematic fashion. In a world of independent states, each with its own laws, customs, and interests, this is impossible. If international trade was entirely a matter of arm's-length transactions between separate and unconnected companies in different countries, the movements of money would also be easier to follow and to control since each company would be operating as an independent entity, subject to whatever local laws and disclosure rules its government imposed. There would be no question of it acting in the interests of a world-wide concern rather than its own.

As it is, the pace and direction of the money movements within each multinational group are directed by the central headquarters of that group. Headquarters lays down the procedures which govern the behaviour of the subsidiaries, and can alter them as it wishes. The subsidiaries themselves have no more freedom of action than headquarters allows, although the extent of that freedom varies considerably from group to group.

Headquarters pursues a global interest. It adjusts its normal business operations in order to try to achieve whatever overriding policy objective the management may have set. This could be the minimization of exchange risks, the maximization of tax avoidance, the maintenance of high profits at home with which to pay high dividends, or the accumulation of large reserves so as not to have to seek outside finance, to name only a few. In most cases a company does not have a single clear objective but rather one that covers a mixture of aspirations that change with circumstances. But whatever the objective it is set by headquarters, and takes precedence over the narrower interests of the individual subsidiaries and the countries in which they are based.

When a subsidiary is not wholly owned the headquarters'

control is necessarily limited, and the position of the subsidiary more complex. If the public owns a proportion of the shares the parent company has to take that interest into account, as well as its own, when formulating policies for transfer prices between affiliates, dividend payments, and profit targets. If two or more companies own a subsidiary their respective interests have to be reconciled. Both these situations give rise to numerous problems. When the subsidiary is a more or less self-contained operation they are tolerable. But when it is engaged in a good deal of trade with sister companies in other countries, and headquarters wants it to operate primarily in the wider interests of the group as a whole, one hundred per cent ownership makes life infinitely easier. Many of the practices described in this chapter are either impossible, or have to be substantially modified where non-wholly owned subsidiaries are concerned. This is one of the main reasons why so many multinational companies operating in the industrialized countries have, in recent years, been buying out the minority interests in their subsidiaries.

The transfer of funds between affiliates gives rise to a running battle of wits between multinational companies and governments. Each government is determined to safeguard its own national interests as it sees them. This usually means ensuring that it secures a fair share of tax from the operations of the multinational companies with operations in its country, and ensuring that those operations are consistent with its broad economic policy objectives. Governments have a powerful armoury of weapons at their disposal, including exchange regulations, the tax laws, tariffs, and the power to impose controls on any aspect of the activities of an enterprise within their jurisdiction. 'We would not knowingly break the rules anywhere,' one managing director told me; 'We always employ one set of experts to tell us what they are, and another set to tell us how to get round them.' 'It is the job of governments to make the rules, and ours to find the loopholes,' said another.

The arguments drag on interminably. It is quite common for companies to have seven or eight tax years still open and subject for audit in any given country. The companies say this gives the governments the advantage since it means they can apply today's rules to yesterday's practices. For their part the governments complain that the companies try to wear down the revenue authorities into agreeing audits which ought not to be passed, and that the companies not only get away with practices that are not always in the national interest, but also retain the use of money which ought to be in the hands of the government.

In financial matters the principal fear of companies engaged in international business is that they will lose their money owing to factors outside their control. They are afraid governments will impose restrictions on the repatriation of earnings from a subsidiary to a parent, and they are permanently worried about changes in the value of currencies. Both fears are quite understandable. Restrictions on the repatriation of earnings from a major subsidiary can seriously disrupt a company's cash flow, and a devaluation can make a nasty mess of a balance sheet. Hoover estimates its losses from the devaluation of the British, Finnish, and Danish currencies in 1967 at over £68m., while Firestone Tire and Rubber Company lost $6.5m. in 1967 and $4.2m. in 1966 owing to devaluations. Other companies have made profits in these and similar circumstances, but this does not diminish their fears of being caught short.

Some companies believe that the best way to guard against this danger is not to allow their subsidiaries to accumulate any surplus cash out of their earnings. A study of the remittance practices of thirty U.S. companies with European subsidiaries, conducted in 1967, showed that a sixth directed those subsidiaries to remit between ninety and one hundred per cent of their earnings back to the parent company each year 'in order to minimise the possibility of exchange loss and any uncertainty about how much control we have over these funds', as one manager put it. A survey* into the behaviour of 115 foreign subsidiaries in Britain, published in 1970, showed a similar pattern. Between 1960 and 1967 thirteen per cent remitted over ninety per cent of their earnings, and a quarter sent back over seventy per cent to their parents. Companies which follow this policy often have to make large loans to their subsidiaries to enable them to maintain reasonable working balances, and to expand. But as governments are less likely to prevent loan repayments than dividends they regard this as a better way of avoiding risk than allowing the subsidiary to retain a greater proportion of its earnings. Some companies also regard the royalties payable by their subsidiaries to head office and contributions to running costs, research, and the like, as providing additional means of draining profits out of their foreign operations as quickly as possible.

Most managements are less scared, and cautious. Instead of thinking only of how much money they can repatriate, they take the needs of their subsidiaries into account, and try to plan their international financial operations on a more rational basis. In practice, this means that the dividend policies imposed on the subsidiaries are much more flexible than those followed by a public company whose shares are quoted on the stock exchange. In a public company every effort is normally made to follow a stable dividend policy. Wholly-owned subsidiaries do not have to worry about stock exchange considerations, or the opinion of the investment institutions and public. Their dividends can be varied as the parent company thinks fit. The variations can be enormous, as this typical example of the British subsidiary of a U.S. office equipment and computer company shows.

In formulating its dividend policy the management of a multinational company considers the industrial and operational requirements of the group and its individual members,

* 'The Strategy of Multinational Enterprise' by Dr Michael Z. Brooke and Dr H. Lee Remmers (Longman, 1970). The authors' research into the financial practices of multinational companies is outstanding.

| Year ended 30 Nov. | Dividend payments (gross) | |
	Amount (£000)	% of issued capital
1956	608·6	1,521·5
1957	747·8	131·2
1958–60	Nil	Nil
1961	3,324·2	583·2
1962	1,399·4	245·5
1963	Nil	Nil
1964	1,012·3	177·6
1965	Nil	Nil
1966	3,596·1	630·9

Source: The Strategy of Multinational Enterprise by Brooke and Remmers.

on the one hand, and the prospects facing the economies and currencies with which it is involved, on the other. As soon as the danger signals appear in a country which suggest that its currency may have to be devalued or additional controls imposed on financial movements, every effort is made to guard against possible loss.

Dividend payments, as one means of getting money out of the country concerned, tend to be raised sharply. In 1964 and 1965, when the devaluation of the pound seemed imminent, Brooke and Remmers found that thirty per cent of the 115 foreign-owned subsidiaries in Britain covered by their survey, which had not paid dividends during the previous three or four years did so. Twenty-five of the 115 remitted over one hundred per cent of their earnings, which meant dipping into their accumulated profits. A few sent home virtually all their retained earnings, and one, whose profits had been running at about £700,000 a year, paid a dividend of £3m. to its parent in 1964 alone. In 1967, when the devaluation of sterling finally occurred, there was another wave of high dividend payments in the months leading up to the crisis in November. The same thing happened in France in 1968 and 1969.

As well as demanding extra large dividend payments, the headquarters management may also insist that the subsidiary should bring forward its royalty and interest payments, and its contributions to general group expenditure, such as head office and research costs. Another useful ploy is the manipulation of transfer prices in sales between subsidiaries. The headquarters management insists that the subsidiary in country X, about whose currency it has doubts, should pay promptly for all imports from other subsidiaries while giving extended credit to those to which it exports. During the 1964–5 sterling devaluation scare and again in 1967 many multinational companies encouraged their European subsidiaries to defer payment to their British subsidiaries by as much as six months.

A characteristic example of a company employing these tactics in Britain occurred in 1965 when a well-known manufacturer of household goods was instructed by its U.S. parent to pay all outgoing service and royalty accounts immediately, while its nine sister subsidiaries were told to delay their payments instead of pumping money into a country whose currency was under pressure. At the same time it was reported that several other U.S. companies were telling their British subsidiaries to settle all transactions on a thirty-day basis instead of the previous ninety days.

In addition to adjusting the flows of money between their subsidiaries, the managements of multinational companies can, like other international traders, make use of the foreign exchange markets. They can switch their surplus funds from one currency to another, and sell short those they do not like in the hope that when the time comes to hand over the money they have sold a devaluation will have taken place.

There is nothing particularly new about any of the activities conducted by multinational companies to avoid foreign exchange losses. International traders have always tried to hedge their foreign exchange positions, and to protect themselves against sudden changes in the value of currencies. So too have individuals with large amounts of capital. Despite the abuse hurled at 'speculators' by politicians and central bankers it is not immoral to do this. Quite the

167

reverse; a company or individual would be foolish not to take such precautions. If by some means they were prevented from doing so the volume of international trade would be much reduced.

There are, however, two new features of the present situation which have far-reaching implications. The first is the sheer size and influence of the multinational companies, and the enormous sums of money at their disposal. The second is the degree of expertise, knowledge, and central control that characterizes their operations.

A typical example of the extent to which they can co-ordinate the affairs of subsidiaries in several different countries has been provided by John Webb, a vice-president of the U.S.-owned USM Corporation, which manufactures shoe making machinery. 'One of our Danish subsidiaries,' he explained, 'had excess cash which it lent to another Danish subsidiary that was receiving goods from the Swedish subsidiary. The Danish company pre-paid its account with the Swedish subsidiary, and this money financed the movement of Swedish product into the Finnish subsidiary. What did this manoeuvre accomplish? If Finland had been required to pay for the goods, it would have had to borrow at fifteen per cent, the going Finnish rate. If the Swedish subsidiary had financed the sale it would have had to borrow at about nine per cent. But cash in Denmark was worth only five or six per cent. Moreover, Danish currency was weak in relation to Swedish; by speeding up payments to Sweden we not only obtained cheaper credit, we hedged our position in Danish kroner as well'.* Until a few years ago few companies would have been able to conduct an operation of this kind. Today it is nothing out of the ordinary.

Except in periods of unusual crisis, or when one is looming, it is unlikely that all or even most international companies would pursue the same policies towards particular currencies. But they have become extremely adept at interpreting economic trends. Ford, for instance, has an econo-

* *Fortune*, 15 September 1968.

mist who, it was reported in 1968, had been right with sixty-nine of his previous seventy-five forecasts of when devaluations would occur. Other companies follow these matters equally closely. The situation is thus becoming increasingly like Wall Street when all the mutual funds with access to the same information follow the same group of go-go stocks. The result is that all tend to want to buy or sell simultaneously, which means that the upward and downward swings are invariably exaggerated. In certain circumstances the same applies to currencies.

A government faced with a run on its currency can retaliate by tightening exchange control procedures and imposing severe restrictions on all exports of money. This causes a good deal of inconvenience to the companies, but does not solve the basic problem.

In the first place the tighter the restrictions the more confidence in the currency will diminish, and so the more speculation against it there will be on the foreign exchange markets beyond the government's control. Secondly, as governments know, restrictions on the export of capital discourage multinational companies from investing in their countries.* Precisely because the restrictions cause so much inconvenience to the companies by forcing them to hold money in a place where they don't want to, and perhaps suffer an exchange loss into the bargain if a devaluation does occur, they become reluctant to increase their investments in plant and machinery in countries which adopt these measures.

Moreover the companies' ability to manipulate transfer prices enables them to get round even the most severe restrictions, at least partially. For manipulation means more than simply making one subsidiary hurry its payments up, and another delay them. It also means varying the prices paid by subsidiaries to each other in their transactions. If the headquarters management wants to run down its reserves in

*For a full discussion of the factors influencing the investment decisions of multinational companies see Chapter 12.

country X, or counteract the effects of exchange control regulations or restrictions on the export of capital, or the repatriation of earnings, royalties and interest payments, it can instruct its subsidiaries to increase the prices at which they sell to the country X subsidiary, while reducing the price at which that subsidiary sells to the others.

An example * of this tactic occurred some years ago when Mexico tried to cut imports and encourage the development of local industries by forcing the U.S. car companies manufacturing in that country to obtain a higher proportion of their components in Mexico. To achieve this aim it forbade certain imports. The companies retaliated by adding the mark-up they would have got on the forbidden imports to those components which they were still allowed to bring in.

The manipulation of transfer prices is one of the most flexible tools in the hands of a multinational company. If handled with care and discretion there is a wide range of uses to which it can be put. But care and discretion are vital. A company which varies its prices frequently and by large amounts is asking for trouble from the revenue and customs authorities in the countries where it operates. The variations must be quite small, say a percentage point or two either way, and should be justifiable by reference to some plausible factor affecting the trade concerned. This could be to market conditions, changes in production costs, or a change in the pattern of supply with a subsidiary in France, say, switching its orders from its sister company in Belgium to the one in Germany.

The most common reason for manipulating transfer prices is what is known as 'tax planning'. This can mean anything from systematic avoidance to ensuring that the same profits are not taxed twice over by two governments, or to taking advantage of an anomaly in the international system.

The European Free Trade Area (EFTA) provides an

* 'The Procurement Practices of the Mexican Affiliates of Selected United States Automobile Firms' by G. S. Edelberg. Unpublished doctoral thesis, Harvard Business School, June 1963.

illustration of the sort of anomaly that may arise. Under the EFTA rules, a duty is applied to a product moving from one member country to another if less than fifty per cent of the value of that product has been added within the EFTA area. But if more than fifty per cent is added no duty is charged. So a U.S. or German company that wants to supply its British affiliate with goods to be used in the manufacture of a product destined for sale throughout the EFTA area is well advised to charge the British affiliate a low price. Then when the finished product is exported from Britain to other EFTA members more than fifty per cent of its value will have been added within a member country, and it will therefore not be subject to duty in the member countries that import it.

In most companies tax planning is carried out with the aim of increasing the company's total effectiveness on world markets, rather than with tax avoidance as the principal object. An example of this approach in practice was described to me by a leading Danish lawyer, who is a director of several Danish subsidiaries of British companies. These companies use their Danish subsidiaries to accumulate profits outside the U.K. with which to finance further expansion in Europe. Each step in the process is completely legal.

Copenhagen has a freeport. This means that a British (or any other) company can export goods to its Danish subsidiary and invoice them in the normal way, but unless the goods are for use in Denmark itself the subsidiary does not have to take them through the Danish customs or pay any duty. It can re-export them at a higher price to a third country on another invoice, and the goods do not even have to touch Danish soil. The Danish subsidiary earns its profit from the difference between the two prices. Naturally it pays tax on this profit, and Denmark gains accordingly. But as Danish company tax is lower than the British, the company gains too.

Although this is a tangible benefit to the company, what

makes the operation really worthwhile is the fact that the Danish authorities are more tolerant than many about allowing companies registered under their laws to help their sister companies in other countries. Thus the Danish subsidiary of a multinational group can provide financial assistance to its sister companies in neighbouring countries. All that is necessary is for the Danish subsidiary to be able to show the Danish authorities that such assistance will be of benefit to itself. As the Danish authorities know that the subsidiary would earn smaller profits, and so pay less tax, if it could not provide this sort of service to other members of its group, they are ready to be convinced.

Another reason for manipulating transfer prices is the fear that if certain subsidiaries show large profits they will come under pressure, either from the local government or their customers, to reduce prices. The fear of government intervention to reduce prices is particularly acute in politically sensitive industries, such as pharmaceuticals, and for those companies which have a very large or dominant position in a local market.

The fear that large profits will provoke large wage claims from the trade unions is an additional reason why some companies like to keep their subsidiaries' profits in certain countries to a modest level. This factor is a matter of special concern in those countries where the local subsidiary has a profit-sharing scheme, or where employee representatives have the right to examine the subsidiary's books. In his study 'Transfer Pricing in Multinational Business' Dr James S. Shulman * describes the practice of a company with a subsidiary in Mexico where the law requires profits to be shared with employees. At the time of his study the employees' rate was set at ten per cent. The company arranged its transfer prices to its Mexican subsidiary with this charge in mind, and tried to ensure that its profits there rose in a gradually ascending curve instead of fluctuating in response to market conditions.

* Unpublished doctoral thesis, Harvard School of Business, 1966.

7) Market conditions themselves can influence the level of transfer prices charged to a subsidiary. If a subsidiary finds itself in an <u>intensely competitive situation</u> so that its selling prices have to be cut to the bone headquarters may decide that the group as a whole should help it in the struggle through the adjustment of transfer prices. Alternatively if a *4)* multinational group wants to <u>hit a rival hard</u> in a particular market it may subsidize its <u>own</u> local subsidiary there in order to enable it to launch and sustain a price war. A decision on these lines could be taken with the hope of forcing the rival to close down its operation in the country concerned, or with the intention of cutting into its profits so as to prevent it from expanding somewhere else.

The manipulation of transfer prices does not mean evading the <u>customs</u>. The customs are not concerned with a company's financial activities, its liability for tax, or where it earns its profits. They are concerned with assessing the value of imported goods, and applying the legal rate of duty to them. So long as a company pays that duty it is fulfilling its obligations to the customs. If the customs consider that goods are being invoiced at a price below their true value for duty purposes, the duty may be based on a higher valuation. It is quite normal for customs to challenge prices which they believe to be too low. The increased assessments may be as high as one hundred per cent, although the range is usually ten to thirty per cent.

Companies complain that they never know where they stand with the customs. Over seventy countries now follow the principles for evaluating goods for duty purposes laid down in the Brussels Convention, but these are applied differently in different countries. The customs in any country may challenge a price accepted by their opposite numbers elsewhere, and by the local tax authorities. Arguments with the customs can take up a good deal of management time, and duty rates are invariably among the factors taken into account by companies when they set the transfer prices between their subsidiaries. But the link between a commodity's price and its dutiable value is indirect and differs from one country to another.

The attitudes of multinational companies to tax avoidance vary considerably. In public all maintain that they act as good citizens everywhere, and this means paying taxes like everybody else. In private, some take it for granted that taxes should always be avoided as much as possible. Others, by contrast, argue that tax considerations should not overrule normal management and marketing decisions, and that if they do the company's structure will, in the long run, be pulled out of shape. A survey of international pricing problems by Business International revealed one company which certainly seemed to have reached that point. 'All of its intracorporate prices,' according to the survey, 'are set by lawyers and accountants, and the head of the international division does not even sit in on the discussions.'*

Some companies try to make use of countries where taxes are very low to minimize their international tax charges. In principle the technique is very simple. Goods are invoiced at a low price to a low tax country where the local subsidiary, without necessarily even taking delivery, re-exports them at a high price to where they are actually needed. The subsidiaries at the beginning and end of the chain make losses, but these are offset by the high profits in the low tax country. Other companies follow a modified version of this technique. They endeavour to arrange the flows of goods and services through their subsidiaries in such a way that the highest tax liabilities are incurred in the countries with the lowest rates.

 Attractive as these operations look on paper they have several disadvantages. They tend to be much disliked by the executives of the companies that are being milked, and the resentment this causes can be so great that the best feel driven to look for jobs elsewhere. In any company one of the most important tasks of central management is to ensure

*'Solving International Pricing Problems'. Prepared and published by Business International, 1965.

that all the subsidiaries are pulling together for the good of the firm as a whole. This is difficult to achieve because each is apt to think first and foremost of its own interest, and only secondly of the whole company. In a multinational company the national differences between the subsidiaries make it harder than ever to create a common purpose, and if some of them see that they are being exploited for the benefit of others the normal problems are compounded.

The long-term planning of investment and sales strategies is also disrupted if too much attention is paid to short-term tax avoidance. Governments change their tax laws and their attitudes towards avoidance suddenly and unpredictably. If a company organizes its affairs with short-term tax considerations primarily in mind it stands to lose badly in the event of a change of policy in the countries on which it relies. Moreover its investment and sales strategies will in due course become increasingly divorced from the economic and other realities of the industry in which it is involved.

For companies that are undeterred by these factors the increasing power of governments to nullify the advantages of the grosser forms of transfer price manipulation is often a conclusive argument against embarking on them. The world has changed a great deal since the 1950s when the companies had things very much their own way in dealing with pricing problems. This was so much so that it was not uncommon for international groups to charge some of their subsidiaries prices that made it impossible for them to earn any profits for years at a time in order that money could be accumulated elsewhere. The parent would then pay the subsidiary a sum of money at the end of each year so that it could show a small profit and pay a modest tax. According to someone who worked in the treasurer's department of the British subsidiary of a major international aluminium company at that time, 'We virtually chose how much tax we should pay each year'. This would now be almost impossible for a large company in a sophisticated country.

The revenue authorities look at transfer prices and the

rates of return on sales and assets of different companies in the same industry, and compare them with each other. They also compare the performance of subsidiary units with those in the same industry that are not part of international groups. If it emerges from these examinations that a subsidiary is either being overcharged for its imports, or is undercharging for its exports so that it cannot earn a reasonable rate of return by the standards of the industry, that subsidiary is liable to be faced with a demand for extra taxes based on the assumption that it has been behaving normally. The Germans have recently been clobbering the oil companies in this way. Another tactic being used increasingly by the revenue authorities is to demand that companies with international links tell them beforehand of proposed changes in their pattern of trade. This not only forestalls possible tax avoidance moves, but opens up new avenues of inquiry for the taxmen.

The revenue authorities in a multinational company's home country have an additional important weapon at their disposal. In most countries there is legislation, which enables them to re-allocate income among the various members of a corporate group for tax assessment purposes. If they think that intracompany transactions within a multinational company have been based on unrealistic prices they can base their tax demands on what they think realistic prices would have been. Not only does this power limit the flexibility of transfer pricing policies, it can result in double taxation. This happens when the revenue authorities in a company's home country re-allocate income after tax has already been paid abroad. By then it may be too late to re-open the accounts in the other country, so that instead of getting away with a low tax, the company finds its profits on a particular operation being taxed twice over. The more this power is invoked in a company's home country, the more risky and less attractive it becomes for the company to embark on large-scale tax avoidance.

The spread of double taxation agreements is another

factor tending to close loopholes. One purpose of these agreements, which are made between governments, is to ensure that companies are not taxed twice over for the same profits. But they have also led to greater disclosure by companies of their activities, and encouraged the more lax taxation authorities to bring their practices into line with the more rigorous. To some extent they have led as well to a greater exchange of information between revenue departments. But as an official of the British Inland Revenue put it: 'When a company is engaged in a practice which lessens its tax liability here, while increasing it somewhere else, albeit at a lower rate, it is expecting too much to suppose that the foreign revenue authority will draw the matter to our attention. It is a case of one man's meat being another man's poison.'

This remark pinpoints one of the principal weaknesses of governments in dealing with multinational companies in financial matters. Each is concerned primarily with its own narrow national interest, so that they do not present a united front. Each company, by contrast, is in a position to pursue a coordinated policy for dealing with governments. Another weakness of governments is that their agencies are usually short-staffed and underpaid in comparison with the equivalent departments in the companies. They have the advantage of being able to invoke the law when they want to pursue a course of action, and they have managed to put a stop to most of the more blatant methods by which the companies have exploited their position. But the game moves fast and the amount of money at the companies' disposal increases rapidly each year. As soon as one loophole is closed the companies have shown themselves able to find others. Moreover the governments know that they have to be careful. They can control the activities of the local subsidiaries within their countries as tightly as they please. But there is a price to be paid. The tighter the controls in a particular country the less willing the companies will be to add to their investments there, and the fewer openings will they provide for the affected subsidiaries on world markets.

In all companies, whether multinational or not, pricing policy is one of the most important prerogatives of top management. The prices both of the final product and of the goods exchanged between subsidiaries are invariably its responsibility. This does not mean that the chairman personally fixes all prices. But it does mean that the principles on which prices are set, and the factors that must be taken into account, are laid down at the highest level. In the case of particularly vital products, or products that are moved in very large quantities, the fixing of the precise price is often set at the highest level as well. In some companies all prices are decided upon by a senior executive committee at headquarters, and subsidiaries have no freedom of action at all.

There are sound commercial reasons why this should be so. Nothing is more crucial to a company's success or failure than its pricing policy. If the final price of a product is wrong, everything else is to no avail. The allocation of costs and profits between the different stages of production, and the prices charged by subsidiaries to each other when they transfer goods between themselves help to determine the final price and are themselves of great importance.

In a multinational company top management's responsibility for pricing policy takes on an additional significance. It enables headquarters to cast each national subsidiary in whatever role it chooses. This is not to say that the local and the wider interest necessarily conflict. But where there is a divergence the interests of the company as a whole come first. However independent a subsidiary of a multinational company may be, or claim to be, this is an area where the extent of that independence is directly controllable by headquarters.

Not surprisingly, pricing policy is among the most difficult subjects on which to gain information from a company. Even the most helpful tend to draw the line at discussing it with outsiders. Those that will talk in anything more than generalities usually insist on remaining anonymous.

One of the most outstanding pieces of research in this field was conducted by Dr James S. Shulman,* and deals with the affairs of eight U.S.-owned manufacturing companies with extensive international interests. In order to preserve their anonymity he has invented fictional names for them, and he provides more information on some than others. The research was completed in 1966 so that some of the companies may have changed their practices since then. But the information they provided to Dr Shulman remains an invaluable insight into the pricing policies of multinational enterprises.

The companies, by their fictional names, are:

PHARMACO, a leading drug and pharmaceutical house, manufacturing ethical drugs, patent medicines, and animal preparations.

FURNCO, a designer and manufacturer of commercial furniture and office equipment.

MACHINECORP, a producer of machinery used in the production of consumer soft goods. It also distributes a limited line of special materials used in the manufacture of products made on its machines.

CONSTRUCTO, a builder of materials handling equipment with a product which is essential and well-known in the construction industry.

EQUIPO, a leading producer of agricultural, road building, and construction equipment.

ELECTRONICS INC, a manufacturer of electronic components and systems. It is an original equipment manu-

*Unpublished thesis for the Harvard School of Business entitled 'Transfer Pricing in Multinational Business'. He has kindly given me permission to draw on his findings.

facturer for scores of companies which make sound, communication and other electronic devices.

APPLIANCE MFG, a world-wide manufacturer of household electric appliances.

SCENTO, a manufacturer of men's toiletries and associated products.

All the companies are integrated concerns with factories in several different countries cooperating with each other. They transfer few finished goods between their various subsidiaries, but a great deal of raw materials and semi-finished products. Most of the shipments are either from the U.S. to the overseas divisions, or between the overseas divisions. There is very little movement from overseas back to the U.S.

Dr Shulman's findings confirm that subsidiaries of multinational companies enjoy practically no effective independence in pricing matters. This is true both of external prices, that is prices to customers outside the group, and of prices in sales between subsidiaries.

To take external prices first: in six of the eight companies these are explicitly the responsibility of head office. In the other two – Appliance and Equipo – the subsidiaries can set their own prices, but they have to act on the 'advice of headquarters'. In Dr Shulman's view that advice is, in effect, a binding decision.

Six of the eight set different prices for their products in different countries, with Furnco and Machinecorp as the two exceptions. Furnco sets a single price for each of its products, and these are allowed to vary only inasmuch as they are affected by purely local conditions, such as customs duties, and transportation, handling, service costs, and the like. Machinecorp is even more rigid. It believes that its customers, which are mainly other international companies, want one price for every product in every country, and acts accordingly.

Transfer prices in transactions between subsidiaries are

also the direct responsibility of the central management at headquarters. Once again there is tight control over the subsidiaries with the notable exception of Appliance.

At Appliance the subsidiaries are free to negotiate with each other on an independent arm's-length basis. They do not even exchange information on costs, although as the final selling price of the machine is known to all, negotiations usually start from that point. All the subsidiaries are free to buy components from outside the group if they wish. But head office is kept informed of what is happening, and can countermand the local decisions if it believes the overall corporate interest demands it. Thus the freedom of action of local managers is considerable, but residual responsibility remains with headquarters, which can exercise it whenever top management decides that it should be.

At Pharmaco the situation is more typical. The company works back from the external price of the final product. Once that has been set the international vice-president establishes the transfer prices for inter-subsidiary sales. The end producer is given a guaranteed mark-up, and there is supposed to be a fair allocation of profits between each link in the production chain. None of the subsidiaries is allowed to buy materials from outside the company.

At Furnco the policy is that each division should secure a full recovery of its costs plus a nominal profit on internal sales. Headquarters tries to ensure that all are equally efficient, but it seems that the result of this policy is that the efficient sometimes subsidize those that are less so. Outside purchases may only be made with the permission of headquarters.

Machinecorp's policy is designed to reflect the pattern of production in the internal transfer prices. The U.S. plants were working at below capacity, so that in order to encourage other subsidiaries to buy from them U.S. prices were based on incremental costs plus a mark-up of only ten per cent. As the British plants had low costs and were working above their rated capacity they were allowed a mark-up of thirty-five per cent. In Germany where costs were higher than in Britain and plant capacity not as fully utilized a mark-up of twenty-five per cent was added. Outside purchases may be made only with head office approval. But when a subsidiary can show that it could buy from outside the group if allowed to, it is permitted 'some independent price negotiation' with the division which normally supplies it.

At Equipo the controller states that company policy is simply 'full cost plus ten per cent' for all internal transfers with the sole exception of one high-volume unit, which is transferred from Britain to the U.S. at full cost plus seven per cent. When a subsidiary has a particularly large requirement it must negotiate for it through headquarters which aims to split the economies of scale equally between the two sides. Except where there is no internal capacity or long delivery delays have built up it is rare for subsidiaries to make purchases from outside the group.

At Constructo transfer prices are fixed by headquarters, and there is a guaranteed profit for each of the manufacturing subsidiaries. Prices are set at material plus labour, plus overheads, plus a mark-up of twenty-five per cent, which covers general and administrative expenses as well as profits. Subsidiaries are required to purchase all their needs internally, unless permitted by headquarters to seek outside sources.

As might be expected, the attitudes towards taxation of the companies in Shulman's survey vary. Constructo says that it does not alter transfer prices in any way to allow for the impact of taxation. 'We could connive on taxes,' it says, 'but the savings would be trivial. We prefer to give full attention to operating our company, and let the tax liabilities fall where they may.' Furnco and Machinecorp say they do not adjust transfer prices for tax reasons if they can help it, but sometimes they are forced to do so by the tax authorities. Equipo maintains that it sticks firmly to its formula of standard cost plus ten per cent regardless of tax rates and customs duties. Electronics Inc. used to adjust transfer prices in order to take advantage of the available opportunities for tax avoidance. But it found that this created so much conflict between the subsidiaries and headquarters that it now refuses to allow income and import taxes to influence transfer prices. Appliance does not usually take tax consider-ations into account in intersubsidiary sales, and this would in fact be very difficult given the wide measure of freedom enjoyed by the local managements. But prices can be adjusted to take advantage of customs variations or to get round duties, and when this happens the company which makes the sacrifice receives a credit back from the head-quarters via the recipient.

Two of the companies pursue a conscious policy of mini-mizing all tax payments. As one of their officials put it: 'We consider it is wasteful to pay higher taxes than is necessary anywhere in the world'. In these companies international tax rates and import duties are under constant scrutiny. They directly affect the transfer prices paid by subsidiaries, and at any given moment a product may sell at widely differing prices to subsidiaries in different countries.

According to the evidence submitted by these companies to Dr Shulman 'the gains have been markedly worthwhile'. The companies have been able to reduce their world-wide tax bill, but they are 'continually exercised over the audit activities of the Office of Internal Operations of the Internal Revenue Service'. Not surprisingly there is a direct correla-tion between the tax minimizing price practices of a com-pany and the severity of the audits to which it is subjected. One executive described the risk of ex post facto govern-ment audits 'as a sword of Damocles hanging over day to day business activity'.

11. Financing

The financing of multinational business is a highly technical operation, but the principles on which it is based are simple enough. In the first place subsidiaries are expected to earn a profit for their parent, and their financial policies are based primarily on the objectives and interests of the parent. Consequently successful subsidiaries tend to be net exporters of capital from their host country, and their access to new capital is dependent on head office approval. Secondly, a company that carries out business on a multinational basis naturally seeks to raise money on an equally grand scale. This has led to the growth of the Eurodollar and Eurobond markets, on which money can be raised from investors of all nationalities and employed in most of the countries of the world. The Eurodollar market alone is now about as large as the domestic money supply of any one of the larger European national economies.

The attitude of companies to their international operations has been clearly expressed by John G. MacLean, the president of the U.S. Continental Oil. 'In the foreign field,' he said, 'we like to see each tub stand on its own bottom'.* In theory each subsidiary should be capable of financing its own needs, either out of its own cash flow or by local borrowing, and be able to provide a continuing profit for the parent. There will be times when even a long established subsidiary must call on its parent for help, but the flow of funds is supposed to be from the subsidiaries to the parent, not the other way about.

* 'Financing Overseas Expansion' by John G. MacLean. *Harvard Business Review*, March–April 1963.

In practice life is more complicated. Mistakes are made that cannot easily be undone, and sometimes management deliberately embarks on a new investment which it knows will not achieve satisfactory financial results when regarded in isolation. When Mr MacLean made the remark quoted above his own company was purchasing distribution networks in western Europe and running them at a loss in order to provide a market for its highly profitable production operations in Libya. Without the distribution networks it would have been dependent on other oil companies for the disposal of its production, and the level of that production would probably have been less. The distribution networks give it a guaranteed outlet, and should, in the long run, ensure that the company's total business is more profitable than would have been the case without them.

In general, however, the tubs do stand on their own bottoms. The most important source of funds for established subsidiaries, as for independent companies, is their own cash flow. After that comes the subsidiaries' own borrowing outside their parent company's country. Subventions from the parent itself bring up the rear.

Even U.S.-owned multinational companies have managed to stick to this pattern, despite the rapid increase in their investments abroad and the enormous number of new ventures they have purchased or started. According to a 1968 estimate* 'in recent years American multinational corporations financed roughly 40 per cent of their overseas operations from cash flow generated abroad, 35 per cent from external sources abroad, and 25 per cent through capital transfers from the U.S.' There is little doubt that since the imposition of tighter controls on capital outflows from the U.S. by the U.S. Government the proportion derived from foreign sources has increased still further. British companies have been subjected to much tighter

* *Eurodollar Financing, a Guide for Multinational Companies* (Chase Manhattan Bank, September 1968).

controls on the export of capital from home than their U.S. counterparts, and for much longer. As a result they have relied to an even greater extent on subsidiaries meeting their own needs. Between 1964 and 1969 British-owned international companies financed at least sixty per cent, and sometimes nearly seventy per cent, of their new foreign investment each year from the unremitted profits of their foreign subsidiaries.

Countries which receive foreign investment must accept that in the long run foreign subsidiaries will be net exporters of capital. Between 1960 and 1967 the outflow of capital in the form of dividends from the 115 foreign subsidiaries in Britain covered by the Brooke and Remmers survey was over one and a half times the inflow of funds from their overseas parents and affiliated companies. It has also been estimated that between 1960 and 1965 the outflow from U.S. subsidiaries in Europe exceeded the inflows by some twenty-five per cent. These figures are incomplete. On the one hand they ignore the substantial sums poured into foreign operations in order to make the initial purchases or to take over minority interests from outside shareholders; on the other they exclude royalties and service payments, which can be very large. But they do show that, once established, foreign subsidiaries are inclined to be considerable net exporters of capital.

This does not mean that foreign-owned subsidiaries simply take money out of a country without putting anything back. If that were the case most governments would not be as anxious as they are to encourage such investment in their countries. In purely financial terms foreign subsidiaries make large contributions to the treasuries of their host countries through the payment of taxes, customs duties, and the other charges levied by governments on industry. In addition they create jobs, introduce new production techniques and management methods, and purchase goods and services from local suppliers. They contribute to the balance of payments by exporting, and they help to increase the level of industrial investment. However, just as a householder pays rent when he lives in somebody else's house and enjoys its amenities, so a country must pay a price for the benefits conferred by foreign subsidiaries. It is up to the government to ensure that the country for which it is responsible gets a reasonable bargain.

There are other implications inherent in a country's reliance on multinational business that are both good and bad. On the credit side is the ability of large companies with access to international financial resources to undertake tasks that are beyond the means of local industry and government.

In 1963, when the French Machines Bull computer concern was heading for bankruptcy, the U.S. General Electric Company proposed to buy a twenty per cent stake in it. General de Gaulle imposed a veto, and ordered his finance minister, Valéry Giscard d'Estaing, to devise a 'solution Française'. The attempt failed, and by the following year it was apparent that France did not have the resources to save the company. The government therefore reluctantly decided that General Electric offered the best available solution, and the American company paid $43m. for a fifty per cent interest.

At about the same time the British Government was faced witht he distinct possibility that Rootes Motors, one of the country's leading car manufacturers, would have to close down owing to lack of financial resources. The newly elected Labour Government, whose leaders while in opposition had opposed previous U.S. takeovers of important British companies, tried to persuade the other British-owned car companies to rescue Rootes. They refused, and it became apparent that the only alternative to closure was for Rootes to pass into the control of Chrysler. Since then only Chrysler's ability to finance its re-equipment and losses with money brought into the U.K. from outside has kept the company (now known as Chrysler United Kingdom) alive.

On the debit side a multinational company may use some of its subsidiaries to help others in a manner that is prejudicial to the country in which the helper is situated. At one point in the late 1960s an American manufacturing corporation found that its Portuguese subsidiary had been under-capitalized and run into trouble. So headquarters asked the British and German subsidiaries to ship components to the Portuguese on open account without taking payment for over a year. This was obviously in the interests of the Portuguese, but not of Germany or Britain. Moreover the policy was in operation at a time when Britain was desperately trying to increase its foreign exchange earnings. Such a manoeuvre is now technically in breach of both U.S. and British regulations, but it would be extremely difficult for the authorities to catch and penalize all the companies that do this sort of thing as there are so many legitimate reasons why a payment might be delayed.

There are other ways in which a multinational parent company can influence the financial affairs of a subsidiary in a manner that is not in the interests of the subsidiary's host country. The parent decides where it should borrow large amounts locally, where it should feed in funds from outside, and where it should keep a subsidiary short of cash. In deciding its strategy the multinational takes the policies of governments into account, and is constrained by the laws and practices of the countries where it operates. But when for some reason, such as exchange risk fears, a large number of companies decide to withdraw funds from their subsidiaries in a particular country, in the ways described in the previous chapter, the implications are far-reaching. Those foreign-owned subsidiaries in Britain (also described in the previous chapter) which remitted over one hundred per cent of their earnings to their parents during the 1964–5 sterling devaluation scare had to rely on local borrowing to carry on. Thus when companies *en masse* are running down their holdings of a currency, they not only help to place the exchange rate at risk. The continuing need of their subsidiaries in the afflicted country for cash gives a powerful twist to the rise in interest rates and the credit squeeze that are the inevitable concomitants of a currency crisis.

An additional hazard for countries that rely heavily on foreign-owned multinational companies is the influence exercised by the companies' home governments on their financial policies. This is an area in which multinational companies are obliged, whatever their own desires, to attach far greater weight to the views of their home government than to those of any other. These governments may insist, as both the British and U.S. have in recent years, that companies based in their countries should limit their export of capital and repatriate a high proportion of their foreign earnings. This inevitably affects the operations of those companies' subsidiaries, and through them the economies of the countries where they are situated.

A classic example of the dangers inherent in this situation occurred in Belgium in 1968 after President Johnson had declared a moratorium on capital exports from the U.S. to the so-called 'Schedule C' territories, which included the entire European Economic Community.

During the preceding years Belgium had become the most favoured location for new U.S. investment in Europe, and between 1959 and 1967 U.S. companies poured about $1,000m. into the country. They became a major factor in the Belgian economy, and in 1966 and 1967 they accounted for more than a third of the country's net investment in manufacturing (excluding depreciation). So when President Johnson made his announcement there was consternation in Brussels. 'The fact is,' said one commentator, 'that foreign investment, American in particular, has become an integrated part of Belgium's long needed industrial renovation.'* If the American companies could not continue their investment programmes the country stood to suffer badly. The government took immediate steps to make

* 'A touch of realism on US investment' by Alain Camu, *The Times*, 31 October 1968.

available alternative sources of finance, and in any case the most restrictive elements in President Johnson's measures did not last for long. So Belgium was able to weather the storm. But the incident shows how when a country becomes very dependent on foreign-controlled companies, it also becomes vulnerable to unilateral decisions taken by the home governments of those companies.

President Johnson's action caused deep concern among those U.S.-owned companies, which had been claiming that they were multinational and so capable of acting as equally good citizens everywhere. As John J. Powers, the president of the Chas. Pfizer & Company chemicals and pharmaceutical concern, said: 'It confirms the worst fears of the host country that the affiliates of U.S. companies are in fact aliens in the national economy'.* The same could be said of the subsidiary of any multinational company, and it applies as much when the subsidiary's affairs are being manipulated for the company's own purposes as when they are being manipulated at the direction of its home government.

Although President Johnson's attempt to curb the capital outflow from the U.S. emphasized the extent to which multinational companies are still in some ways national, it also gave a tremendous boost to one of their more multinational characteristics. This is their ability to raise money from investors all over the western world for use over an equally wide area. The operation is carried out through the Eurodollar and Eurobond markets. Both have grown rapidly in recent years as multinationals of all nationalities have found it increasingly necessary to raise money outside their countries of origin to finance their international operations.

International companies have always been able to raise

*'The Impact of US controls on foreign investment' by John J. Powers. A speech delivered at an American Management Association special briefing on 'New Foreign Investment Controls', New York, 10 April 1968.

money internationally. Wherever they operate they can
borrow from banks, issue bonds, or sell shares in their local
subsidiaries. But each of these possibilities has disadvantages. Governments may impose limits and conditions on
the banks' ability to lend, and they can regulate the terms
and timing of bond issues. When these regulatory powers
are used foreign-owned subsidiaries are liable to suffer discrimination that puts them at a disadvantage against
locally-owned firms. The sale of shares in subsidiaries is also
subject to regulation, although the main objection to it on
the part of most companies is their desire not to have outsiders participating in the ownership of their enterprises.

All these problems can be circumvented by having re-
course to the Eurodollar and Eurobond markets. The Eurodollar market is generally speaking for short-term finance
with loans extending from overnight or a day or two up to
seven years. The Eurobond market is a medium and long-
term capital market for loans of five years or more. Through
these markets it is possible to tap the financial resources of
the world. They supply funds to a wide variety of different
types of organization, including governments, local authorities, and nationalized industries, as well as large companies,
both international and purely national. The only qualifications that all borrowers must have are a sound credit
rating, and the ability to use very large sums of money.
These are not markets for the small concern, and precisely
because they are unregulated the lenders are particularly
interested in a potential borrower's reputation.

A Eurodollar is technically an ordinary U.S. dollar deposited with a bank outside the U.S. It is called a Eurodollar because most of the dealings in this form of money
take place in Europe, and especially London. But it could
just as easily be a dollar deposited with a bank in Japan.
Besides Eurodollars there are Eurosterling, Eurofrancs,
Euromarks, and even Euroyen. In fact any convertible
currency can achieve Euro status. In every case the principle is the same. The currency in question is on deposit

with a bank outside its home country. For the sake of accuracy the market should be called the Eurocurrency market rather than the Eurodollar market, and sometimes is. But because the dollar is by far the most important element in it, accounting for about eighty per cent of the total deposits, the word Eurodollar has become a generic term to cover the whole species.

The market first appeared in the late 1950s and developed rapidly during the 1960s for a number of reasons. The initial impetus came in 1957 when the British Government imposed restrictions on the use of sterling for financing international trade. As sterling was by far the most important currency after the dollar for this purpose, the restrictions led to a substantial increase in the dollars deposited in London and elsewhere to take over sterling's role. In the following year most of the major Western European governments allowed their currencies to become more or less convertible again after the war, which meant that they could be exchanged for each other and for dollars without too much fuss or official red tape. At about the same time the U.S. began to run a trade deficit with the rest of the world, which steadily increased for most of the 1960s. This meant that the dollar holdings belonging to non-Americans also increased. Another major factor was the restrictions applied by the U.S. Federal Reserve Board on the domestic activities of U.S. banks. These enabled foreign banks to offer more attractive terms to both depositors and borrowers of dollars than were available in the U.S.

Apart from the interest rate factor, the usefulness of Eurodollars for those who had accumulated or needed dollars but did not want to go through the U.S. banking system was quickly appreciated. The Communist governments were averse to doing so on political grounds, while international companies and traders were motivated by legal and fiscal considerations. Moreover it is convenient for everybody engaged in international trade that the banking business in the dominant currency should not be confined to the currency's country of origin, but should develop wherever it is needed.

The merchant banks of the City of London with their unrivalled expertise and experience of international financial affairs saw and exploited these opportunities more quickly than institutions elsewhere. This, coupled with the fact that London was in any case Europe's leading financial centre, enabled it to become the centre for the new market. 'The world's only lendable currency,' it was said, 'had come into the hands of the only people who knew how to lend it.' Others from the continent and America have learnt the technique, and it is estimated that about three-fifths of London's Eurodollar business is now conducted by banks with their headquarters in the U.S. None the less London has retained its locational importance, and most banks that want to get into this field establish branches there.

The market's expansion has been phenomenal since its size was first measured in a systematic way in 1959 at something over $1,000m. By the end of 1967 it was put at $17,500m., and at the end of 1968 at $33,000m. In 1969 the rate of growth accelerated still more, and the market entered 1970 worth about $53,000m., of which Eurodollars in the strict sense of the word accounted for $45,000m. and other currencies, notably Euromarks and Euro-Swiss francs, for the rest.

The two main sources of Eurodollars are international companies with spare cash, and central banks that have accumulated large reserves of dollars owing to the U.S. trade deficit. The central banks do not customarily lend in the market directly; they provide their local commercial banks with funds, and the commercial banks then lend them out. The companies use the market in order to earn interest on money they have raised and do not immediately need, and as a sanctuary for profits in preference to the domestic banking systems of the countries where they operate.

Multinational and other companies go to the Eurodollar market for a variety of purposes. They seek funds there to

finance new investments, or to serve as bridging finance,
as did Pan American World Airways which borrowed
$166.8m. to help with the purchase of ten jumbo jets in
1970. They use it as a source of export credits to cover the
gap between shipping goods and receiving payment. They
borrow to repay debts, or to rearrange the pattern of
internal debts and credits among their different units depending on international interest rate considerations and
their view of the prospects for different national currencies. In addition banks employ Eurofunds to back their
general operations, and other organizations seek money
there. The Hungarian state-owned pharmaceutical industry, for instance, borrowed $30m. from a consortium of
western banks in 1970 to finance new developments.

For whatever reason money is needed the Eurodollar
market can provide it. The market's great advantages are
its sheer size and flexibility. Deals can be fixed up in a
matter of hours over the telephone, though obviously the
larger they are and the longer the period the money is
needed for, the more complicated the arrangements become. The minimum size of a loan is usually about $500,000,
but amounts of well over $100m. can be raised by a single
borrower dealing with a group of banks. Pan American's
$166.8m. loan was provided by a consortium of twenty-six
banks led by the British Bank of London and South
America.

The growth of the Eurodollar market is a source of widespread concern among both governments and the bankers
who operate it. This is partly because of the lack of controls
and recording procedures. Money flows into it and out
again at a tremendous rate, and the same deposit may be re-
lent several times. It is feared that if one link in the chain
of borrowers and lenders should fail a rash of crises could
spread through the international banking community.

Europeans particularly are worried about the extent to
which the market connects their national interest rate
structures with that of the U.S. The implications of the tie

were dramatically illustrated in 1969 when the U.S. imposed a credit squeeze and U.S. banks started to borrow dollars from the Eurodollar market in order to replenish their domestic reserves. As a result interest rates in that market were driven up from about seven per cent for three months deposits to eleven per cent. Consequently money was sucked into the market from other countries which in turn had to raise their own interest rates in order to prevent a rush of money out of their currencies. The market also 'lubricates the channels of international speculation', as one commentator has put it. During the 1969 Deutsche Mark revaluation crisis $4,000m. flowed into Frankfurt in a single ten-day period of which more than half came from the Eurodollar market. This enormously increased the pressure on the Germans to revalue, while simultaneously intensifying the pressure on those currencies which were being sold by speculators in order to buy marks. After the Germans had revalued the money flowed quickly out again thereby causing concern in Germany. But instead of returning to other currencies much of it stayed in the Eurodollar pool.

The market has grown up so fast that nobody – governments, bankers, or academics – has yet had time to evolve comprehensive theories about how it works, and how it should. From time to time governments impose controls designed to regulate the flow of their currencies into the Eurodollar pool, and in the United Kingdom there are permanent restrictions on domestic residents. But all governments are committed to the principle of free movement of capital both for political reasons and in order to encourage world trade. It is universally recognized that the Eurodollar market, by helping companies to finance their international operations, has encouraged the flow of trade and investment between countries on which the prosperity of national economies depends.

The Eurodollar market has given rise to the Eurobond market where companies and other organizations raise

long-term finance. A technical description of a Eurobond
is 'an international bond issue, which is underwritten by an
international syndicate and sold to purchasers who are able
to pay in funds not subject to exchange control with the
result that the proceeds can be freely remitted by the
issuer'.* Most of the outstanding issues are in dollars, but
other currencies, especially the Deutsche Mark, are used as
well. The standard denomination is $1,000, and the bonds
are issued in bearer form so that the purchaser receives an
imposing piece of paper as proof of his investment.

A vital characteristic of Eurobonds is that the holder
should receive his interest and the repayment of the principal without the deduction of any withholding tax. For the
company it is equally important that the money raised by
the sale of Eurobonds should be readily transferable across
frontiers to finance the operations of its various subsidiaries
or, until it is needed, to earn interest in the Eurodollar
market. Consequently companies usually handle these issues
through special finance subsidiaries established in countries
with favourable tax laws. Luxembourg, Holland, and the
Dutch Antilles are favourites, and U.S. companies also
make extensive use of Delaware.

The market originated in 1963. Before then New York
was the leading international centre for the raising of long-
term finance through bond issues. Companies, local
authorities, governments, and nationalized industries would
float their new bond issues there, and these would be
offered for sale by American investment bankers. Many
were purchased by non-Americans, but the use of the New
York market for this purpose led to an outflow of money from
the U.S. The government therefore introduced an interest
equalization tax, which did not prevent Americans from
buying foreign securities but penalized them for doing so.
The result was to make it impractical for foreigners to make

* 'Eurobonds', by Dallas Bernard, a managing director of Morgan
Grenfell. Given at the *Financial Times* Conference on Eurobonds and
Eurodollars, December 1969.

further new issues, and thus to create an obvious need for an alternative source of finance. Even without the tax, however, the Eurobond market would probably have developed, though less rapidly than it has. Several European banks had noticed that as much as fifty to seventy-five per cent of the foreign bond issues made in New York were purchased by non-residents of the U.S. Moreover, said a director of S. G. Warburg and Company, the London merchant bank, 'We found that if we secured large amounts of bonds from New York we could distribute them to other banks and brokers on the continent. It was a ludicrous situation.'* In July 1963 Warburgs led a group of other banks with an offer of $15m. on behalf of Autostrade, the Italian state highways authority. The birth of the Eurobond market is generally dated from that offer.

At first only non-American concerns tapped this new market. But in 1965 the U.S. Government launched a programme of voluntary restraint on the transfer of capital out of the country, and Mobil Oil became the first U.S.-based company to raise a Eurobond. Others quickly followed, and in 1968 when the voluntary programme was replaced by a mandatory one U.S. international and multinational companies plunged headlong into Eurobonds. During 1968 alone their sales of newly issued Eurobonds amounted to almost $2,100m. compared with a total of $1,200m. for the previous three years put together.

Because of their large size and outstanding credit ratings U.S. companies are frequently able to command lower rates of interest than other borrowers including some governments. In September 1967 the American advantage was rather dramatically highlighted when the international financing subsidiaries of Procter & Gamble and National Biscuit floated fifteen-year dollar issues at 6.61 per cent and 6.66 per cent respectively, while the governments of Finland and Portugal had to provide their ten-year bonds with yields of 7.21 per cent and 7.24 per cent respectively.

* *Men and Money* by Paul Ferris (Hutchinson, 1968).

Differentials of this sort arise because investors in the Euro-bond market attach particular importance to the name of the borrower, and its commercial rectitude. They trust large U.S. concerns partly because of their size and prosperity, and partly because they know that a U.S. company would never welsh on its debts if it could help it, and would suffer the direst consequences if it did. History shows that governments have a less good record in this respect, and are much more difficult to call to account.

Not a great deal is known about who buys Eurobonds. But many of the investors are believed to be individuals from Europe, South America, the Middle East, and the Far East who seek refuge from inflation or political risks in their own countries or who cannot find investments of similar quality at home. Traditionally people of this sort have relied on Swiss banks to hold their accounts, and advise them on financial matters. Not surprisingly therefore Swiss banks are among the largest purchasers of Eurobonds, although only a small part of these are for Swiss residents. Pension funds, insurance companies, and other institutional investors play a relatively small part in the market since their activities can be easily regulated by governments which wish them to keep their money at home. However, a number of investment and unit trusts (mutual funds in American parlance) have been organized to take advantage of Eurobond opportunities.

It is difficult to generate much enthusiasm about the people who purchase Eurobonds. They are not concerned with broad concepts about uniting the world's economy or spreading the ownership of multinational companies among the peoples of the countries where their subsidiaries operate. The banks of London, Frankfurt, Paris, and other financial centres are similarly realistic and unromantic. Yet the fact remains that the purchasers of Eurobonds, the banks that sell them, and the companies that issue them have succeeded in creating the freest and most international capital market ever known. Along with the Eurodollar market, it provides a far more successful example of international economic cooperation than most of the schemes sponsored by governments. It also forms the foundation on which it may one day be possible to create a system of multinational ownership for multinational companies. But that is a long way off.

12. Finding the Right Place for the New Plant

Large multinational companies, like large animals, tend to be very shy. Each subsidiary tries to merge as far as possible into the background of its surroundings and to assume a local character. They hate to draw attention to their size and influence for fear that it will provoke the animosity of governments, small businessmen, and the general public. They realize, in the words of Unilever's chairman, Dr Ernest Woodroofe, that 'to be big and to be loved seems to be against nature',* and that internationalism arouses suspicion. Whenever possible they deny that their activities result in decisions affecting a country's economic welfare being taken outside its frontiers. L. E. J. Brouwer, the senior managing director of the Royal Dutch Shell Group, dismisses the idea as 'a rather romantic concept, reminiscent of feudal Europe',† but having 'no substance in fact'. Even Brouwer, however, admits that 'internationalism gives us the ability to choose where and when we will invest'. A government can prevent a new investment in its country, but it cannot force an international company to build or expand. The company, for its part, can select whichever country offers the best industrial, economic, sales, and political prospects for its new plants and facilities.

This freedom of action has serious implications for governments. Whatever their policies in other respects, most are anxious to secure a high and rising level of new industrial

* *The Times*, 4 November 1969.
† 'The Oil Industry – Fact and Fiction'. Speech to the Netherlands Chamber of Commerce for Switzerland, Zurich, 5 March 1970.

investment. This means they must, in effect, compete with each other for the favours of international companies. Some countries are more dependent than others on these companies, and the extent of their dependence in any case varies from industry to industry. But the general position has been well put by the British Government's Economic Development Committee for the chemical industry. 'Since so many companies in the industry operate internationally,' it said, 'it follows that the U.K. is competing as a home for new investment with other countries. The actual level of investment depends on the investment climate in each of these countries'.* The same is true, in varying degrees, of most other countries, and many other industries.

In motors, for instance, the Ford of Britain shop stewards have begun to realize that their freedom to disrupt the company's production whenever they wish is matched by Ford's ability to expand its activities on the continent more rapidly than in Britain. When Henry Ford II visited Britain in February 1970 they questioned him anxiously about the implications of a recent statement he had made to the effect that he preferred to do business in Germany than in Britain. They feared that a number of major projects for new models to replace existing ones being made in British factories would be allocated to a new plant at Saarlonis in Germany.

For Ford both Britain and Germany are foreign countries, and it can assess their investment climates on an equal footing with no difficulty. Most companies are still inclined to favour their home country for new investment in the sense of accepting a lower rate of return before going ahead than for projects in foreign countries. In 1968 *Fortune* reported† that a survey of 92 U.S. companies with substantial direct investments overseas revealed that 53 ex-

* 'Industrial report by the Chemicals EDC on the Economic Assessment to 1972' (National Economic Development Office, February 1970).
† 15 September 1968.

pected a foreign project to yield a higher rate of return than a domestic one before they would undertake it. This bias is not the result of beneficent patriotism; it arises from the fact that management understand their home country better than any other.

Increasingly, however, the most experienced multi-nationals are drawing no distinction between foreign and domestic investment alternatives. In 1970 David Barran, chairman of Shell Transport and Trading (the British end of the Anglo-Dutch Royal Dutch Shell Group) said: 'When it comes to investment to serve an international business, exactly the same criteria are applied in Britain or the Netherlands as in, say, New Zealand or Japan'.* This is still a minority view, but by the end of the decade it will be assumed as a matter of course by virtually all companies with international interests.

In view of the dominant position of multinational companies in many of the most important and technologically advanced industries, these criteria assume considerable significance. Naturally there are variations between industries, and between companies in the same industry. But such research as exists on the subject, which draws overwhelmingly on the experience and practice of U.S.-owned concerns, suggests that there is a good deal of common ground.

The normal approach is less scientific than might be supposed. Management does not live in an ivory tower endeavouring to construct theoretically perfect investment models. Their deliberations must always take place within the framework imposed by their company's existing pattern of interests, operational needs, and availability of executive and financial resources. They must think always of the company as it is, and as they would like it to be. Thus a new investment which, considered in isolation, yields a very low

* 'The Anatomy of a Decision' by David Barran. Speech to the Economic Research Council Dinner at St Ermin's Hotel, London, 25 February 1970.

rate of return may make a lot of sense if it secures a supply of vital raw materials. Similarly companies often make seemingly uneconomic investments in order to ensure an outlet for some other part of their total operation. An example is the construction of a refinery by an oil company to provide an outlet for its crude oil production. Companies also undertake new investments to safeguard their existing interests. This happens when a car company introduces a new model for which there is an uneconomically small demand so as to provide a full range, and thereby close off an opportunity for a rival to establish a bridgehead in the market which might later be expanded. Equally a company which sees an opportunity to establish such a bridgehead may jump at it, and be prepared to sustain substantial losses over quite a long period in the hope that it will eventually be able to capture a profitable share of the business.

In a study* of a hundred leading U.S. manufacturing companies the National Industrial Conference Board found that 'most companies do not have a master plan for international investments arrived at through a careful evaluation of the various possibilities of employing capital so as to maximize the return on it.' The great majority consider each proposal on its individual merits, and in the light of the contribution it could make to the company's overall position and prospects. The crucial point in these considerations is the effect the proposed investment is likely to have on the company's sales. 'The various managements are primarily moved, of course, by their responsibility to improve earnings,' says the study. 'But their decisions must accommodate the various – often conflicting – elements of finance, production, and marketing. The study showed that among these, marketing strategy was clearly the dominant element in investment decisions.'

Most multinational companies use highly sophisticated

* 'U.S. Production Abroad and the Balance of Payments: A survey of corporate investment experience' by Judd Polk, Irene Meister, and Lawrence A. Veit (National Industrial Conference Board, 1966).

methods for the financial evaluation of their investment projects. If the results are poor the project may be killed before a penny is spent. But the Board found that financial evaluation is generally not a determining factor in the decision-making process. It is usually employed to show how a new investment should be financed rather than whether it ought to be undertaken. The attitude of executives questioned in the survey is expressed by the phrase, 'if a project is good we find ways to finance it'. When asked what is meant by good, their replies invariably refer to marketing opportunities rather than to anticipated rates of return. Indeed a senior executive of a leading but anonymous U.S. consumer goods company is quoted as saying: 'If we can look forward to a certain level of sales, we won't hesitate to invest, for our profit will justify any amount of investment needed to support such an operation.'* In short the aim of most of the hundred companies covered in the board's survey is to sell more rather than to earn more.

Marketing opportunities can refer to sales in the proposed new investment's domestic market or to exports to other countries, but management's overriding concern with this factor gives a built-in advantage to large, prosperous, and rapidly growing economies in the competition between countries for the investments of the multinational corporations. As the British Economic Development Committee's report on the chemical industry, referred to earlier, pointed out: 'The U.K.'s relatively slow economic growth and small market size act as overall deterrents to chemical investment,' compared with the European Economic Community. Many plants which might have been sited in Britain, had it been a member of the Community, have instead been built within the Community and export their surplus production to Britain.

If a country offers highly attractive marketing opportunities companies are prepared, up to a point, to accept

* In context this statement referred to a situation in which no unusual investment risks were anticipated.

certain other disadvantages, such as government interference in industry, political instability, an unreliable currency, and perhaps even controls on the repatriation of earnings. But if the marketing opportunities are significantly less than in neighbouring countries, a government must be prepared to provide generous incentives. If its policies bring any disadvantages in their wake, their deterrent effect on potential corporate investors will be compounded. It must offer an especially attractive investment climate in other ways.

The assessment of an investment climate can be an extremely complicated affair. As a rule the marketing opportunities in one country are not strikingly better than those in all the neighbouring countries, nor is there usually some other crucial factor, such as access to raw materials, to be taken into account. A company must balance out a host of conflicting points and arguments before deciding where to place its new investment. This is particularly true of the European Economic Community, which constitutes a single large market, yet whose members still retain quite different internal political, financial, and social characteristics.

Some companies are very simple in this respect. In a study* of forty U.S.-owned international companies, Robert Stobaugh of the Harvard Business School found that there are still some which base their decisions on whether or not to invest in a country on an examination of only one or two factors. As an example of this approach he cites a statement by the planning manager of the international division of a large U.S. chemical company. 'We have not considered investing in Brazil,' said the manager, 'because we have experienced foreign exchange losses in the de-

* 'How to analyse foreign investment climates' by Robert B. Stobaugh, Jr. *Harvard Business Review*, September–October 1969. Mr Stobaugh is Lecturer in Business Administration at the Harvard Business School before which he served with Monsanto, Caltex, and Standard Oil (New Jersey).

How one company assesses a country's investment climate

EXHIBIT I. Corporate rating scale for determining a country's investment climate

Item	Number of points	
	Individual subcategory	*Range for category*
Capital repatriation:		
No restrictions	12	0–12
Restrictions based only on time	8	
Restrictions on capital	6	
Restrictions on capital and income	4	
Heavy restrictions	2	
No repatriation possible	0	
Foreign ownership allowed:		
100% allowed and welcomed	12	0–12
100% allowed, not welcomed	10	
Majority allowed	8	
50% maximum	6	
Minority only	4	
Less than 30%	2	
No foreign ownership allowed	0	
Discrimination and controls, foreign versus domestic businesses:		
Foreign treated same as local	12	0–12
Minor restrictions on foreigners, no controls	10	
No restrictions on foreigners, some controls	8	
Restrictions and controls on foreigners	6	
Some restrictions and heavy controls on foreigners	4	
Severe restrictions and controls on foreigners	2	
Foreigners not allowed to invest	0	
Currency stability:		
Freely convertible	20	4–20
Less than 10% open/black market differential	18	
10% to 40% open/black market differential	14	
40% to 100% open/black market differential	8	
Over 100% open/black market differential	4	

	Number of points	
Item	Individual subcategory	Range for category
Political stability:		
Stable long term	12	0–12
Stable, but dependent on key person	10	
Internal factions, but governments in control	8	
Strong external and/or internal pressures that affect policies	4	
Possibility of coup (external and internal) or other radical change	2	
Instability, real possibility of coup or change	0	
Willingness to grant tariff protection:		
Extensive protection granted	8	2–8
Considerable protection granted, especially to new major industries	6	
Some protection granted, mainly new industries	4	
Little or no protection granted	2	
Availability of local capital:		
Developed capital market; open stock exchange	10	0–10
Some local capital available; speculative stock market	8	
Limited capital market; some outside funds (IBRD, AID) available	6	
Capital scarce, short term	4	
Rigid controls over capital	2	
Active capital flight unchecked	0	
Annual inflation for last 5 years:		
Less than 1%	14	2–14
1%–3%	12	
3%–7%	10	
7%–10%	8	
10%–15%	6	
15%–35%	4	
Over 35%	2	
Total		8–100

Source: Harvard Business Review: September–October 1969.

valuation of foreign currencies, and these upset our board of directors. Therefore we made the decision not to consider investing in Brazil.' Other companies attach an equally pre-eminent significance to other matters, such as labour relations, political stability, or government intervention in industry. In every case their attitude is understandable, yet far too simple to be right. Even if a country has some fatal flaw, it does not preclude a company from turning the situation to advantage and making money out of it.

Most companies are, however, more sophisticated. Stobaugh found that about eighty per cent of his sample use a method which he calls 'premium for risk'. In essence this means that management classifies countries into a number of categories, and requires investment projects in some to aim for higher post tax returns than those in others. In its simplest form this could mean that projects in industrialized countries are given a target rate of return of ten per cent compared with fifteen per cent for those in developing countries. Alternatively, each country may be classified separately. One company, for instance, has a cut-off point of thirteen per cent for one particular country, as against fifteen per cent for another, which it considers to have a slightly inferior investment climate.

The assessment of an investment climate involves the study of numerous different aspects of the country concerned. To enable their managers to formalize the process some companies have prepared detailed rating scales, a typical specimen of which is reproduced on pp. 206–7. It is easy to work. The international planning division just goes through each of the sections awarding points on the basis set out in the scale. When that has been done it adds up the total, and sets the target rate of return for a project in that country accordingly.

This method has many advantages. It enables a company to assess a country's marketing opportunities in the light of other relevant information. It can then balance different considerations off against each other. Thus it may be that the willingness of a government to grant extensive tariff protection to a new plant and to allow freedom to repatriate capital would give a relatively small economy a higher rating than a larger but less compliant neighbour for a particular project. In many cases it is very difficult to determine where the balance of advantage lies. This is especially true when political and economic considerations have to be considered together. Like any system for assessing form, whether for horses, women, or countries, the premium for risk method must be used with care. If the points scale is wrongly drawn up in the first place, or if the marketing opportunities are incorrectly forecast, the whole exercise will be a waste of time. But if the initial homework is good, the system can provide a useful guide to action.

None the less it has certain inherent disadvantages. One is that it sets absolute standards whereas the various elements in the rating scale may in reality have different effects on different projects. Thus the profitability of a plant built to serve the export market would depend less on the granting and continuation of extensive tariff protection than would a plant designed to serve the local market. Another is that the situation in a country may change radically during the life of a project following a change of government or a new piece of legislation. Efforts can be made to overcome these difficulties by assigning different weights on the rating scale to different projects in the same country, and by employing a discounted cash flow technique in which a different discount factor is used for each year of a project's life. But 'in practice', as Stobaugh points out, 'such corrections become so complicated and arbitrary that they mainly serve to highlight the difficulties in assigning proper weights and in selecting a proper risk premium'.

In an attempt to surmount these difficulties some of the more adventurous and sophisticated companies try to forecast how the future may develop, and the effect that possible future developments may have on the proposed new plant's ability to meet its targets. The planning division looks at all the influences bearing on each factor on the rating scale in order to determine the range of possible changes that could occur. Having established this range it assesses the relative probability of each of the possible changes, and the impact each would have on the profitability and viability of the project. In most cases the planning division takes the life of the project as the basis for these complicated calculations. But some go a stage further, and try to work out the probability of each of the various possible changes occurring in year one, year two, and so on of the project's life.

All these calculations depend on the use of the most modern computer facilities. But computers alone are only as good as the information fed into them. 'If you put garbage in, you get garbage out,' as the saying goes. Consequently companies devote a good deal of effort to finding out as much as possible about the national life of the countries where they operate and where they are thinking of investing.

In the purely economic sphere this is not too difficult. If a company wants to assess the chances of a change in the value of a currency all the relevant information is freely available. It can study the currency's past record, and by consulting the official published documents it can discover all it needs to know about the trend and pattern of the country's imports and exports and the level of its reserves.

The study of the political environment in which economic and other decisions are taken is more difficult. But several companies are devising new techniques for this purpose. One is Du Pont, whose researchers have identified fifteen to twenty interest groups per country ranging from small landowners to private bankers. Each group has a 'latent influence' depending on its size, educational level, and ability to make its views felt. Du Pont considers how likely it is to feel strongly, and to mobilize its resources on issues that would affect the company, such as pollution or the foreign ownership of local industry. This is called the 'group cohesiveness'. The 'latent influence' and the 'group cohesiveness' are expressed in figures and multiplied together, and the result is then multiplied again by another figure representing the government's receptivity to the group's influence. The final result helps the company (it should not be put stronger than that) to judge how seriously to take any political controversy that may blow up around its operations or proposed investment.

In this way a multinational company reduces all the interlocking, complementary, and conflicting strands in the national life of the countries in which it is interested to a set of figures that can be fed into a computer. The subsequent print-out from that machine does not absolve management from its responsibility to decide between a number of alternative courses of action. Nor does it necessarily provide an accurate forecast of events. Politics and human behaviour remain, thank goodness, too unpredictable for a computer to anticipate in advance. But it does help to get executives away from basing their decisions on such gut reactions as 'we don't like their trade unions', or 'their currency is unsound'. It forces them to examine a country in depth, and to think systematically about the balance of advantage and disadvantage in each of the various possible options.

Market research and the analysis of investment climates show what could be done by management if the company was starting with a clean sheet of paper. But in the real world the final decision on where to expand and where to put down new investment must be taken in the context of the company's existing interests. This means that additional points have to be taken into account. Some have been mentioned already, such as the need to safeguard existing investments, or to secure a raw material supply, or to provide an outlet for the production of another plant.

Others are of a more political nature. A company that

already looms very large in the country where it would most like to expand may feel that if it gets any bigger in relation to the total size of the local economy it will arouse nationalistic resentments. Accordingly it lays down the new production lines elsewhere. Alternatively it may feel that it ought to invest in its third or fourth choice country since its imports into that country are having an adverse effect on the balance of payments, and unless something is done to rectify this the government may act to curtail its sales. Yet another possibility is that the government of the country in which the management would most like to invest will not allow it to build on the site it wants. So rather than take a second choice site in the first choice country the management goes to another country altogether.

A typical example of how extraneous factors can influence a company's investment decisions is an experience of Standard Oil (New Jersey), usually known as Esso, when planning its European refinery expansion programme a few years ago. Esso Europe, which coordinates all the company's European interests, decided not to extend German Esso's refinery at Hamburg. German Esso, however, pointed out that Hamburg would in any case need an extensive overhaul to combat its pollution problems. Consequently the plant could be extended for a relatively small additional cost. Moreover if nothing was done about pollution it would have to close down entirely. This in turn would mean that the company would have to invest in the construction of new terminal and transport facilities to enable it to bring refined oil into the area to meet the demand currently supplied from the refinery. In these circumstances Esso Europe decided that Hamburg rather than the plants it had originally favoured should be expanded.

Companies can not only use market research and the analysis of investment climates to guide their own decisions. The results can also be employed as a lever to play governments off against each other. Most chairmen deny vigorously that they would ever do any such thing. They argue that they can never talk to governments on equal terms since it is the governments which lay down the rules within which companies have to operate. This is true, but if a government is very anxious to secure a large investment running into several hundreds of millions of pounds, the rules of the game may change.

As Arnaud de Vogue, the president of the French-owned St Gobain, has pointed out, the multinational company can use its extra-territorial nature to great effect in dealings with a particular country. 'There is a little game,' he says, 'which consists of a multinational company doing the rounds of all the European countries to find out which will offer the most advantageous conditions for a given implantation. The states in question find themselves competing with each other.'*

There are signs that competition between governments to attract the investments of international companies will grow more intense during the 1970s. For some years national and local governments have advertised the advantages of their territories for new industrial investment in newspapers and business magazines. Now some are taking this technique a stage further by calling attention to the tax concessions they are prepared to offer, and comparing these with the more restrictive attitudes of the taxmen in a neighbouring country. This rather charming and whimsical advertisement produced by the Irish Development Authority, which shows how companies can avoid taxes by moving from Britain to Ireland is a striking example of the new approach. In view of the contribution international companies can make to raising the level of industrial investment it is obviously sensible that governments should take their interests into account in framing tax policy. A small country situated next door to a large one must be more prepared to do this than others. None the less there are grave long-term dangers inherent in governments using

* 'Multinationals in a Market Economy' by Arnaud de Vogue. *International Management*, January 1970.

Get up & go

E & OE, two taxmen.

OE: *British,* *acidulated, vindictive.*   E: *Irish,* *acidulated, vindictive.*

their tax system to compete for the favours of international companies.

U.S. experience shows what can happen. Under U.S. tax law the interest payment on bonds issued by states and municipalities are exempt from federal income tax. Consequently their rates are much lower than those on bonds issued by industrial companies. In the early 1950s some cities hit upon the bright idea of attracting new investment by issuing bonds in their own name, and then allowing the money that was raised to be used by companies who were prepared to set up in their areas. These came to be called Industrial Development Bonds. By 1956 cities in three states were using the device, and total industrial development bond issues came to about $2m. Ten years later cities in twenty states were issuing such bonds, and their total exceeded $500m. The pioneer cities derived great advantages from the scheme, and undoubtedly attracted new investment they would not otherwise have received. But once it had become a general practice it ceased to have much influence on companies' decisions about where to place their new plants. Moreover the cities were forced to raise their interest rates in competition with each other, which meant that they lost some of the advantages of whatever new investment they continued to receive. Eventually the Treasury had to step in to limit the use of funds borrowed by municipalities to subsidize industrial development.

If competition of a similar nature should develop between countries there would be no central authority capable of restoring order. The only beneficiaries would be the international companies who could take a global view of the opportunities open to them, while the countries cut their own throats in pursuit of a rapidly diminishing short-term national advantage.

13. Trade Union Problems

Trade Unions in the industrialized countries are becoming increasingly concerned about the problems arising from the rapid growth of international companies. In essence they are in the same boat as governments: they are national institutions facing an international challenge. In the opinion of Charles Levinson, the secretary-general of the International Federation of Chemical and General Workers' Unions, usually known as the ICF, 'a revolutionary new situation has been created'.

In some circumstances the disruptive power of the individual trade unions has been enhanced. The effects of a strike are no longer confined to a single country. If work stops at a crucial factory supplying a company's plants in other parts of the world, it can cause disruption simultaneously in several countries. Thus when Ford of Britain was hit by a month-long strike in early 1969, it lost production worth $26.4m. in Belgium and Germany as well as $89m. in the U.K. The more companies rationalize their production processes so that their operations in different countries become increasingly inter-dependent, the greater the unions' ability to dislocate those operations will become.

At the same time the structure of the international companies and their flexibility threatens the very heart of trade union authority. This is based on the assumption that a union leader can negotiate directly with the top management of a company, and, in the event of a deadlock, stop the company's production lines by calling his members out on strike. In an international company a national union leader can talk only to the head of the local subsidiary. If he calls a strike, the company can retaliate by threatening to switch production and new investment to its plants abroad, or by building up stockpiles at its other plants with which to supply customers in the strike bound country.

Generalizations are impossible. The manufacture of some products may be switched easily from one plant to another, or it may be relatively easy and inexpensive for a company to maintain a reserve capacity in several plants or to accumulate stocks as an insurance against a strike at the main production centre. In such a case the company has the whip hand in dealings with a national union. In 1966, for instance, the U.S.-owned Goodyear Tire and Rubber Company built up a stockpile at its Swedish subsidiary before the start of negotiations with its unions in the U.S. Partly because it could then show the unions that it could withstand a stoppage at its U.S. plants it was able to deter them from calling one. In 1967 the stockpile proved equally useful in dealings with the unions in Germany. But this tactic is not always open to a company. For other products a rapid switch of production from one plant to another may be very difficult, and the cost of maintaining spare capacity or a stockpile impossibly high. On those occasions the balance of advantage lies with the unions.

There are, however, two strong cards invariably to be found in the hands of an international company when it negotiates with national unions.

In the first place it can threaten that if a strike takes place, or if it is forced to concede more than it wishes, it will concentrate its expansion and new investment elsewhere. The Canadian Massey-Ferguson publicly threatened its Canadian employees in this way when they demanded equal pay with their U.S. counterparts in 1968. In public, union leaders affect to despise threats of this sort, arguing that once a company has created a large investment in one place it is locked in and must continue to expand it. There is some truth in this in the sense that Ford, for example, could not simply close down its British plants and transfer their work to Belgium or Germany. It has an investment in Britain which it must protect, and this is likely to lead to continued expansion in almost any circumstances. But in private union leaders admit that a company can, over a period, significantly alter the pattern of its operations by building up some subsidiaries faster than others. As this happens the bargaining power of the unions in the less favoured locations declines in line with the relative importance of their plants in the company's world-wide scheme of things.

The international company's second ace is that only its management knows the full details of its interests in different parts of the world. It knows which plants are crucial, and which are not; it knows where it intends to expand its existing investments most rapidly and to make new ones, and where it does not. Finally it knows where it can afford to make substantial concessions and where it would find a prolonged stoppage or overtime ban the lesser of two evils. In short, when an international company negotiates with a national trade union it is in full possession of the facts whereas the union representatives are not. Their detailed knowledge is confined to the local subsidiary. They can only guess at its true position in the company, and they do not know the international strategy of the management at the corporate headquarters.

Theoretically the unions should have no difficulty in countering the challenge of the companies through co-operation with each other. From their earliest days the trade union and socialist movements have used the language of internationalism, as typified by slogans such as 'workers of the world unite, you have nothing to lose but your chains'. Karl Marx argued that workers everywhere had common interests that transcended national frontiers, and similar arguments have been repeated by their leaders ever since. Reflecting this attitude trade unions formed international organizations long before governments established the League of Nations. The International Metalworkers' Federation (IMF) was established in 1893 when metal-workers in several European countries 'decided to join their efforts in the fight for an eight-hour day'.* The International Federation of Chemical and General Workers' Unions (ICF) dates from 1907.

On paper these federations have for long looked most impressive. Their membership is composed of national trade unions, and is numbered in millions. The IMF claims about ten million and the ICF some three million.† They are now the most important international bodies striving after practical trade union cooperation in industrial affairs, as distinct from those pursuing more general political objectives.

The reality of their power and influence has, however, never been commensurate with their size. Their members lack a common purpose, and have always been primarily interested in securing their own national objectives. Just as real power in the British trade union movement lies with the individual unions rather than with the Trade Union Congress, so on a world scale it lies with the national unions. It is they who conduct negotiations with the employers, and who are responsible for maintaining and improving the pay and conditions of the men and women on the shop floor. The international federations provide a useful machinery for the exchange of information and ideas, but they cannot act without a mandate from the members. The secretariats are the servants of the membership, and their ability to act depends entirely on the extent to which the members are prepared to follow their advice and guidance.

Old habits of mind die hard. Despite their mounting

*'What is the IMF?' (International Metalworkers' Federation).

† The unions join the federations through affiliating themselves on behalf of those of their members who work in the relevant industries. Thus a union with members in both the chemical and car industries could join both. The IMF charges the affiliated unions 9·3 U.S. cents per member per year, and the ICF 6 U.S. cents per member per year.

concern over the activities of international companies, union leaders still think primarily in national terms. They recoil from the idea of delegating the formulation of policy to an international federation. The concept of matching the power of international companies by an international union with a multinational headquarters staff and branches in different countries is far beyond contemporary thinking.

For the present the principal international interest of most union leaders is to ensure that unions in different countries should cooperate to the extent necessary to prevent companies from using their international facilities to bring pressure to bear on national negotiations, as Goodyear did with its stockpiles, or to break national strikes. This sort of cooperation has been practised for many years, but it is now greater than ever before. In 1969 there was a strike at Belgian Ford's plant at Genk not far from the German frontier. While it lasted workers at German Ford's Cologne plant promised not to allow men to be sent to Genk, or work usually conducted in Belgium to be switched across the frontier. If the company had tried to send work to Ford of Britain, the British workers would undoubtedly have adopted the same attitude as the Germans, and it would be nothing unusual for the dockers and railway workers in Britain and Belgium to have refused to handle the transfer of goods between the company's plants.

Useful as such cooperation is its scope is limited. For a while men at one plant will forgo extra work and earnings to help their foreign colleagues at another. But if a strike in a foreign country means that they are laid off or lose money, their solidarity is unlikely to last for long. Nor are workers anywhere disposed to prevent a company from expanding their plant and improving their prospects just because it is being done at the expense of foreign employees of the same company. If a company decides to expand the capacity of its Belgian plants, for instance, at twice the rate of its British and German factories and to transfer certain operations from Britain and Germany to Belgium, the British and

German workers may object but it is inconceivable that the Belgians would join their protests. Similarly if a company has to cut back production it is very difficult for the unions to maintain a united front: each is above all concerned to ensure that its own members suffer least, and the devil take the hindmost.

None the less the winds of change are beginning to blow. In both the IMF and the ICF the first tentative steps have been taken on the long road towards international collective bargaining.

In the words of the assistant general secretary of the IMF, Daniel Benedict, 'the challenge of multi-national companies has led to the first new structural adaptation of international trade unionism in decades: the formation of world councils or working parties of workers in specific companies around the globe'.* The first were established in 1966 for Ford, General Motors, Chrysler, and Volkswagen-Mercedes Benz. In 1968 the principle was extended to the electrical and electronics industry with the formation of a council for the U.S.-owned General Electric Company. The purpose of the councils is to enable workers' representatives from a company's plants all over the world to meet regularly to exchange information, discuss plans, and consider possible avenues for cooperation, and for the coordination of their negotiations. The work of these councils is buttressed by industry committees, which bring together workers in a particular industry, such as, for instance, the European motor industry.

As they have no executive authority it would be easy to dismiss these councils as no more than talking shops, but that would be a mistake. To begin with their mere existence makes it difficult for a company to grant concessions in one country without, in due course, having to concede comparable terms everywhere. The unions compare their

* 'Workers and Managers in Multi-national Giant Companies'. Speech by Daniel Benedict to a seminar of the Irish Transport and General Workers' Union, Dublin, 14–16 November 1969.

wages, job security provisions, holidays, retirement benefits, and other terms of employment, and there is an inevitable tendency for them to demand parity with the best
available in the company's world-wide operations. This does
not mean that they all press for identical contracts; national
habits, tax, welfare systems, and housing arrangements vary
far too much for this to be practical. But it does mean that
they will increasingly want contracts, which, taking local
conditions into account, are as good as those to be found
anywhere else in the company. Moreover, given time, the
councils will lead to the creation of an environment in
which all the different national unions concerned with a
particular company share a set of common assumptions.
As it develops, the concept of coordinating their negotiations and pursuing certain common objectives will evolve
naturally.

Already there are signs that this is happening. It was no
coincidence that in 1969 and 1970 motor workers throughout Europe clamoured for the elimination of regional wage
differentials within their countries. In Britain this meant
securing equality for all plants with the Midlands, and in
Belgium equality with Antwerp. The elimination of these
differentials was among the subjects most discussed and the
targets set at the IMF's conference for world motor workers in Turin in 1968, and at its European motor workers'
conference in Paris in 1969.

The coming together of national trade unions in pursuit
of common objectives and sharing the same basic set of
assumptions will be hastened if more companies follow the
example of the Dutch Philips Electrical of talking to unions
on a multinational basis. The Philips top management at
Eindhoven has accepted the right of IMF members' unions
representing its workers throughout the European Community to discuss with it matters of common interest. At
the first meeting the threatened closure of a plant in Berlin
was considered, and, in response to union pressure, the
company produced an alternative plan to keep it open. At

the second a more general exchange took place about such matters as how to set up a procedure for giving the unions advance warning of developments affecting employment.

Although acutely aware of the problems raised by the rapid growth of international companies, the secretariat of the IMF is modest about its own ability to initiate new policies in this field. Its general secretary, Herr Adolph Graedel, a veteran leader of the Swiss Metalworkers and Watchmakers' Union, points out that despite the increasing importance of the motor and electrical companies to his member unions, only about three million of their ten million members work for international companies. The rest are employed in industries, such as steel, shipbuilding, and engineering, which are, for the most part, organized on national lines. Moreover many of his member unions are extremely powerful and independent–minded bodies. The largest is the German IG Metall with nearly 1.9m. members, and several have memberships running into the hundreds of thousands.

'We cannot aspire to set their policies or interfere in their affairs,' says Graedel, 'nor would they welcome an attempt by us to coordinate their activities'. He believes that the unions themselves must initiate action when they see the need for it. The secretariat should confine itself to drawing attention to possible needs, putting forward ideas, disseminating knowledge, and providing active assistance to members only when asked. In the context of the IMF this is undoubtedly the right policy.

The Canadian secretary-general of the ICF, Charles (always known as 'Chip') Levinson, is more adventurous. For his three million members international companies are by far the most important employers. The companies are in industries which are highly capital intensive, and where a break in production, or even a reduction in the level at which the plants are worked, is extremely expensive. They employ relatively small numbers of people who are frequently quite highly qualified. The result is that the unions are smaller and less traditionally minded than those of the IMF. The structure of their industries forces them to think internationally, and they find it less difficult to accept the implications of doing so than their opposite numbers in older industries. For these reasons Levinson believes that the ICF is well placed to pioneer new ways of dealing with international companies.

He eschews the more peaceful approach of the IMF, as demonstrated by its dialogue with Philips. 'We will make contact with the top management of international companies and win their respect through conflict,' he says, 'talking is no good.' His long-term aim is to harmonize the activities of his member unions to the point where they coordinate their negotiations, and seek common objectives. He realizes that it will be many years before this becomes possible on a large scale, but he is not a visionary. Already he has helped to coordinate a number of negotiations on an international scale. The most notable concerned the French-owned St Gobain glass and manufacturing company, which, at the time, had interests in twelve countries.

In 1969, St Gobain workers in France, Italy, Germany, and the U.S. were due to re-negotiate their agreements with the company. On March 29 of that year delegates from the ICF unions concerned met at its headquarters in Geneva to coordinate their strategy. They were joined there by representatives from the company's plants in Belgium, Norway, Sweden, and Switzerland. The participants at the conference reached agreement on five points:

(1) To establish a standing committee to coordinate the negotiations in France, Germany, Italy, and the U.S.
(2) That no negotiations should be concluded in any country without the approval of the standing committee.
(3) That in the event of a strike in one country all unions would provide financial assistance if needed.

(4) That if the strike was prolonged, overtime would be stopped at other St Gobain plants.

(5) That if the company <u>tried to move production from one country to another</u> in order to break or weaken a strike the <u>move would be resisted</u>.

Several days later the German union, IG Chemie-Papier-Keramik, began negotiations with St Gobain's German affiliate. It was offered a handsome package deal, including an effective eleven per cent pay rise plus various attractive redundancy and job security provisions. These not only represented a substantial advance by the German affiliate, but also provided ICF members with a useful precedent for negotiations with other St Gobain subsidiaries. With the standing committee's approval, the union promptly accepted, but warned the company that its promises to the unions in other countries still held good.

In Italy negotiations began on April 22 only to be broken off the following day until May 8. In the interim the Italian unions heard, through the ICF, that the U.S. St Gobain workers intended to call a strike in three plants. They asked that it should be delayed until May 8 to coincide with the resumption of their talks with the company in order to subject it to a double pressure, and the Americans agreed. When the Italian negotiations re-started an impasse seemed imminent, and the unions called for a 72-hour strike. However, before the action took place a breakthrough was achieved, and a settlement reached, which, the unions claim, represented 'virtually a 100 per cent result in comparison to initial demands'.* It included pay increases, a new basis for calculating production bonuses, and, most significantly, recognition by the company of the unions as the responsible bodies for negotiations on a company-wide basis.

In the U.S. St Gobain claimed that it could not concede the demands of the Glass and Ceramic Workers on the

* *ICF Bulletin*, June–July 1969.

grounds that the U.S. subsidiary had failed to earn profits from 1966 to 1968. Accordingly the I CF sent the union details of St Gobain's world-wide profits, which had risen sharply over the period, and the details of the agreements reached in Italy and Germany. Armed with this information the union argued that large concessions could also be made in the U.S. After a strike of twenty-six days negotiations were resumed, and the union secured a three-year contract with wage increases of nearly nine per cent a year, and various other benefits.

Only in France, St Gobain's home country, did the I CF have no practical effect. This was because the main French union, the Communist-controlled CGT, did not participate in the overall plan. It accepted an offer of a 3.5 per cent pay increase, and left the I CF member unions in France high and dry.

Thus the St Gobain affair, as it is often called, resulted in only a partial victory for the unions. Moreover they were only coordinating their negotiations; they were not attempting to pursue common objectives. Nor did a crisis occur in which I CF member unions were called upon to make sacrifices on behalf of their colleagues in foreign countries. Nevertheless it would be difficult to deny Levinson's contention that he had proved that trade unions can tackle an international company on a collective basis and achieve more than would have been possible if they had acted singly.

He has also demonstrated his ability to mobilize the power of a large union in an international company's home country in support of a small union in conflict with a subsidiary. In May 1969 the Turkish Chemical Workers' Federation called a strike against the local affiliate of the German Hoechst. The I CF called in I G Chemie-Papier-Keramik, which represents Hoechst's German workers, and it intervened on the Turks' behalf at the company's Frankfurt headquarters. The combined pressure of the two unions led the subsidiary to put forward a promising offer, and in

June Karl Kupper, a vice-president of IG Chemie and director of its Collective Bargaining Division, flew to Turkey to help the local union negotiate on it. Soon afterwards a satisfactory settlement was reached.

A dispute does not have to occur before international resources are mobilized for negotiations with an international company. An example of a company accepting the right of its home union and the ICF to set standards for a subsidiary is the Norwegian Borregaard, a major producer of pulp and paper products, industrial chemicals, and a wide range of household items. In 1969 the company started to build a vast new pulp mill and subsidiary installations at Porto Alegre in Brazil, where unions are weak and ill-informed. From the outset the Norwegian unions and the ICF cooperated with the Brazilians in direct negotiations with the company's head office over the working conditions for the Brazilian workers. On this occasion the ICF cannot claim much of the credit for initiating the discussions. As Borregaard is relying heavily on Norwegian government funds for the project, and has very good relations with its domestic unions, those unions would probably have been consulted regardless of the ICF. But it is through the establishment of precedents like this that the ICF can subsequently tackle more intractable companies elsewhere.

Levinson's aim now is to move another step towards full collective bargaining on an international scale. He wants to persuade his member unions to demand parity with each other on a number of specific matters. By this he means that several unions should simultaneously ask a company for the same redundancy provisions, for instance, or for the same industrial training rights. The ICF would first find out which of the company's subsidiaries already provides the best terms; then member unions, working in conjunction with each other, would try to get them introduced on a world-wide basis. He sees this as a gradual process to be tackled company by company and issue by issue. But once the precedents have been established, a growing number of companies will treat their workers in different countries alike on a growing number of issues.

Eventually Levinson would like his members to demand the same rates of pay, and identical contracts that would be varied only so far as was necessary to take account of differing national tax and welfare arrangements. He recognizes that it will be a long time before unions can even begin to think in these terms. But, like the IMF, he is attempting to create a common environment through the formation of world company councils and industry committees to bring together workers with the same interests and the same employers from different countries.

Should the Common Market's expansion be followed by the evolution of far-reaching common economic, tax, social, and industrial policies, the task of the ICF and the IMF will be made much easier. Within Europe at least the breakdown of national barriers will force unions to think beyond their own frontiers. But Europe is only one part of the world, and the operations of international companies extend far beyond it. To persuade unions in Europe, North America, and Japan, to name only three industrial areas, to cooperate will be much more difficult.

Whether the more aggressive policies of the ICF or the more peaceable methods of the IMF prove most effective remain to be seen. But whatever happens both will encounter some major obstacles along the road to unity. In an international company there is a central headquarters responsible for identifying and sustaining the corporate interest. If the national interests of the subsidiaries should interfere with it, the central headquarters can and, in the end, usually does impose its will upon them. In the trade union movement the ultimate authority will continue to rest with the individual national unions. Their attitudes will have to undergo a fundamental change before they are prepared to make sacrifices on behalf of their fellow workers in another country or another part of the world.

Indeed some of the impetus behind the present move towards more trade union cooperation comes from unions who are pressing for their own rather than any common interest. The motor industry provides a case in point. When the U.S. United Auto Workers sends representatives to Europe to encourage European motor unions to demand better terms, they are not motivated by a simple desire to help their brother workers. They are worried by the rising volume of foreign car imports into the U.S., and they believe that one way to tackle this problem is to try to push up European labour costs. In the long run, as international companies standardize their production processes the world over, it will be in the interests of the unions to present a united front to the employers. Only in this way will they be able to prevent the companies from playing them off against each other. But in the short run situations can arise in which workers in some countries will gain more by moderating their claims. By so doing they will encourage the company to increase its investment in their subsidiary, and thus improve their own prospects.

In the last resort an international company can always decide where it wishes to invest, and which subsidiaries it wants to encourage. If the company as a whole will gain through making concessions in one place in order to stand firm in another, the management will do so. A union has no such choice. All its interests and responsibilities are in one country. None the less if they are to be safeguarded in the long run the unions will have to remember Benjamin Franklin's remark to John Hancock at the signing of the Declaration of Independence on 4 July, 1776, when the individual and rebellious American colonies were confronted by the international might of Britain: 'We must indeed all hang together,' he said, 'or most assuredly we shall all hang separately.'

14. White Negroism

Multinational companies cannot yet claim to be citizens of the world. They earn their profits, build their factories, and sell their products in many different countries. Their home country is only one among many whose interests they take into account. But one important aspect of their activities remains firmly national in character. The vast majority still appoint only citizens of their home country to their top management positions. However multinational a company's interests may be in every other respect, it is extremely rare to find a foreigner with executive responsibilities as a member of the main parent board at headquarters. During the 1970s the companies will come under increasing pressure to provide equal opportunities to reach the top for all their employees, and there will be widespread discussion about how to achieve this objective.

The companies' failure to multinationalize their senior management is in marked contrast with their usual policy towards their subsidiaries. In the developed countries these are often almost entirely run by local nationals.

There are several reasons why this should be so. One is the companies' desire to merge into the environment of the countries where they operate. Their ambition is always to become accepted as part of the local scene, and for it to be forgotten that they are controlled from abroad. To achieve such identification it is vital that most of their local executives should be citizens of the countries where they work. It is also more practical to employ locals. They know more than expatriates about the manners and mores of their own countries. Thus, so long as they have the necessary technical expertise and authority, they will be more effective salesmen, factory managers, and negotiators with government. Moreover, even the largest companies do not have unlimited reserves of executive talent in their head offices and domestic operations. So the sooner a foreign subsidiary can build up an indigenous management capable of standing on its own feet the better, both for itself and for its parent.

(3) In addition, it is usually much cheaper to employ a local than an expatriate. The expatriate and his family cost money to move from one country to another, and need special help with housing and schooling in their new location. They frequently have to be paid a premium over their normal salary to compensate them for living abroad, and to enable them to maintain their pension, mortgage, social security, and other commitments at home. As well as being expensive, the employment of expatriates gives rise to other practical financial problems. Every country has its own tax and salary structure, and its own scale of fringe benefits. In 1969 Associated Industrial Consultants estimated that a Frenchman earning £7,500 a year kept 86.2 per cent of his salary, a German 72 per cent, and a Briton 66 per cent. Whereas it was rare for Britons to receive Christmas or holiday bonuses, 65.7 per cent of German executives got one at Christmas and 47.3 per cent when they went on holiday. By contrast 79.3 per cent of the British got subsidized lunches compared with only 20.9 per cent of the Germans. These and a host of other complications have to be ironed out so that the expatriate executive feels that he is being fairly treated both in comparison with his local colleagues and with what he would have received if he had stayed at home.

Despite the difficulties, companies are moving executives from one country to another to an ever-increasing extent. In every major commercial city there are large colonies of expatriate businessmen; Americans are the most numerous, but most European nationalities are strongly represented.

It has become commonplace for able and ambitious young men in international firms of their own nationality to assume that they will work abroad for part of their career. A growing number employed in foreign-owned subsidiaries are beginning to think the same way.

The moves take place for a variety of reasons. As a company's foreign interests expand it becomes desirable for the senior executives at headquarters to have had foreign experience, and for the men in charge of the subsidiaries to know how head office works. The dissemination of knowledge, experience and new techniques similarly demands that men should move about the world within the company in order to teach and learn. Sometimes too a subsidiary, or even the parent company, may find that it has nobody suitable for a certain job, and must seek help from another part of the organization. But there is a significant difference between movements such as these, and a genuine multinationalization of top management. The most a foreigner can usually hope for is to run the local operation in his own country, or to carve out a career in the regional organization of which his national subsidiary forms a part. In all but a few companies the doors to the most senior offices at headquarters are closed to him.

'You have to accept the fact that the only way to reach a senior post in our firm is to take out an American passport',* a British executive of a U.S.-owned company once told Professor Howard V. Perlmutter, an authority on international business. When *Business Week* conducted an inquiry† into why able young Europeans were leaving U.S.-owned subsidiaries to work for locally-owned companies, it was told by a Belgian that Europeans are subject to a form of discrimination which he described as 'white negroism'. It is unfair to single out U.S. companies as

* 'The tortuous evolution of the multinational company' by Howard V. Perlmutter. *Columbia Journal of World Business*, January–February 1969.
† *Business Week*, 7 June 1969.

objects for quotations of this sort. Similar criticisms can be levelled at most international and multinational companies, regardless of their country of origin. The former chairman of a British multinational once told me why he would not have foreigners on his main board in London. 'We have to be able to speak freely together, and trust each other implicitly,' he said; 'if we had a foreigner here his loyalties would be divided. He might sometimes be tempted to give undue weight to the interests of his own national subsidiary, or to tell his home government of our deliberations.' Other chairmen emphasize that the top directorate of a company should be a closely-knit group of men who understand each other absolutely. It is difficult enough to create this kind of relationship between men of the same nationality and background; when they do not share these links the normal problems are compounded.

They are not, however, insurmountable. At Shell and Unilever, Britons and Dutchmen have been working together for generations. At Shell three nationalities are in fact represented on the committee of managing directors, which controls the company, since one of its members is Monroe Spaght, an American. Because of their dual ownership these companies have no choice but to be multinational. So perhaps a better example is Nestlé where 'it's an accepted fact . . . that because you're Swiss you won't succeed any faster than, say, a Frenchman or Italian'.* With the exception of the chairmanship a foreigner can aspire to any position.† Among the executive grades at its headquarters at Vevey on Lake Geneva about a third are non-Swiss. The managing director, who is the operational

---

* 'The Full Cream Life of the Nestlé Man' by Norris Willat. *The Director*, October 1969.

† Nestlé's policy reflects the unusually international nature of its business. Some 97·5 per cent of its turnover is earned outside Switzerland, and its products are to be found throughout the non-Communist world. But its ownership remains firmly Swiss. In order that it cannot be taken over by a foreign concern, only Swiss nationals are allowed to buy its voting shares.

head of the company, is a Frenchman, Pierre Liotard-Vogt. Before he took over, his responsibilities were shared between two men, an Italian, Enrico Bignami, and a Swiss, Jean-C. Corthesy. As well as Liotard-Vogt, there is an Englishman, R. S. Worth, on the parent board, and of the seven general managers, one is Dutch and another French.

Some companies simply do not believe that it is necessary to follow Nestlé's example. They are apparently content that their multinational commercial empires should be run by citizens of their home country. The U.S.-owned Gulf Oil, for instance, says that, 'While it has proved useful to transfer certain U.S. citizens from nation to nation to deliver (and obtain) new insights and techniques, it seems doubtful that a multinational manager type of class is developing, or is needed.'* There are other companies who share Gulf's view, while feeling that it would be tactless to express it in public. But more and more are becoming worried about the need to multinationalize their top management.

They are being pushed in this direction by their younger executives. Claude Henrion, a Frenchman on the board of the British subsidiary of the Canadian Massey-Ferguson, expresses the aspirations of many ambitious and able young men working for international companies in these words: 'He must feel,' says Henrion, 'that if he has the ability he can aspire to any job in the company, apart perhaps from the presidency. It may be that when he is faced with the prospect of going on to the main board, and so spending the rest of his working life outside his home country, he will decide to reject the opportunity. If so that will be his decision. But he must feel that his nationality does not, of itself, disqualify him from aiming for the stars.'

Henrion is fortunate. In 1959 Massey-Ferguson re-organized its corporate structure in order to separate the head office from the North American operation with the aim, among others, of opening its top management to

* *Successo* (English language edition), February 1970.

people of all nationalities on an equal footing with North Americans. But the experience of Massey-Ferguson shows how long it can take to multinationalize top management. After twelve years its highest echelons are still largely North American with a sprinkling of Britons. Within the company it is thought that it may not be until 1980 or so that the full implications of the 1959 decision are felt.

Obviously everything could be speeded up by reserving certain jobs for particular nationalities, or by the introduction of a quota system to ensure that each subsidiary fills a given number of posts at headquarters. That is how organizations such as the European Commission and the United Nations overcome national rivalries. But in a commercial firm these expedients would be unsuitable. They would mean that men received promotion who were not properly qualified. This would be bad both for profits and for the morale of those passed over in favour of less able colleagues. National animosities would be intensified rather than the reverse. The only way for a company to proceed is to promote individuals on the basis of ability and qualification, and it takes a long time to groom and test a potential top executive.

In Shell, for instance, the aim is to identify the men who have group managing director potential when they are in their early thirties. They are then launched on a career pattern in which they are given jobs that will simultaneously prepare them for the top and test their suitability for it. They have to gain experience over a wide range of the company's activities, and to be prepared to spend not just a few years but much of their life abroad. This pattern will be quite different from that of a man whose ultimate potential is considered to be within the compass of a subsidiary. Consequently many years must elapse from the moment a company decides that its top management should be open to all, until the effects of this decision become apparent in the board room. In the intervening years, however, an increasing number of foreigners will begin to appear at headquarters and in the ranks immediately below the top. As this happens so the character of the company will undergo a gradual but distinct change.

There are many problems to be overcome during this period. Among them is the attitude of the potential senior executives themselves. The aspirations of men like Henrion have something in common with the claims of women for equal pay and opportunity. On the one hand women want these things, while on the other they want to retain the freedom to change their responsibilities and even their jobs in response to the prior demands of their domestic life. Similarly, the international executive wants equality of opportunity with his company's home country nationals, while retaining the option to jump off the promotion ladder if he finds at the end of the day that he does not want to take up permanent residence abroad.

The desire to retain this option is perfectly understandable. For a man and his wife to spend a few years abroad when they are young and their children are young is one thing; it is quite another for a couple in their late forties or early fifties, the normal age for the top-level management appointments, to decide to spend the rest of their working life in the foreign country where the headquarters of the man's company happens to be. To do so may involve having to choose between educating their children in that country or being separated from them as they continue their studies at home. It also involves separation from the rest of their family and friends and living in an alien atmosphere. These considerations are especially serious for the French and southern Europeans who attach far greater value to family ties with aunts and uncles, grandparents and cousins than do the British and Americans. Whereas a man may be prepared to sacrifice these ties in the interests of his career, his wife is likely to be far less amenable.

Even at a relatively early stage differences in national attitudes towards living abroad become apparent, with the Latins on the whole being less mobile than the nordic peoples. As a result it is extremely difficult for a company to devise a staffing policy that will simultaneously give equality to all while furthering its own best interests. It is always hard to pick out and train the top managers of the future; a vast amount of time, money, and effort has to be spent on developing their careers and skills. The majority who are spotted in their early thirties fail to stay the course. If those who do, at the expense of others, decide to quit before the company has secured an adequate return on its investment in them, the job becomes even more difficult. Companies can therefore be forgiven if they prefer to rely on men who are unlikely to drop out of the race, and these are more likely to come from their home countries than any other.

Another major problem is language. An international company must have a *lingua franca* in which instructions go out from head office, and reports returned, in which information is filed, and in which men of different nationalities converse with each other. If a man does not have a thorough command of that language he cannot hope to be promoted to a really senior position outside his own country.

For English speaking companies – that is principally the Americans, British, and Canadians – the problem is less serious than for most. English is now the most widely spoken language in the industrialized countries. More Europeans speak it as a second language than anything else. For other companies language constitutes a serious communications barrier between different parts of their organization. It was in an attempt to overcome this, and to ensure that non-Swedes are not placed at a disadvantage when going for top jobs, that SKF has adopted English in place of Swedish as its company language.

It is difficult to imagine a French, German, or Italian speaking company adopting such an attitude. Even the Dutch, who are far more internationally minded than most, boggle at the idea. Philips Lamp, for instance, is anxious to internationalize its top management, and on 1 January

1969, welcomed the first non-Dutchman, a Belgian, onto its main board at Eindhoven. When the president, Frits Philips, was asked* if there was any reason why more foreigners should not follow, he replied that there was none, but added the crucial proviso that they must be able to speak fluent Dutch. It is perfectly reasonable and understandable that a company should expect men who want to rise within its organization to speak the language of the country in which it is based, and from which most of its senior executives are drawn. But the importance of this obstacle to the multinationalization of the top management of multinational companies is one that should not be underrated.

Yet another obstacle, which is frequently overlooked entirely, is that the style in which companies are run reflects the national characteristics of the people of the country in which they are based. The directors of Ford, British Petroleum, Philips, and SKF assess the problems and opportunities facing their companies on the basis of their own corporate interest rather than any national interest. But they do so as Americans, Britons, Dutchmen, and Swedes with the characteristic national attitudes, standards and prejudices of those countries. Although the tools and methods of management are becoming increasingly standardized the world over, each nationality has its own quirks and manners that have grown out of its own particular social structure, educational system, and cultural heritage. 'What differentiates one international enterprise from another comes, not so much from financial resources and techniques, but rather from the people who work in the company',† says Professor Howard V. Perlmutter. Jacques G. Maisonrouge, the French president of the IBM World

*'The Lamp Glows Brighter' by Timothy Johnson (*Sunday Times*, 19 January 1969).

†'The International Enterprise, Three Conceptions' by Howard V. Perlmutter. First published in French in *La Revue Économique et Sociale*, Lausanne, Mai 1965, Numero 2.

Trade Corporation (which coordinates the company's foreign operations) agrees. He believes 'that we always under-estimate the role of cultural background in management. We are oriented towards our own national cultures, and it takes time and dedication to understand how others react'.*

Even when a man speaks a foreign language perfectly it does not necessarily follow that he will fit easily into the environment of another country. For all his ability as a manager, lack of social confidence and his unfamiliarity with the way things are done may make him vastly less effective at head office than in his own national subsidiary. Governments have found to their cost that successful businessmen do not transplant easily from industry to politics and government service. Qualities that achieved enormous success in the manufacture of cars or washing machines somehow often turn out to yield less impressive results in the different atmosphere of Whitehall, Washington, or Bonn. When men are moved from one country to another they can be equally unpredictable.

Finally there is the question of money. Just as it is more expensive to employ an expatriate than a local national in a subsidiary, so it is to bring a foreigner from a subsidiary onto the main board at head office. Indeed the amount of money involved is very much larger since the potential top executive earns more and has greater pension and other commitments than a subordinate. If a company really wants an individual to do a particular job, then, within reason, the cost is of little consequence. But if a company finds that a policy of preparing foreigners for top management positions and employing even a small number at headquarters adds substantially to its salary bill, it must be convinced that there is an overriding reason why the additional expense should be incurred.

That overriding reason will be the need to attract and

*'The Evolution of International Business' by Jacques G. Maisonrouge. Speech to the American Bankers Association, 15 May 1968.

retain the best available executive talent of all nationalities. International companies which reserve their top jobs for nationals of their home country will face, on a larger scale, the same difficulties as family companies which reserve their best jobs for members of the family. More and more executives will adopt the attitude of Claude Henrion and others like him that a man's nationality should not, of itself, disqualify him from aiming for the stars. Companies which refuse to promote foreigners beyond a certain point will find that many of their best men leave, and that they cannot recruit their fair share of able and ambitious young men for their subsidiaries.

As the *Business Week* inquiry into why Europeans leave U.S. subsidiaries in Europe shows, this is not a fanciful prediction. Companies are already aware of the problem. During the next decade or so it will become more acute. As the influence of international companies spreads, and their importance in the economic life of nations increases, a growing number of the best young men entering business will wish to embark on careers which hold out the chance of eventually helping to run them. A top position in a multi-national giant will represent the ultimate reward and challenge of a business career; to be barred from even aspiring to that position simply on grounds of nationality will be intolerable.

An important role in moulding the views and aspirations of young businessmen will be the business schools, both in Europe and the U.S., which are attracting an increasing number of non-Americans. At these schools they will learn to regard business as an international activity in which qualifications and ability count for more than anything else. They will also learn to assess their career opportunities by comparing the prospects offered by different companies on an equal footing regardless of nationality, and to go to those which offer the best opportunities.

The difficulties facing a company that wishes to multi-nationalize its top management will not disappear, but they will diminish. Another effect of the business schools will be to create an <u>internationally recognized qualification</u>, and to accelerate the move towards <u>common standards</u>. The problems of national differences and the necessity of learning foreign languages will remain, but in the new context they will be less significant. It will no doubt be a long time before the rising generation of top executives can emulate the scholars and film stars who move from one country to another in pursuit of their careers without losing their national identity. But the trend will be in that direction.

15. Conclusion

We are now at the half-way stage between the end of the war and the end of the century. The years behind us saw the establishment of the foundations and superstructure of the contemporary international business system. The years ahead will see its completion. Important changes will also take place in the nature of the nation state, and in the relationship between states. But at this stage it seems highly unlikely that national political systems or international political federations will develop at the same pace. The central feature of our politico-social system will remain the nation state, to which people look for the management of the economy, the constant improvement of their standard of living, defence against internal disorder and external attack, and the solution of political and social problems. His country and his sense of nationality will remain the focal points of a man's loyalty, while international companies, as a group, become an ever-increasing source of industrial power and influence. It is in the interests of both companies and governments to appreciate the realities of the situation. Only then can they hope to be successful at finding ways to reconcile their respective aspirations and interests in order that they may work together as harmoniously and effectively as possible.

In some quarters it is suggested that the rate at which the companies' power and influence is increasing will accelerate dramatically, and that we are rapidly moving into an era of super-giant firms. A leading exponent of this theory, whose ideas have widespread support among industrial leaders, is Professor Howard V. Perlmutter. He believes that by 1985 world industry will be dominated by 200 or 300 very large international companies responsible for the greater part of industrial output.* There will still be small companies, he suggests, exploiting new inventions, providing special services, and carving out niches of their own. But the middle-sized group will virtually disappear.

It is difficult to believe that the reality will be quite so startling. Enormous agglomerations of power always call forth countervailing social and political forces. In international business these † will probably have the support of governments, which already tend to create or support national enterprises whenever they fear that an important or strategic industry will otherwise fall into completely foreign hands.

However, the trend is clear. The leading multinationals have for some time been increasing their production and sales faster than most countries can expand their gross national products. Each year new companies join the international ranks. The value of goods produced by international companies outside their home countries is rising more rapidly than the value of world trade. A growing proportion of the imports and exports of all industrialized countries is accounted for by the internal transactions of international companies, and the same applies to the movement of funds through the world currency markets. There is no doubt that in absolute terms these companies will account for a much larger share of world production and trade in 1985 than today.

In some industries this trend will be accomplished by a sharp reduction in the number of competing companies. The large multinationals will grow even larger, while their rivals merge so that a small group of mammoth companies is left to carve up world markets. Fiat's chairman, Giovanni

*'Super-giant Firms in the Future' by Howard V. Perlmutter, *Wharton Quarterly*, Winter 1968; and numerous other writings.

† For an interesting discussion of this point see 'Big Business in the late 20th century' by Andrew Shonfield, *Daedalus*, Winter 1969.

Agnelli, believes that this will happen in the European motor industry. 'Eventually,' he says, 'there will be the three American companies, and one British. The rest will wind up together – as one or two companies.' * In view of the fact that only three companies account for almost the entire U.S. car production, Agnelli's vision is not unreasonable. His company has indeed started to work towards its fulfilment through its partial acquisition of the French Citroen. But as it presupposes the ultimate merger or disappearance of about a dozen companies in Italy, Germany, France, Sweden, and Holland, it is still pretty dramatic. Another industry where equally far-reaching moves towards concentration are expected is chemicals. N. G. S. Champion, who is in charge of planning at BP Chemicals, suggests † that over the next few years the eighty or ninety leading European chemical companies could be whittled down to ten. In computers too there are signs that the various European companies are moving towards the conclusion that the most effective way of competing against IBM is to pool their efforts. At the same time they are putting out feelers to the smaller U.S. companies engaged on the same difficult task.

Mergers and attempted mergers always attract a good deal of publicity, and there is a tendency to assume that when a number of industries are being concentrated into fewer units, the same thing will happen everywhere. This is not the case. In some important industries there is a clear trend the other way, towards greater competition. Oil, for instance, was dominated from 1945 until the late 1950s by the so-called seven sisters – Standard Oil (New Jersey), Shell, Texaco, Mobil, Gulf, Standard Oil of California, and British Petroleum. According to much contemporary business theory they should have spent the 1960s forming themselves into three or four vast all-embracing groups accounting for virtually the whole international industry. Instead, they not only remained apart, but throughout the

Fortune, 15 September 1968.
†*Daily Telegraph*, 30 January 1970.

decade saw their percentage share of production, refining, and sales diminish as newcomers from the U.S., France, Italy, and Germany, as well as the producer countries, elbowed their way in.

Oil is the longest-established international industry, and its experience is therefore relevant to all others. It demonstrates that such an industry need not be dominated by an oligopoly, and that when an oligopoly has been formed it can be broken. But it is significant that the successful challengers were themselves either extremely large in their domestic market before they expanded abroad, or enjoyed access to government funds and the support which went with it. U.S. 'independents', such as Continental and Phillips, fall into the first category, and the Italian ENI and French ERAP into the second. Both groups realized that if they were to hold their own against the multinational giants at home, they had to compete everywhere.

In the long run oil rather than motors, chemicals, or computers is likely to provide the best guide to the future. This is partly because governments will not wish to see their whole industrial structure controlled by foreign-owned firms, and will support national enterprises that fight back. To have any chance of success these enterprises, like the newcomers in oil, will have to be prepared to compete across the world.

Another reason is that purchasers of every sort of industrial raw material and manufactured product never want to be dependent on a very small group of suppliers. They know that the smaller the group the more likely are price rings and other restrictive practices, and the more vulnerable they are to having their supplies disrupted by strikes and stoppages. So regardless of their own status and ambitions, they try to encourage competition in those industries that supply them. The car companies, for example, have learned from bitter experience that dependence on a small group of component manufacturers invariably leads to production holdups as a result of strikes in strategic factories. Consequently Volkswagen is increasing the proportion of its components bought outside Germany, and the badly hit British Leyland is buying more from the continent. Sometimes large buyers positively encourage their suppliers to go international, as happened with the U.S.-owned Eaton Yale and Towne, whose president says it expanded abroad, 'because our major automotive customers rather strongly suggested that we establish manufacturing facilities in the various countries where they proposed to build trucks and cars'.* This kind of thing will happen much more in the future.

Regardless of the way in which their own industry may develop, the extent to which all international companies integrate their activities across frontiers will increase. The necessity to secure the greatest economies of scale will drive them to concentrate production of particular products in a small number of plants designed to serve several national markets. In some cases the eventual finished product, such as a car or computer, will be the culmination of work carried out in up to half-a-dozen different countries. In others, each national subsidiary will produce one or two complete items in the company's product line for international distribution, and rely on its affiliates to provide it with the rest for its own home market. Some companies already operate on these lines, of course. By 1980 it will be the rule rather than the exception.

The integration of national economies through the activities of international companies will also be increased by the spread of central purchasing of supplies by a head office or regional office on behalf of several of its subsidiaries. Again the oil industry provides an indication of the shape of things to come. For many years it has been customary for the companies to offer a comprehensive bunkering service throughout the world to substantial customers. After one set of negotiations the price and terms of delivery to an individual shipping line at every major port, or airport for an airline, can be arranged. The terms of the contracts vary

*See Chapter 2.

from line to line, but for each line they are based on the same agreement the world over. The possibility of this principle being extended to other products and commodities is very real. For some time the British Steel Corporation has believed that in due course steel will be purchased in this way by the major users. The car companies have talked about negotiating for the purchase of some components for their European subsidiaries on a centralized basis with the individual suppliers. In practice this would mean that the head office or European office of, say, Ford, would deal direct with SKF for bearings, and negotiate a contract for the terms by which SKF would supply all their factories. The purchaser might stipulate where each subsidiary's supplies should come from and in what proportion, or it might leave that to the seller to decide. But either way the freedom of action of the various national subsidiaries of both the buyer and the seller would be further reduced.

In this context the relationship between international companies and their professional advisers also has important implications. Just as companies like Eaton Yale and Towne expanded abroad in order to provide a world-wide service to their big domestic customers, so have banks, advertising agencies, accountants, and numerous other providers of professional and specialist services. The advance of the multinationals can be likened to that of an army with a large band of camp followers. When the company settles in a new market it likes to have familiar faces around it, and to seek advice from the local subsidiaries of the same firms who provide it at home. Thus the Chrysler and Gulf Oil subsidiaries in Britain, for instance, employ the U.S.-owned Young and Rubicam for much of their advertising and public relations, and Young and Rubicam in turn has an account with the London branch of the First National City Bank of New York.

International companies do not, of course, confine their patronage to banks and advertising agencies from their home country. For a variety of reasons they often employ local ones as well. They want to integrate themselves into the local community, and to maintain a wide range of choice. Sometimes they find that a local concern is simply better or more suitable in a given situation than any other. But the final choice of whom a subsidiary employs either lies with head office or must be acceptable to it. Banks, advertising agencies, and the rest find that this means they must secure the confidence of the companies' head offices, which can only be effectively accomplished by establishing themselves in the countries concerned. So the spread of international companies affects those who service them in two respects. In the first place it forces them to internationalize, either from the head office country to the subsidiaries, or vice-versa. Secondly it leads to the gradual evolution of a common mode of behaviour and set of practices.

As the role and influence of international companies increases, their tensions with governments will become worse. Some will arise from the scale of their operations, the flexibility inherent in their position, and the difficulties faced by governments when trying to maintain a check on them. Others will result from the companies acceding to the wishes, laws, or policies of some governments, and thereby offending others. The companies themselves will in general continue to try to be good citizens everywhere. But their overriding commitment to their own profits and self-interests on the one hand, and their need to choose between the conflicting demands and aspirations of several governments on the other will create inevitable problems.

The first category of tensions stemming from the nature of the companies has three potentially explosive aspects. These are the companies' power to allocate markets, their freedom of choice about where to invest, and their ability to move vast sums of money between different countries and currencies.

Even the most tolerant and liberal governments are becoming resentful of the international companies' ability to allocate markets. They feel that it is wrong that a subsidiary

249

occupying a prominent place in the domestic economy should be barred from attempting to export to certain markets just because its parent has decided that they should be served by another affiliate. The subsidiary in question may justifiably claim that despite the restriction it has a good export record, but this leaves it open to the riposte that if it was a free agent it could do better still. If the export record is bad the government is likely to blame the parent company's restrictions, even if the fault really lies with its own economic and industrial policies, low productivity, or persistent strikes. Governments also dislike seeing the subsidiaries of international companies being forced by their head offices to import components that could be purchased locally. Sometimes the subsidiaries can answer that the imports are cheaper than comparable local products, with the result that their own finished products are cheaper and more competitive than would otherwise be the case. But governments are often reluctant to accept this, especially if they see that the subsidiary in question happens to be spending more on imports than it earns in exports. As the integration of international companies' activities across frontiers increases, and the practice of giving each subsidiary a specific and limited role in the total operation spreads, the problem will get worse. It will be intensified by the growing dependence of many industrialized countries on international companies for the bulk of their exports. By 1980 foreign-owned internationals will account for about half the total exports of many Western European countries, and locally-owned internationals for much of the rest.

The allocation of markets is closely linked with the question of investment, since a decision to build a new plant or to reorganize existing ones usually precedes export planning. We have already seen (Chapter 12) how governments are beginning to compete with each other to attract the investment favours of international companies. This is a contest which once begun will be difficult to stop. Although governments may recognize that it is bound in the long run to lead to diminishing returns, its short-term attractions are enormous. A company like Shell now announces investment plans of £200m. at a single stroke, which is enough to make a sizeable impact on any Western European country's annual level of industrial investment, and creates orders that flow throughout the economy. Moreover, the country which can secure the largest share of an international company's new investment is well situated to pick up its best export markets. The successful countries in these situations are bound not to want to do anything to deter the goose with the golden eggs. But the less successful are equally bound to become resentful. If a government finds that not only is its country's level of industrial investment lagging behind those of its neighbours, but that a sizeable proportion of its total and of its neighbours' is provided by the same group of companies, this resentment could reach formidable proportions. This will be so even if much of the fault lies with the government's own policies, as would probably be the case.

Moreover, investments which have been 'purchased' at a high price in terms of tax concessions have a habit of creating political difficulties. The Irish experience with Gulf Oil provides an illustration of what can happen. At first when the company decided to take advantage of the tremendous concessions and inducements offered by the government to build its massive crude oil trans-shipment facilities in Bantry Bay instead of elsewhere in Europe, the Irish public was delighted. But later when it became apparent that the company was operating on more favourable terms than it could have secured in other countries, criticisms developed. The government was accused of having been outsmarted, and the company of having taken advantage of a small country's ignorance. The upshot was that the government began to look for ways of squeezing more money or other benefits out of the company.

The importance of the international companies' ability to move money between different countries and currencies is closely linked to the scale of their activities. As these increase, the influence of their financial operations grows. By the time they are accounting for the greater part of the western industrialized countries' trade in manufactured goods and for much of the investment it will be considerable. If for some reason they should lose confidence in a particular currency, and simultaneously set out to drain their subsidiaries in the country concerned, the effects would be far-reaching. The subsidiaries' outward dividend payments would be increased, and their royalty payments brought forward. They would have to settle their liabilities quickly, while money due to them from their parents and affiliates would be delayed. As the process gathered momentum the unfortunate country's reserves would rapidly diminish and confidence in its currency would drain away. A vicious spiral would have been set in motion that is very difficult to stop. Alternatively, if the companies believed that a currency was in line for revaluation they would run down their other balances, and buy it on a large scale. Much of the money that flowed into Deutsche Marks in the autumn of 1969 when the German government was pressured into revaluing against its will was generated in this way. In both sets of circumstances the companies are not responsible for creating the situation in which their actions take place, but the weight of their money is so great that they can drive it to extremes.

The existence of the Eurodollar market helps to make this possible. Its main purpose is to enable the companies to raise and invest money with which to carry on their business. By mid-1970 it was estimated to be employing funds equivalent to well over half the stock of international currency reserves. Its size, flexibility, and freedom from controls have enabled the companies to expand rapidly, but these same factors also mean that it acts as a sort of lung, sucking in money from some currencies, and pumping it out into others. When companies want to speculate against a currency they sell it to buy Eurodollars, and when they want to speculate in its favour they sell the Eurodollars in order to buy it. The speculation would take place in any case, and used to do so before the Eurodollar market was invented, but its existence makes the process much quicker and more efficient than would otherwise be the case.

The second category of tensions are those stemming from the companies acceding to the wishes, laws, or policies of some governments and thereby offending others. The most potentially explosive crises in this area are likely to arise over attempts by a government to limit trade with another country. In the past the most obvious example of this has been the U.S. boycott of China. There are innumerable examples of U.S.-owned subsidiaries in Western Europe and Canada refusing to trade with China in direct contradiction to the wishes of their local host government for fear of contravening U.S. laws. Sometimes, too, non-U.S. companies have preferred to follow the U.S. line on this issue rather than risk the possibility of action being taken against their U.S. interests. China is not an isolated example. In 1966 the U.S. Government prevented Control Data from exporting two computers to France for use in a French nuclear weapons laboratory. These computers were to have been shipped from the U.S., but there is little doubt that the U.S. Government would have at least attempted to prevent their sale even if they had been manufactured by one of Control Data's foreign subsidiaries. In the 1970s several governments, notably the Swedish, but possibly the U.S. and British as well, may decide to impose a limited trade boycott on South Africa. Once this principle is accepted there will always be suggestions that it should be employed in other situations, and the more moral issues are brought into political and commercial policies the greater will be the danger of this practice spreading.

Anti-trust and competition policies are another fruitful source of disagreement between companies and governments. Again the long arm of the U.S. is the likeliest source of trouble. The Americans claim universal jurisdiction in these matters over companies that operate in their market.

Consequently any company with U.S. interests, even if it is not American-owned, may be inhibited from a merger or trading practice in another part of the world for fear of falling foul of U.S. law. In doing so it runs the risk of countervailing action being taken by the local government to offset the U.S. claims. This problem has been a constant irritant in Canadian–U.S. relations. With the growth of U.S.-owned companies in Europe and of European investment in the U.S. there are fears that it could spread across the Atlantic.

Having discussed a problem over many chapters, the occupational hazard of all authors is to produce a straightforward solution. It completes the book in a tidy fashion, and provides the readers with something to latch on to and remember. Unfortunately there are no adequate straightforward solutions to the problems raised by international companies. They are far too complex.

To suggest one would presuppose that all governments on the one hand, and all companies on the other, have identical interests, and that it is only necessary to reconcile the tensions existing between the two groups. In reality each government has its own interests, fears, and hopes, some of which it shares with others, and some of which are particular to itself. The same applies to the companies. In these circumstances proposals for an international agency to regulate the companies' investment activities, and for an international ombudsman to which they could appeal against the conflicting demands of governments, are quite simply irrelevant. They are favoured in some American academic circles,* and they have the merits of straightforwardness, but they do not meet the needs of the situation. The same can be said of the 'Yankee go home – we will build up European companies of our own' approach, that is sometimes heard on the other side of the Atlantic.

* See *American Business Abroad* by Charles P. Kindleberger (Yale University Press).

It is, however, desirable that governments should encourage international direct investment by their own nationals. Some of the worst problems in the relationship between companies and governments occur when a country feels that its industry is falling under foreign control, and that it has no stake of its own in the growth of international business. When the flow of inward direct investment and the expansion of foreign-owned international companies in the domestic economy is accompanied by the spread of locally owned international companies in foreign markets, the relationship between the government in question and the international companies tends to be far easier. The corrosive and embittering feelings of nationalism and distrust of the foreigner are less likely to break out, and the government and public opinion are better informed about the whole question. It is only necessary to compare the relatively objective and relaxed approach of the British, Dutch, and Swiss governments towards international companies with the suspicious nationalism of the French to appreciate the strength of this point.

For their part the companies should try to involve the nationals of the countries where they operate as much as possible in their senior management. It is all very well to allow them to run their local subsidiaries, but that does not go nearly far enough. If a company is to be really multinational it must provide opportunities for people of all nationalities to reach the highest positions at its head office and to participate in the most important decisions. For as long as the present apartheid systems practised by most companies continue, it will be difficult for international enterprises to win the full confidence of public opinion and of governments in the countries where their subsidiaries operate. Because of the long and complex training required to become a top executive in a major industrial company it will be many years before a reasonable number of them can claim that their senior management is as multinational as their investments. But a start should be made immediately.

Quite apart from the political considerations, it will become increasingly necessary for international companies to consider people of all nationalities on an equal footing if they are to continue to attract the ablest men into their organizations. Such men will not be satisfied if an artificial ceiling is placed on their chances of promotion, and will look for better opportunities elsewhere. The researches carried out by *Business Week* and Professor Howard V. Perlmutter, among others, show that U.S.-owned companies in Europe are already running into this problem, and it applies just as much to European-owned multinationals. It is significant that a Belgian executive should have used the term 'white negroism' when telling *Business Week* of the discrimination practised against non-Americans by his U.S.-owned multi-national employer. The arguments in favour of equality of opportunity that have become so familiar in countries with depressed racial and religious minorities will be heard in business circles. In Italy there has even been a case of mutiny by a subsidiary of a U.S.-owned company – the Compagnia Tecnica Industrie Petroli belonging to Arthur G. McKee of Cleveland. The managers tried to change its ownership without the parent knowing under the slogan 'Let the profits go where the brains are'.* This was an exceptional event. The simplest course of action for those who feel dissatisfied is to vote with their feet by leaving.

Besides providing openings for its nationals, a company can associate itself with a country by selling shares in its local subsidiary. The British-owned Rio Tinto-Zinc mining and metals group does this as a matter of policy wherever it can. It believes that once the initial exploration and development stages have been overcome local participation is of vital importance to its operations. If the public can own shares they are less likely to be suspicious of the company's profits or trading policies. It also becomes easier to win and to hold the trust of governments as the necessity to pay dividends, to safeguard the shareholders' interests, and to publish inform-

* For details see *Time*, 25 July 1969, and *Financial Times*, 31 July 1969.

ation in the annual report provides a constant reassurance that the country is being fairly treated. Most non-American international groups encourage the American public to buy shares in their U.S. subsidiaries, but otherwise the prevailing fashion is against minority shareholders. Indeed over the last few years several companies have spent large sums of money buying them out. General Motors' chairman, James M. Roche, says flatly that, 'we have no partners in our foreign subsidiaries',* and a director of a leading U.S. chemical company once told me, in response to a question on this subject, that 'nobody wants lodgers in their home if they can get along without them, but if lodgers are the only way you can keep the house or build an extension you will take them in. We feel the same way about having outsiders in our company.'

As was pointed out in Chapter 3, non-American companies with subsidiaries in the U.S. usually do not have the resources of executive talent or money to build up their enterprises unaided. Most of them feel that without lodgers they could not survive in that alien and desperately competitive environment. Moreover, their U.S. subsidiaries are largely self-contained operations. They may import raw materials, semi-finished products for further processing, or complete manufactures from their parents or affiliates, but they are designed exclusively to serve the U.S. market. Consequently the parent can offer the public a shareholding in a complete enterprise all of whose activities take place within the legal and fiscal jurisdiction of the U.S. Most of Rio Tinto-Zinc's mining and related ventures, the bulk of which are in the U.S., Canada, Australia, and South Africa, are similarly self-sufficient.

The situation in Europe is quite different. To an increasing extent the activities of national subsidiaries are being integrated with each other across frontiers. The individual subsidiary is no longer a complete enterprise. It is merely a cog in an international operation whose role and facilities

* *Time*, 29 December 1967.

would make no sense if it was cut off from its affiliates. It would therefore be difficult for the parent companies to offer the public a satisfactory shareholding in their subsidiaries in the same way as Rio Tinto-Zinc can in its mining ventures or non-American companies can in the U.S. If it tried to meet the investing public's requirements it would not be able to integrate the subsidiary in which the shares were sold fully into its international operations. As a result that subsidiary would become a low priority area in the company's empire and suffer accordingly in the allocation of new funds and export markets. The shareholders would get their dividends, but the country would not get the volume of investment and trade over a long period to which it could otherwise aspire, as the parent would favour those subsidiaries over which it had complete control. Where a group of subsidiaries forms a relatively self-contained unit it would make sense to sell shares to the publics of the countries involved. But the differences in national legal and fiscal procedures, and stock exchange regulations, would prove an insurmountable obstacle.

However, even if it is impractical at present, the device of local shareholdings provides a clue to the way forward towards establishing a satisfactory relationship between companies and governments. Now that their operations play such an important role in national economies, the companies should be prepared to consider the governments with whom they deal as if they were a mixture between shareholders and partners. This means that they should be prepared to provide them with far more information about their international activities and plans than has hitherto been considered necessary. For their part the governments should set out to accumulate knowledge about those international companies that are important to their economies with the same dedication that they devote to finding out about the internal affairs of friendly governments. Before friendly governments embark on international negotiations they go to considerable lengths to find out all they can about each others' interests, aspirations, and strengths and weaknesses. The same effort should be devoted to finding out about the world-wide operations of the international companies.

As with international diplomacy, summit meetings are not the best way of dealing with the matter. It may be desirable that the cabinet minister responsible for industrial affairs and the men who run the international companies that play a major role in his country should be personally acquainted with each other. On rare occasions they may be the only people who can settle a particularly intractable problem that has been a long-standing source of dissension. But as a rule they will find it difficult to exchange more than generalities in their inevitably brief and rare meetings.

Ideally a procedure should be agreed between each government and the international companies with which it is concerned whereby the two sides maintain contact with each other, and the government can check on each individual company's activities. This already sometimes happens informally between governments, and locally-owned companies, and between governments and the local subsidiaries of foreign-owned companies. Where governments are dealing with locally-owned companies it is relatively easy for the two sides to maintain contact and for government to find out anything it needs to know. But a subsidiary is like a battalion in a great army, and its chief executive is merely a colonel whose role is laid down by headquarters. If the government is to know what is really going on it must deal with the headquarters, not just the subsidiary.

The procedure should take the form of an annual review of each company's activities. The company would explain to officials from the relevant ministry the outline of its plans, and show how its local subsidiary would fit into them. There would be an emphasis on investment in new plant and machinery, the proposed sources of raw materials and components for the various factories, the allocation of export markets, and the proposed financial movements into and out of the subsidiary. The procedure would be informal. The officials would respond to the company's presentation with an account of their government's hopes and plans, and make counter-suggestions to the company's proposals if they felt that their national interest was being insufficiently taken into account. There would be no question of the company asking for permission to proceed or the government refusing it. Each side would simply be keeping the other in touch with its plans for and views of the future. As at present the company would only seek official permission when it wished to embark on a specific project for which the law lays down that official permission is required.

It might be argued that, since most countries already require companies to seek permission for a wide range of projects, there is no need for an additional review. But at present government departments inevitably deal with a company's requests on a rather *ad hoc* basis as and when they are made. The officials can see how they fit into the national scene, and form a view on their merits and defects in that light, but they do not have a clear picture of the company's world-wide operations. If a regular review or some other similar procedure were instituted and backed up by intensive information gathering conducted through the government's embassies abroad, there would be a far greater equality of knowledge between the two sides. The government would be in a better position to ask relevant questions, to impose conditions, and to seek assurances that would be both practical for the company and in the national interest. The conditions and assurances would be designed to help the balance of payments, and to ensure that the proposed new investment fitted satisfactorily into the government's own plans.

The reviews would have to be conducted in complete confidence to be of any value, but it would not be enough for governments to deal with companies on a unilateral basis. They must also exchange information between themselves when their common interest demands it.

The exchanges should take place between departments, such as the tax authorities and the customs and excise, and between the central banks. They should be concerned with the details of corporate behaviour with regard to the transfer of funds, prices in inter-affiliate deals, tax declarations and the like. At present the companies have a considerable advantage in their dealings with these agencies because they deal with each on a national basis, telling them what goes on only in the local national subsidiary. Once again therefore the officials find it difficult to judge a company's behaviour in the light of its international activities. One purpose of exchanging information would be to warn of impending danger, as for instance when a large company starts to run down its holdings of a particular currency and to milk the relevant subsidiary of funds, so that the government concerned could take countervailing action. Another purpose would be to assist in the rooting out of attempts by some companies to evade their obligations in different countries. They may, for instance, tell the tax authorities in country X that they earn most of their profits on a particular process in countries Y and Z, and the governments of those two countries that their profits come from country X. Alternatively they may mislead governments about the sources of their exports and imports by shipping goods through third countries instead of direct from one to another. There are numerous other devices employed by companies anxious to avoid irksome payments and restrictions, most of which are as old as international trade itself. Taken together their potential scale is now too great for governments to continue to tackle them on an individual basis.

There is finally a need for governments to agree among themselves on a code of conduct to cover certain aspects of their industrial policy. The objects would be to prevent companies from playing one off against another, and to establish a framework within which the companies could work on the same footing everywhere. For many years governments have accepted international rules on export

261

incentives, and the extent to which they can offer preferential trading terms to other countries. They do so in order to guard against destructive trade wars on the pre-war pattern. The new need is to guard against a potentially equally destructive competition to secure the favours of the great multinational corporations when they allocate their new investment projects, and determine the terms and patterns of trade between their affiliates.

The most urgent need in this context is for rules to govern investment incentives. Governments are already bidding against each other in their efforts to attract new investment, and unless something is done quickly this competition could get out of hand in some places. Codes of conduct for the setting of transfer prices between sister companies, and the allocation of export markets, are also needed. As with most successful international regulatory systems the rules governing the conduct of international companies and governments would not go into infinite detail. They would set broad principles to which the individual national rules and regulations would have to comply.

With the European Economic Community enlarged to include Britain and the other applicant countries it will become easier in the long run to tackle the problems surrounding the relationship between governments and international companies. Nine of the leading European countries will be united in the Community, and working increasingly closely together in a multitude of political, economic, and industrial matters. Their policy towards international companies will be correspondingly easier to evolve. But a self-contained Community system is out of the question since any satisfactory arrangement would have to include the U.S. and other non-members, such as Canada, Sweden, and Switzerland. Moreover, this problem cannot wait to be tackled until the Community has moved further towards reconciling its internal differences. For many years to come the members of the Community, will remain quite separate political entities, and even if they should ever cease to be so, other independent industrialized states will remain. Meanwhile the power and influence of the multinational and other international companies will continue to grow, and the erosion of national economic independence as a result of their activities will gather momentum.

The position of the companies is, in some ways, analogous to that of the Catholic Church in the past. Kings and emperors frequently felt their positions to be overshadowed by its international organization, its influence on national policies, and its immense buildings and tracts of land. Eventually the tensions were overcome in two ways. Some countries broke with Rome altogether and set up independent churches of their own. Others negotiated concordats with the Pope defining their respective spheres, and establishing a framework within which they could work together in harmony. No advanced industrialized country can cut itself off completely from the multinational and international corporations, and those that try will suffer for it by losing the advantages the corporations can confer. Multinational industry is an economic and political reality of the modern world. If countries are to secure the benefits which flow from it and minimize the costs, they must be prepared to work together, and to establish a new industrial concordat between themselves and the companies.

Appendix

The memorandum reproduced below was prepared in February 1928 by Mr (later Sir) John Hanbury-Williams of Courtaulds, and addressed to his board of directors. Courtaulds was at that time the leading producer of rayon, also known as viscose or artificial silk, in both Europe and the U.S., where it owned the American Viscose Corporation. Hanbury-Williams was responsible for most of the company's negotiations with the other rayon producers. The memorandum therefore gives a clear idea of the sort of difficulties in the way of establishing an international cartel as they appeared to a participant. It was first published in the company's history, *Courtaulds: An Economic and Social History*, Volume 2, by D. C. Coleman (Oxford University Press), and is reproduced here by kind permission of the Clarendon Press, Oxford.

MEMORANDUM REGARDING LIMITATION OF WORLD
PRODUCTION OF ARTIFICIAL SILK YARN – (VISCOSE)
(By J. C. Hanbury-Williams)

In June 1927 the chairman and Sir Thos. Latham spoke to me regarding the price arrangements which we have with our Continental friends and pointed out that such arrangements might work satisfactorily when times were good but were in danger of breaking down when a slump came or when production exceeded demand. I was instructed to bear this in mind and at the same time try to devise some means of safeguarding our interests and the interests of the trade as a whole during any future discussions which might take place with the Continental producers. Since June I have had an opportunity of meeting some of the heads of the most important Continental producers and both Mr F. Williams and myself have gone to some pains to obtain their views and to ascertain what collaboration we might expect in the event of definite proposals being put forward.

Whilst it is admitted that some form of control of either production or prices or both is desirable, no scheme has yet been put forward which is satisfactory and agreeable to all.

There are three ways in which one might deal with the situation, none of them in my opinion satisfactory but I give them as briefly as possible under headings 1, 2, and 3.

1. *Control of production by nozzles.* It has been suggested that if the most important producers of Viscose yarns were to state the capacity of production of their existing factories and also those under construction at the same time giving the number of nozzles employed, one might arrive at a quota for each producer which would be subject to mutual modification when trade warranted. There would however be serious difficulties in agreeing on a 'Quota' of production and one would have no guarantee that even if quotas were agreed upon that same would be carried out and we should all find ourselves in the same position as under existing price agreements. Further trade might be good in some countries and bad in others and the producer in a country where trade was good might be placed in a position of being unable to deliver the required weights owing to his quota having already reached the agreed limit. In many countries control of production would not only be unenforceable but illegal as being in restraint of trade. Then there is the difficulty of standardization of quality and this in my opinion is one which at present cannot be got over; the trade might require only the best qualities and such producers as ourselves would be unable to supply requirements if our quota were filled resulting in a benefit to the producers of inferior silk.

2. *Control of production by limiting exports to agreed countries.* This system whilst having some of the disadvantages of No. 1 would at least allow each producer to satisfy the requirements of his own country.

It might be possible by ascertaining the consumption of a non-producing country to agree on a division of exports to that country but here again the question of quality plays a big part and we might again find ourselves in a position of having to refuse orders to the benefit of producers of inferior grades and also to those who were not parties to the agreement. Snia propose that this difficulty should be overcome by allowing the contingent to be exceeded provided a fine of so much per kilo be levied, the total sum accruing from such fines to be divided pro rata amongst those who had not exceeded their share. This to my mind is unsound, it being in the nature of a premium on the production of good silk. In any case if such an agreement were made, the question of the form it should take, the law by which it should be governed and the means whereby it could be rendered enforceable in the various countries in which the parties were operating would be a matter of special consideration and enquiry in conjunction with the legal representatives of those interested.

3. *Central Sales organization.* This would perhaps be the most suitable of the three methods, it would take the form of a separate Company and it would probably be necessary that all the producers who were agreeable to effect their sales through its organization to figure as shareholders, either each for the same interest or with holdings proportionate to their production. Such a company could probably be formed in Bruxelles or Paris and would work on a small commission to cover its overhead expenses, each producer still retaining their agents or selling organizations but all orders would pass through the selling company. It would be undesirable for collateral agreements to be entered into between the selling company and the producing companies as its organization could not be directly utilized either to limit production or to control prices; the producing companies might however enter into separate agreements between themselves undertaking to give the selling company the exclusive right to sell their products on a particular market or markets; the agreement would further provide for the fixing of prices at stated intervals and in the event of the agreements being in any way broken the offenders would automatically cease to be members of the selling company.

To sum up neither of the three methods are in my opinion suitable at any rate under present conditions and I am inclined to believe that whatever arrangements are entered into the question of supply and demand will always regulate both prices and production. I do feel however that the existing price agreements with our Continental friends have been and still are of great value. If the Board wish to pursue the matter further I would recommend for your consideration either the formation of a separate company or the formation of an Information Bureau, the upkeep of which would be guaranteed by those producers parties to an agreement which would provide for the following: Each producer to declare at stated intervals his production giving deniers and any other information considered desirable; also to send to the Bureau facsimile copies of invoices to all agents and customers other than those in the countries of the producers parties to the agreement.

If such a company or Information Bureau were formed to receive such information the larger producers of Viscose yarns would be in a much better position to deal with any slump in trade or over production in an amicable manner and it would by frequent meetings cement the friendly feelings which already exist.

In suggesting these proposals for your consideration I realize that at present they may not be in our best interests but with increasing competition we may in years to come find such an organization of great value.

Bibliography

The History of Unilever in two volumes by Charles Wilson. Cassell.

The American Invaders by F. A. McKenzie. Grant Richards, 1902.

The American Takeover of Britain by James McMillan and Bernard Harris. Leslie Frewin.

Cartels in Action by George W. Stocking and Myron W. Watkins. Twentieth Century Fund.

Oil: The Biggest Business by Christopher Tugendhat. Eyre and Spottiswoode.

Courtaulds: An Economic and Social History in two volumes by Dr D. C. Coleman. Oxford University Press.

Transatlantic Investments by Christopher Layton. Second edition, January 1968. Atlantic Institute.

The Role of American Investment in the British Economy by Professor John H. Dunning, P.E.P. Broadsheet 507, February 1969.

The Problem of International Investment: a report of a Study Group of Members of the Royal Institute of International Affairs. Oxford University Press, 1937.

Some Patterns in the Rise of Multinational Enterprise by Jack N. Behrman, Research Paper 18. Graduate School of Business, University of North Carolina.

Management and Merger Activity by Gerald D. Newbould. Guthstead.

Men and Money by Paul Ferris. Hutchinson.

The Strategy of the Multinational Enterprise by Dr Michael Z. Brooke and Dr H. Lee Remmers. Longman.

Transfer Pricing and Multinational Business by Dr James S. Shulman, an unpublished doctoral thesis for the Harvard School of Business.

British Economic Prospects by Richard E. Caves and Associates. A Brookings Institution Study. George Allen & Unwin.

American Business Abroad by Charles P. Kindleberger. Yale University Press.

European Advanced Technology by Christopher Layton. Published on behalf of P.E.P. by George Allen & Unwin.

The Multinationals

The International Transfer of Corporate Skills by Peter P. Gabriel. Harvard University.

Effects of U.K. Investment Overseas by W. B. Reddaway in collaboration with S. J. Potter and C. T. Taylor. Cambridge University Press.

Politics and the Multinational Company by Louis Turner, Fabian Research Series 279.

U.S. Production Abroad and the Balance of Payments by Judd Polk, Irene W. Meister and Lawrence A. Veit. National Industrial Conference Board.

The Proposal for a European Company by Dennis Thompson, European Series No. 13. Chatham House and P.E.P.

Concentration or Competition: A European Dilemma? by D. Swann and D. L. McLachlan, European Series No. 1. Chatham House and P.E.P.

The Growth and Spread of Multinational Companies, Q.E.R. Special No. 5, the Economist's Intelligence Unit.

Britain in Europe, a second industrial appraisal by the Confederation of British Industry.

Unilever 1945–1965 by Charles Wilson. Cassell.

The International Corporation, a symposium edited by Charles P. Kindleberger. M.I.T. Press.

International Business Enterprise by Endel J. Kolde. Prentice Hall, Inc.

The Worldwide Industrial Enterprise by Frederic G. Donner. McGraw-Hill.

After Imperialism by Michael Barratt-Brown. Heinemann.

The New Europeans by Anthony Sampson. Hodder & Stoughton.

The American Challenge (Le Défî Americain) by Jean-Jacques Servan-Schreiber. Hamish Hamilton.

Foreign Ownership and the Structure of Canadian Industry, report of the Task Force on Canadian Industry, prepared by the Privy Council, Ottawa.

The International Corporation. Background report by Sidney L. Rolfe for the 22nd Congress of the International Chamber of Commerce, May/June 1969.

Industrial Policy in The Community, memorandum from the Commission to the Council, generally known as the Colonna Report, published March 1970.

Business in Britain by Graham Turner. Eyre & Spottiswoode.

The New Industrial State by J. K. Galbraith. Hamish Hamilton.

NEWSPAPERS, MAGAZINES AND PERIODICALS

Much of the most up-to-date information about international companies is published in newspapers, magazines and periodicals. I have found the *Financial Times*, the *Harvard Business Review*, *Fortune*, and *Management Today* particularly helpful. I have also drawn heavily on *The Times*, the *Sunday Times*, the *Wall Street Journal*, the *Columbia Journal of World Business*, the *Director*, the *New York Times* and *Business Week*.

Index

Index

Immigrants, and U.S. industrial revolution, 64

Imperial Chemical Industries (ICI), sales compared with GNP Norway, 20; foundation of comprehensive scheme, 40–41; cartel case v. U.S., 53–4; U.S. subsidiary, 76; profitability, 100; and SKF, 111

Industrial Development Bonds, 216

Industrial Revolution (U.S.), capital requirements, 64–5

Industrial Reorganization Corporation (IRC), 88–9; abolition, 89

Industry, small role played by international companies (1914), 37; drop in post-war demand, 40; sacrifices cooperation to sales, 44; increasing internationalism in U.S., 55; infected by foreign investment, 58; needs of research and investment programmes, 82, 86; expansion through mergers, 86; defence of home market, 86; performance of small companies, 100; accelerating pace of change, 101; slow transnationalization, 107, 119; manufacture of components, 141; advances in international cooperation, 150; unsuccessful transfer to government service, 240; reduction in competing companies, 244–5; fear of foreign control, 255

Institut de Development Industrial (IDI), 89

Instituto per la Recostruzione Industriale (IRI), 93

Insurance companies, 32, 113

Interest payments, way of moving funds, 161, 167

Internal Revenue Service, 183

International Chamber of Commerce, 1969 Congress, 21 n., 29–30

International Combustion, 88

International companies, relationship with governments, 9, 22, 24, 137, 200–202, 212, 243, 249,

255, 258–9; dearth of reliable statistics, 9; secrecy over figures, 9–10; rapid staff changes, 10; variation in accounting methods, 19–21; value of foreign-produced goods, 21; overriding corporate aims, 22; influence on public affairs, 23–4; dangers of public discussion, 29–30; historical background, 30–44; trans-Atlantic movement, 36–7; inter-wars expansion, 38–9; compared with cartels, 42; head-office-subsidiary relationships, 46, 229; trend towards inter-related plants, 47; value of local plants, 56, 72–4; losses incurred be latecomers, 58; expansion through takeovers, 60; new-comers challenge the field, 67–8; cause a merger boom, 82–3; disappointing performance, 95; promotion ladder, 101–2; as employers, 110–11; global interests, 130; influence on economic policy and scene, 136–7, 167; trading patterns, 138; effect of financial cuts, 145; allocation of new investment, 151 and n., 201 3; and transfer of funds, 161–83, 251–2; and economic trends, 168–9, 209–10; and large ventures, 187; remain nationalistic, 190; and Eurodollar market, 193–4; distinction between foreign and domestic investment, 201–2; use of computers, 211; threat to union authority, 217–18; negotiating position, 218–19, 230; and world councils, 222–3; failure to multinationalize management, 231, 234–5, 255; need to attract top talent, 240–41; integration of trans-frontier activities, 247–8, 250; and their professional advisers, 248; relationship with host country, 253, 256–9; suggested consultation procedure, 259–61; compared with R.C. Church, 263. *See also* Multinationals

Index

Index